BENEATH
THE
FALLEN
Stars

NEW YORK TIMES BESTSELLING AUTHOR

KAYLEE RYAN
USA TODAY BESTSELLING AUTHOR
LACEY BLACK

BENEATH
THE
FALLEN
Stars

Chapter 1

Ford

THERE WAS NEVER A DOUBT THAT I WOULD BE A SOLDIER. THE Gregory family tree is full of them, and I grew up listening to my dad and my grandad talk about the brotherhood and the satisfaction of serving our country. I wanted to be just like them. When I turned eighteen, the three of us, along with my mother, went to the Army recruiter's office together. An hour later, I was enlisted.

I will never forget that day, or the feeling of doing something good, something bigger than myself.

Basic was hell, but I expected it. The purpose was to tear us down, only to build us back up again. I knew that, and mentally I was ready. There were many who weren't and many who didn't make the cut. I wasn't one of them.

What I wasn't prepared for was the loneliness and the longing for home. I miss my family with a fierceness I didn't know I was capable of. They write all the time, and Mom is constantly sending me and my platoon care packages. My buddy Chad benefits the most. When I call home, he's always there chiming in and laying on the charm when it comes to Mom. She's already fallen for his charisma.

Chad and I made it through basic together. Unlike me, Chad is a first-generation soldier. His parents were supportive, but it took them some time to get used to the idea. The way he tells it, it's just him and his little sister, Cassie, and their cousin Shayne to carry on the family name. That was an issue for his family, but they've since accepted his desire and need to be a soldier.

"Two more days," Chad says from his spot next to me.

We're stationed overseas. It's been a long nine months, but we're finally going home. If all goes well, we'll be home for a while before we get shipped off again. Regardless, when we get our orders, we'll go. We're soldiers. That's what we do.

"Two very long days," I say, tilting my head back and looking up at the night sky. It's a quiet muggy night here in the desert, but the stars are bright, and this time next week, we'll be stateside.

"You're still coming home with me, right?" Chad asks.

"Yeah. Mom and Dad are on a cruise, so I'll stay with you for a week or so before heading home to Ohio."

"You mean until we head home to Ohio," he jokes.

"You're really only going to visit with your family for a week?" I ask him.

"No. I'm going to visit them for a week, then I'm going to follow your ass home to make sure you make it okay. Your momma would have my ass if you detoured and got hitched or something." He laughs. "Besides, I'm just a few hours from home. You do know that Kentucky and Ohio border one another, right?"

"Ha ha, very funny, smartass. Yes, I'm aware. As for Mom, she'd probably be thrilled if I got hitched. Just as long as she got to meet her and there were talks of grandkids in the future."

"Nah, Momma Gregory would want to be there." He taps his temple. "I know these things."

"Sure, she might be disappointed, but the happiness of the potential for a grandchild would win out."

"You think the stars are shining this bright back home?" he asks after a few minutes of silence passes between us.

"In some spots," I say. "As long as it's outside of the city."

"I grew up on a farm, and I don't ever remember the stars being this bright."

"We took them for granted." I didn't grow up on a farm, but we do live in the country. I never took the time to look up at the stars, but out here in the desert, there's not much else to do. It's still stifling hot at night, so Chad and I have gotten into a routine of sitting outside the tents when we're not on patrol.

"Does your mom know I'm coming home with you?" he asks.

"Nope, but she's not going to care. I wasn't certain you'd made up your mind the last time I spoke to her. What about yours?"

"Yeah, I told her not to make fun of your ugly mug," he says, laughing at his own joke.

"Come on now. You know the panties will be dropping when I walk into the room," I quip.

"Dude, my hometown is so small. You're going to be disappointed."

"I'm good with small. Chasing women in the big city is not my style."

"All this panty-dropping talk, and then you come back with that it's not your style."

I can feel his gaze on me. "I'm being real. I'm not one to play the field. Sure, I could get my dick wet, but I want more than that. Pussy is pussy, man. You don't need to sample them all. You just need one that is attached to a good heart, and take it from there."

"Damn, Gregory. What's got you all sentimental?"

I shrug, keeping my eyes on the night sky. "Missing home, but that isn't what made me say that. That's just me, man. I'd rather find someone I know I can lean on. Someone I know that, when I come back to this godforsaken desert, she's still going to be waiting on me back home." I'm a military brat. I've moved and lived all over, but the one constant in my life was the love between my parents and the love they had for me. Maybe it makes me a pansy, but that's what I want.

I know finding that person is like finding a needle in a haystack, but I'm not giving up hope. Besides, it's not like I can meet a woman and fall in love in a two-week time frame. That's how long we're on leave.

"I don't know. Rosie is exhausted," he says, holding up his hand.

"Fuck off." I laugh. "I don't need to know that shit."

"Like you don't." He scoffs. "I know damn good and well that you beat the meat just like the rest of us."

"I'm not denying it. But fuck me, I don't need to hear about it."

"No thanks, I'm good with Rosie. You're not my type," he fires back, barely containing his laughter.

"Ha ha." I shake my head.

"For real though, two weeks stateside. You're really not going to get yourself any?"

"I've never had a one-night stand."

"What? You're twenty-one years old, and single, and in the army. How in the hell is that possible?"

"Serious girlfriend in high school. We broke it off when I enlisted."

"Sara, right?"

"Yeah." Sara was my high school sweetheart. We dated for two years. She was pissed when I enlisted. That's on her. From the moment we started dating, she knew joining the army was my plan. She had this silly idea that she could change my mind. I cared about Sara and loved her even, but she wasn't my forever. She didn't support me in my choices. She was irate that I didn't discuss them with her. That's the issue, though. I did discuss it with her. I talked about it all the time. She was just stuck in her head thinking that us being together for two years would change my mind.

"It's been a while since she's written."

"Yep."

"I guess she's no longer pissed?"

"Oh, the last letter she made it known that she was pissed. Apparently, I ruined her life or some crazy shit like that. I stole her youth."

Chad barks out a laugh. "Are you shitting me? I didn't get to read that one. How long ago was that?"

"Nah, I tossed into the fire as soon as I was finished. It's been about a year since I've heard from her. She's pissed I didn't bow down to her and change my life plans. I know that makes me sound like a dick, but it is what it is."

"That's why relationships are a pain in the ass, and random hook-ups are where it's at."

"Not relationships, not if you find the right person."

"How did I not know my ride or die is a closet romantic?"

"You never asked."

"Right." He snorts. "Because that's a dude question." He changes his voice to sound deeper. "Hey, bro, you into fucking random chicks, or are you a one-woman kind of guy?" he says, making me burst out in laughter. The sound fills the muggy night air around us.

"Fuck off." My words have no heat, and we both know it.

"I'm just giving you shit. I'd be good with it. Someone to come home to." There's a wistfulness to his voice I've never heard. "Just don't see how we're going to meet anyone stuck in this hot hole."

"If it's meant to be, it will be."

"Waxing poetic now, Gregory?"

"Just stating the facts. You don't find love. Love finds you."

"Really? Who the hell are you, and what have you done with my best friend?"

"I admit that was a little cheesy. It's something my grandma used to say when I was growing up. My sister, Faith, used to claim she was in love with every new guy she would meet."

"How is Faith?" he asks.

"She's off-limits."

"Testy testy," he fires back. "I was just inquiring as to the well-being of my best bro's little sis. Is that a crime?"

"Let's see, Mr. One-Night Stands Are Where It's At. What do you think?"

"I think it was very friendly of me." I don't have to see his face to know that he's smirking.

"She's good," I finally answer. "She's in her third year of college, working on her teaching degree."

"Yeah, sexy teacher fits Faith for sure."

"Seriously?"

"You've seen your sister, right? I mean, how is it possible that the two of you are twins? She's smoking."

"Change of plans. You're not coming home with me. You're going to have to stick it out in Kentucky and deal with your family being upset with you. I'm not letting you anywhere near my little sister."

"Little? Just because she's shorter than you doesn't mean you can call her your little sister."

"No, but the fact that I was born five minutes before her does." This is information that he already knows. I know he's just trying to get me worked up. If I'm being honest, Chad is one of the best guys I know. I trust him with my life, and my *little* sister could do much worse than my best friend.

"You know what I'm looking forward to?"

"What's that?" I'm almost afraid to ask. You never know what's going to come out of Chad's mouth.

"Chicken wings. Spicy, messy chicken wings, and a nice cold beer."

"Let's move that to the top of the list," I tell him, my mouth watering at the thought.

"My cousin Shayne works at the bar in town. Best wings around."

"We're definitely going to have to check that out," I tell him.

Chad doesn't talk about home much, not in the sense of family. Everyone has accepted his choice, but something tells me there's still a strain there from his decision to enlist in the army. His parents, his sister, and his cousin Shayne are really the only people from back home that he talks about. He mentions a few friends here and there, but it seems as though none are permanent in his life.

Hell, I'm sure he's in the same situation that I am. My buddies didn't write and don't keep in touch now that I'm enlisted. They all went off to college to do their thing, and they don't understand why I felt the need to go the army route. I think it's because they don't have any experience or firsthand knowledge of anyone who has served. If they did, they would understand. This was just something I needed to do.

Much like Sara, they didn't understand, and it's my guess they never will. I'm not torn up over it. True friends would be there to support me no matter what. Friends like Chad, who I've known since our first day of basic, and who I trust with my life, that's the kind of relationship you need out here in the desert. It's not just Chad. There isn't a single member of our unit I wouldn't say the same thing about.

We're more than a unit, more than friends. We're family.

We may not share the same blood, but we're all fighting to defend our country so that our loved ones can continue to live a life of freedom.

That means something.

"Shayne will hook us up."

"Perfect." My stomach grumbles just at the thought. "I'll take first watch," I tell him, lying back on the artificial grass, my eyes focusing on the millions of stars.

"You sure?"

"Yeah. I'm good." Technically we shouldn't be sleeping out here.

We take shifts watching the sleeping tents, but it's stifling hot. Instead, we look out for one another, sleeping in shifts. Believe it or not, we get more sleep this way than we do sleeping in the hot-as-fuck tents. Sometimes others join us, but today was a long-ass day, and everyone crashed. Chad and I stuck to the routine no matter how tired and sore our muscles are. This is where we both wanted to be.

Lying beneath the stars.

Chapter 2

Shayne

"CONNOR JORGESON, GET YOUR ASS OFF THE TOP OF MY BAR!" I holler down to the far end after catching movement out of the corner of my eye.

"I didn't do anything," he replies over the classic Alabama song pumping through the speakers.

I turn quickly to see him trying to swing a leg up without kicking the row of glasses perched on the edge of the bar. "Do it, and I'll be required to remove you from the bar top with force, buddy."

He gives me a huge wolfish grin. "I love it when you talk dirty to me," he replies, making his friends laugh.

I arch a single eyebrow heavenward. "Don't make me call Jet over," I threaten, referring to the owner of the bar I work at four nights a week.

Jet's Pub and Pool Hall is known for cold beer, the best chicken wings in town, and an endless supply of locals willing to throw a few bucks onto the felt in a friendly game of pool. Jet found his love for billiards in his twenties, when he would travel to bigger cities and hustle men twice his age out of their hard-earned cash. Now, there's no hustling involved. Everyone knows he's unbeatable, but that doesn't stop them from trying.

"All right, all right, sweet thing," Connor pleads, throwing both hands in the air. "I'll be a good boy. But, you know, if you want me to be bad for a little while, you just tell me when to meet you in the supply closet." His friends laugh once more.

Morons.

I can't stop my eye roll. Connor has been trying to get in my pants since he returned home from college just a short year ago. He had a brand-new finance degree, which he thought equaled success and money, and was jonesing to screw the town whore.

"Not going to happen, Jorgeson," I state bluntly, grabbing a Miller Lite and popping the top before sliding it across the bar and collecting the offered cash.

"Don't act like you don't want it," he replies, winking as he takes a drink of his Jack and Coke.

I shiver, but it's not a good reaction. In fact, the thought of Connor Jorgeson putting his hands on me causes bile to rise in my throat.

We went to school together, but he barely paid me any attention. I was the girl from the wrong side of the tracks. With my mother in and out of trouble and a father never around, I didn't have many friends, but the ones I had were loyal. We lived in the same trailer park together, which was why Connor only noticed us on the rarest of occasions. He was town royalty—Daddy owned the bank and Mommy a stay-at-home mom who volunteered for everything—and I was, well...not.

My only slice of normalcy was when I'd get to spend time with my aunt, uncle, and cousins. They often delivered extra meals to make sure I ate. Lord knows my mom wasn't too worried about making sure there was dinner on the table when I got home from school. It was Aunt Joan who taught me how to do laundry and cook the basics, and Uncle Henry showed me how to change the oil in my old car.

Then there's Chad and Cassie, my cousins. Even though they're younger than me by a few years, I've always considered them more siblings than anything else. I knew if I ever needed them, they'd have my back. Cassie is away at school, but she still pops in every now and again to catch up and have some chicken wings, and Chad is serving in the army. He's been gone way too long overseas but just arrived home for a brief leave.

I can't wait to see him.

Connor, on the other hand, I'd be completely fine if he just up and disappeared.

Once Connor—aka the Golden Boy—moved back home last summer and started working at his daddy's bank, he took an interest in me. I'd like to say it was because of my sparkling personality and my killer rack, but that's not true. Well, my rack really is great. What I mean is, that's not why he's so enamored with me. You see, I'm a challenge to him. One he's still trying to conquer.

And by that, I mean sex.

When he returned, the rumors were already flying about my "sexual promiscuity." In other words, I was labeled a slut. A whore. Lock up your husbands, ladies, because Shayne Danner was on the prowl for a new man, and young Mr. Jorgeson thought he was it.

Unfortunately for him, he most definitely is not *it*.

Nor is anyone else in this damn town.

So that's why he—Connor, if you're not keeping up—is here, again on a random Thursday night, and offering me a quick little romp in the storage closet. A *storage closet*. Gross.

Never going to happen.

The song changes to some Garth, and the bar starts to liven up as everyone sings about a young couple running off to get it on in the back seat of a car. I run food orders from the window out to a table and refill their drinks on my next pass, all while ignoring the asshole squad at the end of the bar who are leering at my ass.

I head for the pool hall side of the building, where Jet is perched on a barstool beside one of the pub tables. "All good over here?" I ask, collecting the dirty glasses to take back to wash.

"We're fine, Shayne. You know you don't have to clean up after us. I'll get it," the big burly man says, a fatherly smile on his face.

I wave off his comment. "I know, but I was out, so I thought I'd stop by and see if you guys needed anything."

"I'll come get another round shortly," he replies, keeping his eyes locked on the man circling the table, looking for the best shot.

"Holler when you're ready," I state quickly, turning to head back to the front to wash up the dirty drink glasses. I also know he will do no such thing. Jet won't use me as his personal servant. He'll make his own drinks, even take care of those he's playing against.

Jet's my backup when it comes to needing help. Friday and Saturday nights, he's behind the bar with me, slinging drinks and pouring drafts. I know he keeps one eye on me and the bar, even when he appears to be completely focused on his game. If I start to get behind, he'll be there in a second, helping serve waiting customers.

Everyone loves Jet's. It's not too rundown, but not fancy either. The stools and counter are marred with age and a little abuse but are in great shape. The lights are low wattage custom-made mini whiskey barrels, and the walls are covered with beer and alcohol signs.

If you play pool or even throw darts, this is the place you do it. Four tables and two dartboards fill the second room. You'll find all levels of skill too, not just the pros like Jet. He loves taking young guys under his wing and teaching them about angles and English.

But what we're really known for is our wings. Yeah, there's hamburgers on the menu too, but that's not what people come to Jet's for. Honey barbecue, parmesan garlic, pineapple teriyaki, and Cajun jerk are the most popular. However, if one of those doesn't strike your fancy, we have eight additional flavors on the menu.

When I first started here more than two years ago, a week after turning twenty-one, we only served food Thursday through Saturday, but as the months went on, and seeing how many orders came through those nights, I worked to convince Jet to add more days. Sunday was first and the most popular, especially during football season. With wings available, I noticed baseball, hockey, and even NASCAR seasons started to see an increase in food orders. Eventually, we went seven days a week and serve enough nightly to keep a cook busy for hours.

Once the patrons at the bar have refills, I turn my attention to washing the dirty glasses. I'm bent over the sink, scrubbing each one inside and out, when the heavy wooden door opens and slams closed. I hear a few offered greetings but keep my focus on finishing my task. Only two more glasses to go...

"How in the hell do you get a drink around this place anyway?"

I know that voice.

It's loud and laced with humor, and when my eyes fly up and meet his happy hazel ones, I let out a little squeal. Then my legs are carrying me, away from the soapy dishes and the running water and toward one of my favorite people ever.

"Chad!" I bellow, rounding the corner of the bar and leaping into his outstretched arms. He catches me easily, holding steadfast and barely making a grunt as I slam into his chest.

"Hey, Shay," he whispers, holding me tight against his chest.

After a few seconds, he releases his hold on me and allows my feet to return to the floor. "I can't believe you're really here," I say, my face hurting from smiling so widely.

"Are you kidding me? My feet barely landed on US soil, and I couldn't wait to rest up and walk through that old door," he says, hitching a thumb over his shoulder in the direction of the door.

But that's not where my eyes go.

Oh, no.

They lock on the tall man standing behind my cousin. Crazily fit body, scruffy jaw, and buzzed dark hair. His alluring green eyes are the perfect shade of freshly dewed grass under warm, rich sunshine. They're twinkling with eagerness and mischief, and maybe even a promise or two of dirty things. At least that's the way my dried-up lady parts dissect them. He's just a hint taller than Chad and sports the same buzz cut and Army Proud green T-shirt.

"Hey, Ford, this is Shayne," Chad says, taking a step back to allow room for his friend to join our close circle.

His eyes widen with shock right before they take a leisurely perusal of my body. When they finally return to my face, he seems even more confused than moments ago. "You're Shayne? But...you're a woman."

I glance down at my chest, at the hint of cleavage peeking out of the fitted V-neck T-shirt I'm wearing. "Uh, yeah, I'm definitely a woman."

Chad barks out a laugh and hits his friend on the back. "I told you that, didn't I?"

The impossibly gorgeous man turns to my cousin and shakes his head. "No, I'd definitely remember...her."

"Oh, well, sorry," Chad replies with a shoulder shrug. "Come on, let's grab those two seats at the bar."

He takes off, but Ford doesn't move. He's still looking at me, those green eyes assessing and observing. It starts to make me feel a little uncomfortable under his intense scrutiny, but it's quickly washed away when he steps forward, extends his hand, and says, "Ford Gregory."

His hand is rough, warm, and sends sparks of lust bolting through my bloodstream. Like little zaps of electricity, they land firmly between my legs, leaving me a little achy and breathy.

What the hell?

"Shayne Danner," I reply, allowing him to hold my hand for way longer than normal. "Female," I add, unable to help the little dig.

He smiles perfectly white, straight teeth. Of course he does. A man this pretty wouldn't have a stained, crooked grin. "Sorry about that. You were just a…surprise."

I wave his comment off. "Believe it or not, you wouldn't be the first person to be shocked by my lack of a penis."

He barks out another laugh and shakes his head. As he opens his mouth to respond, we're interrupted by a holler. "Yo, Ford, quit hitting on my cousin and get over here! I've been thinking about these wings for nine long months."

"I guess I should…" he starts, leaving his statement hanging open.

"Yeah." I clear my throat and turn to head back behind the bar. Only, we're still holding hands. The realization is both startling and comforting. I didn't even notice he still had my hand in his. I pull it out of his grip and give it a little shake, as if I could vibrate the warm sensations prickling my skin where his hand once rested away.

"I'll j-just—" I stammer but stop immediately. I'm acting like a lunatic who hasn't seen a gorgeous man before.

You haven't met one who makes you all breathless and tingly before.

I force my legs to carry me away and back behind the bar and turn off the water I left running, completely ignoring Connor and his cronies as I go. I stop and grab another Michelob for a regular sitting at the bar, taking the three dollars out of his stack of cash in front of him. Then, I make my way to where Chad and Ford sit. "What can I get ya?" I ask, tossing two coasters in front of them.

"Miller Lite," Chad states.

When I look at his friend, I'm again struck by the intensity of his green eyes. "Bud Light, please."

"And grab the new guy a menu too, Shay," Chad adds with a side glance at Ford, as I reach down to grab two beers from the cooler.

I pop the tops off the bottles and set them on the coasters before wiping off my hands and grabbing a menu. And by menu, I mean a laminated index card with the hamburger and wing selection.

"Thank you," he replies politely, taking the offered card and glancing at it. He flips it over, surprised when the back side is blank.

"You either order a hamburger, which no one gets, or wings. I recommend the parmesan garlic," I suggest, leaning against the cooler with my hip.

He sets the card down and nods. "Then that's what I'll get."

I take their orders to the kitchen and deliver a few more plates to a nearby table. As I'm walking back to the bar, I jump as a hand slaps my ass. Hard. I ignore the stinging on my cheek and whip around, ready to throw punches with whoever just touched my ass. Only, when I turn around, I'm not in the least bit surprised by the smirking features I come face-to-face with.

"What's wrong, sweet thang?" Connor asks innocently, his words slurred from the alcohol he's been consuming for the better part of two hours.

"What's wrong? Don't touch me, Jorgeson. Ever," I seethe through gritted teeth.

Movement catches out of the corner of my eye, and I already know it's Jet approaching. He has a keen eye for trouble, especially where I— or any other bartender—is concerned. But before Jet can make it up to the bar, a large figure slides stealthily between myself and the jackass. I have to look up—*way* up—until I see the back of his head. It's not Chad, his big egg-shaped noggin I'd recognize anywhere.

"Did you put your hands on the lady without her permission?"

I recognize the voice instantly. It's Ford, and he's in Connor's face.

"Hey, Green Giant, I didn't mean no harm, friend," Connor replies with a drunken laugh.

I step to the side just as Ford steps forward, his nose practically touching Connor's. "Touch her again and lose your hand forever, *friend*," Ford growls, his eyes narrowed into little slits. I'm only beside them, but I can still feel the anger, the authority, and the threat oozing off my cousin's friend.

Connor seems to sober up a little and squints up at Ford. "Yeah? You gonna do something about it?"

"Put your hands on her one more time and see what fucking happens," Ford snarls.

"All right, settle down," Jet states, pushing his own big body between the two going toe- to-toe. "Connor, I think you've had enough to drink. Maybe it's time to call it a night."

"What? Me? He just walked in here and started threatening me, Jet!" Connor whines, his glassy eyes pleading at my boss.

"He only stood up because Connor slapped my ass again," I argue, immediately coming to Ford's defense.

"Again?" Ford asks, those wide, green orbs locked on mine. I see the mix of fury and disdain flash within them.

I shrug, placing my hand on his forearm. It tenses under my touch, but his entire body seems to relax instantly. "Yeah, well, I work in a bar. Sometimes, the assholes get a little handsy."

His jaw ticks. "Unacceptable, Shayne. No one should touch you without your permission."

I smile at his insistence. "Thank you, and I do agree. All I'm saying is sometimes the alcohol causes them to do something they shouldn't. I can usually handle them, though. Or Jet," I reply, nodding at the man leading Connor and his posse toward the front door. "He's the owner. He'd never let anything happen to me."

Ford seems to relax even more and walks beside me back to his barstool. Chad is there, standing and watching the entire scene.

"Thanks for coming to my rescue," I tease my cousin.

He snorts. "Are you kidding? I barely knew what was happening before G.I. Joe jumped up and was over there. I knew you were in the most capable hands ever, so I wasn't too worried," he replies as he takes his seat.

Capable hands.

My mind flashes to all the places I'd love to feel those "capable hands" on my body.

A flush sweeps up my neck, but before either can ask about it, the bell rings in the kitchen. "Order's ready. I'll be back." I scurry off, away from the big man who makes my body heat with desire just with his mere presence.

Yes, I could definitely use a little distance from Ford.

Between those eyes and his no-nonsense attitude, he screams trouble. The type of trouble that could easily get a girl like me into a whole heap of it.

Again.

And trouble's the last thing I want or need.

No, the best thing I can do is stay away from Ford Gregory.

Chapter 3

Ford

SLIDING MY ASS BACK ONTO THE BARSTOOL, I FIGHT LIKE hell to appear unaffected. I don't want her to think I'm an asshole, but the minute I saw that prick's hand connect with her ass, red-hot anger ignited in my veins. I was on my feet and on my way to her before I could think better of it.

"I knew you were in the most capable hands ever, so I wasn't too worried," Chad says from his seat beside me.

Capable hands.

Flashes of what I could do to her with my hands filter through my mind. I shake my head, trying to jolt the thoughts, but it's no use. They're there, front and center like a fucking movie reel. My cock even agrees as it painfully presses against my zipper.

Never before have I seen a more beautiful woman. Not in a magazine or on TV, and certainly not standing before me with her long dirty-blonde hair and those striking blue-green eyes. I allow my gaze to travel over her slender neck and briefly stare at the V-neck of her shirt, showing off what I'm sure are the greatest set of tits in all the world.

"Order's ready. I'll be back," the beautiful Shayne says as she turns on her heel and scurries back to the kitchen.

"You all right there, man?" Chad asks. I don't have to look at him to know he's smirking. I can hear it in his voice.

Turning my head, I see that I'm right. "You didn't tell me Shayne was a *female* cousin." My voice sounds accusing even to my own ears. What I'm not saying is that he never told me his cousin Shayne is a fucking knockout. I'm also aware that this is the second time I've stated the fact and that I'm starting to sound like a broken record.

"Huh," he says, placing his bottle of beer to his lips. "Must have slipped my mind." I watch as he takes a healthy drink.

"You might as well let me have it," I say, taking a huge drink of my own beer. From the way he's talked about Shayne over the years, I know they're close. Now that I know Shayne's a girl, well, I'm sure I'm about to get the "she's family and off-limits" speech. Come to think of it, he's never given me that speech about Cassie either.

"What exactly am I giving you? Bro, you know I'm batting for the ladies' team, right?" He huffs out a laugh.

"Fuck off," I grumble.

"Here you go," Shayne says cheerily, setting a plate of wings in front of each of us. "Here are some extra napkins." She reaches under the bar and places a large stack in front of us. "Can I get you anything else?" Her eyes flash from me to Chad.

Your number.

"No. Thank you, Shayne. These look great."

Her smile grows at my compliment. It's funny how I want to beat on my chest and roar like a caveman from the smile I got out of her. I don't know what the fuck is wrong with me. Maybe it's being stateside for the first time in almost a year. Although, I've been gone the same amount of time in the past and never had this kind of reaction to a stranger.

Only she's not a stranger. Not really. I know she's worked here for two years and that she is close to Chad's immediate family. I know she spent more time at his place growing up than she did her own. I know she sticks to herself and that she means a lot to my buddy. I knew all those things about her when I thought *she* was a *he*. Her gender doesn't change that. What it changes is now I've met her, now I've laid eyes on her, I want to know more. I want every tiny morsel of information I can learn about her.

It's fucked up, and I don't understand why I feel this way. I just do.

"Here." Chad hands me a napkin.

"What's that for?" I ask, confused. I've yet to take a bite of my wings.

"The drool on your chin." He laughs.

"I blame you for that."

"Me? How in the hell do you blame me for you drooling over my cousin?"

"You could have warned me."

"She's just Shayne to me. Sure, she's beautiful, but I just see her as my cousin." He shrugs. "As far as Shayne goes, she's good people. The best. She's had a hard life. She was dealt a shit hand in the parent department. She's family...might as well be my sister. You're my best friend. I'd lay my life down for you, and I have not a single doubt in my mind that you'd do the same for me. If you're interested in her for more than just getting your dick wet, then go for it."

"Is she seeing anyone? I mean, how would that work? We're home just under two weeks. Fuck, I'm only here for a week," I ramble.

There are a million and one questions filtering through my mind. I know that starting something when we have to go back to base is a bad idea. While we're stateside and shouldn't be deployed again for a while, this is the army, and you never know when that's going to change. We could be called out tomorrow and have to go back. It's not fair to start something and leave her. That's what one side of my brain is saying. The other is telling me that I've never had a reaction to a woman like I have to Shayne, and I need to hold tight and never let go. My head is a fucked-up jumbled mess of what-ifs right now. Not to mention, I'm still thinking about what I could do to her with my hands.

"Nope. You're not getting any more intel from me, my friend. If you're interested in Shayne, you're going to have to work for it. She deserves that and so much more."

"Come on, man. You at least have to tell me if she's seeing someone."

"Who are we talking about?" Shayne asks, appearing in front of us. She opens a fresh bottle of beer, setting it in front of me, before doing the same for Chad. "I pretty much know everyone in this town."

"You," Chad tells her. "Ford here was just asking me if you were seeing anyone."

I watch her closely as her mouth forms an O, her jaw slackening, and her eyes widen. "Me?" She blinks a few times before closing her mouth and looking between Chad and me.

I open my mouth to say something, anything to redeem myself, but I can't seem to find the words. Instead, I sit here on the barstool looking like a damn fish, opening and closing my mouth over and over again.

"Damn, Shay, you've rendered my boy speechless." Chad claps a hand on my shoulder. "Ford here's interested in knowing more about you. I told him that my lips are sealed."

I turn to look at my best friend, shrugging his hand off my shoulder, and watch as he pretends to zip his lips and toss the key over his shoulder.

What are we, ten?

"Ford." Her sweet husky voice says my name, and my head turns back to face her, giving her all my attention. "Ask me," she says, tilting her head to the side. She's the epitome of calm, cool, and collected, all except for the towel in her hands that she's twisting over and over again. When she bites down on her bottom lip, I swallow back the groan that tries to escape. She's sexy as fuck, add in the lip bite, and she's downright irresistible.

Reaching for my bottle of Bud Light, I take a long pull before placing it back on the bar. My eyes lock on her blue-greens, and I'm lost in her. "Are you seeing anyone?" I manage to form the words to the question that's been eating at me.

"No." She shakes her head with her words, and her hands are still twisting that towel.

I nod. "I'm here for a week," I tell her. It's important that she knows that upfront. That I'm not here to stay. "I'm going home to Ohio to see my family next week." Maybe I can convince her to come with me? I mean, Chad's coming, so it's not like it would just be the two of us. I shake my head at the thought. I barely know this girl. Sure, I know of her and about her, but I don't *know* her, and I'm already thinking about taking her home with me. This tour really fucked with my head.

"Wh-What are your plans while you're here?"

"You tell me." I'm willing to do anything she wants just to spend time with her. I don't know why. I can't explain it, but I'm drawn to her, and I think she's worth getting to know. Maybe we can write when we go back to base and even when we deploy again. It's inevitable that it's going to happen. We just don't know where or when.

"I'm off in an hour." She glances at the clock. My eyes follow hers and see it's just a little past eight in the evening.

"My place or yours?" Chad asks, once again entering the conversation after throwing me under the bus. I'm beginning to wonder if I should trust him with my six after all.

"Uh, yours," Shayne replies with a flush to her cheeks.

"Everything good?" Chad asks her.

"Yeah. My place is just small, so yeah, yours is better."

"You know Mom and Dad would love to see you," he tells her.

"I just had dinner with them the other night." She smiles at Chad. He nods. "Good."

There's something there, something I'm missing. I know Chad said she had shit parents and that she was dealt a rough hand growing up. Is she safe?

No. Stop it, Gregory, I mentally chastise myself. Chad and his parents would never let her be in a situation where she wasn't safe. I'm just apparently losing my fucking mind over this girl.

"We'll just hang out here until your shift is over." Chad peers around the bar, and the crowd is already starting to thin compared to when we got here.

"All right, but no more of these if y'all are driving." Shayne points an index finger at each of our beers sitting in front of us on the bar.

"Yes, ma'am." Chad salutes her, making her laugh. I wish I could bottle the sound and carry it with me always. The sound of her laughter sure could brighten up the hot sandy desert we spend so much time in.

Over the next hour, Chad and I devour our wings and switch to water at Shayne's insistence. Chad tells me stories of him and Shayne and his sister, Cassie, growing up and the hell they used to raise. Apparently, when he was sixteen, he and Shayne, with Cassie in tow, dropped a round bale of hay in the center of their small town and set it on fire. How they didn't get hauled off to juvie for that one, I don't know.

"All set," Shayne says from behind us.

I turn to look over my shoulder and suck in a breath. Her hair that was pulled up is now down, hanging over her shoulders. It looks like it's silky soft with the way it flows down her back. I want to touch it. No, I need to. Unable to stop myself, I reach out and rub a piece of the silky strands between my thumb and index finger.

"So soft," I murmur. I hear her quick intake of breath as her eyes land on mine. I can't pull my eyes away from her. My breath stalls in my lungs as I allow myself to get lost in her gaze.

"Come on, Casanova," Chad jokes as he places his hands on my shoulders and guides me out of the bar.

"I'll follow you," Shayne tells him.

"Wait. Shouldn't we follow her? What if she breaks down?" I ask Chad, watching Shayne walk away. I don't tear my eyes off her until she reaches a silver older model Honda Accord and climbs inside.

"She's a big girl, Ford. Get in the truck," he orders. His tone is filled with humor. "Seriously," he says once we're in the cab of his truck. "Shayne has lived here all of her life."

I nod, forcing myself not to turn and gaze out the window to make sure she's behind us. Instead, I look into the side mirror, hoping Chad will think I'm taking in the sights.

"Enjoying the scenery?" he asks after we travel about halfway to his house in silence.

"Yep."

His laughter fills the cab of his truck. "It's dark out, Gregory," he points out. "You can't see shit."

He's right, and I know I'm busted. Running my hands over my face, I groan. "What the hell is wrong with me?"

"You've been hit by the bug."

"The bug? What do you mean, *the bug*?" I ask, thoroughly confused.

He slows down to turn on what I recognize is his road. He glances over while he waits for a car to pass. "The looovvee bug," he sings.

"Fuck off. I'm not in love with her."

"No?"

"No, but damn, man, she's gorgeous."

"Of course she is. She has Anthony blood running through her veins. What did you expect?"

"A man, for starters. Fuck, you should have told me what I was walking into."

"And what do you think you walked into?"

"A bar to meet your cousin, who just so happens to be the most beautiful thing I've ever laid eyes on. And while we're on the subject, why didn't you defend her?" I hate the thought of no one looking out for her. I would have thought that Chad would have had her back.

"Trust me. I was keeping an eye on the situation. I was ready to intervene, but you beat me to it. I trust you with my life, so in turn, I trusted you to take care of it. I was watching and listening if you needed me."

"I could have taken them with my eyes closed."

"That's my point. You were there. She didn't need me."

Did she need me? No, she didn't, but damn if the thought of her needing me doesn't have my heart beat an erratic flutter in my chest. It figures I finally meet someone I wouldn't mind getting to know better, and she lives a state away from my family, and I'm only home for two weeks. It's back to the base for us, and who knows where after that. That's not fair to her. Fuck, it's not fair to me.

For the first time since enlisting, I wish I was at a normal nine-to-five, just so I could have the chance to get to know her better.

I don't understand what's happening to me.

Chad pulls into the driveway and climbs out of his truck. He greets Shayne while I sit here, wiping my sweaty palms against my jeans and pull in deep, even breaths into my lungs. A knock sounds on the door, and I startle. Turning, I see Chad and Shayne standing, looking through the window at me. Luckily, it's dark. That's my only saving grace that neither of them can see me freaking out.

Why am I freaking out? Right, the beautiful woman who just smiled and waved at me through the window. Lifting the handle, I push open the door and climb out.

"You good?" Chad asks.

I can hear the concern in his voice. We've seen things that neither of us likes to talk about, but that simple question tells me he's making sure that it's not just my infatuation with his cousin that had me sitting in the truck like an antisocial loner. "Yeah, I'm good," I assure him. Funny, I haven't thought about our most recent deployment at all since I walked in and met the beautiful Shayne.

She's the perfect distraction.

Chad throws his arm over my shoulder and the other over Shayne's as we walk toward the house. He pushes open the door and enters, Shayne behind him and then me. I'm not going to deny the fact that I let my eyes roam over her. My cock twitches when I take in her ass in those jeans. Fuck, her in those jeans should be illegal.

I'm jolted out of my thoughts when I slam into the back of her. My hands immediately go to her hips to steady her. Is it just me or did she lean into my chest? "You all right?" I ask, my lips next to her ear.

"Y-Yeah, I'm fine."

"Damn, Ford, you just about mowed her over." Chad chuckles. He knows exactly what had me distracted if the glint in his eye is any indication.

"Sorry, Shayne," I say softly. My hands are still gripping her hips, and my hard cock is now pressing against her ass. I know I should release her, but I can't seem to get my hands on board with that plan.

"Shayne, what a nice surprise," Joan, Chad's mom, says as she enters the living room. "Are you kids hungry?" Her eyes flash to my hands on Shayne's hips, and reluctantly, I release Shayne. I miss her heat instantly.

"Nah, we had wings at Jet's," Chad answers.

"Speak for yourself," Shayne says, stepping next to Joan and giving her a hug.

"Well, you're in luck. I just so happened to pull two homemade peach pies out of the oven."

"Aunt Joan, you know I can't say no to your peach pie."

"You should have started with that, Mom," Chad says, moving toward the kitchen. "I'm always hungry for your peach pie."

I trail along behind the three of them. With my hands shoved into my pockets, I watch as Chad and Shayne take a seat at the island as they've done, I'm sure, countless times. I'm envious of all the time he's been able to spend with her.

"Ford?" Joan asks, holding up a plate with a huge slice of peach pie.

"Thank you." I nod and slide onto the empty barstool next to Shayne, who takes a bite of her pie and moans. I have to swallow hard to bite back a groan of my own, but it has nothing to do with the pie and everything to do with her.

This woman is going to be the death of me.

Chapter 4

Shayne

I'M COMPLETELY ENTHRALLED BY THEIR STORY. I'VE BEEN LISTENING to Chad and Ford carry on together around the campfire, sharing how they met in basic training and tales of mischief and comradery. They've pretty much monopolized the conversation since we moved from the kitchen to out here, but I haven't minded. In fact, I've discovered I really enjoy listening to Ford talk. There's just enough Ohio twang that I could hear him recite the owner's manual for my car and never get bored.

"I had to get really drunk to scrub the image of Hunt streaking naked through that field out of my mind," Chad says, a disgusted shiver sweeping through his entire body as he pulls a face.

I giggle quietly, only so I can soak up the sound of Ford's deep, hearty laugh. It sweeps through me like an ocean wave, calming and with just enough force to knock me on my ass if I'm not careful.

"Sorry, we've kinda monopolized the conversation," Ford says, taking a drink from his beer bottle. His eyes are like laser beams across the fire, direct and intense. I can feel them through the heat of the dancing flames, which only causes more warmth to flood between my legs. "So, tell me who that jackass was at the bar."

Sighing, I spin my empty bottle in my hands. Fortunately, I'm saved from having to answer right away because Chad jumps in.

"He's a douchebag. Connor Jorgeson. Thinks he owns this town and is above everyone in it. He was a prick back in school, and it appears he hasn't changed in the least."

"No, he definitely hasn't changed. His dad owns the big bank, which is how he got his job," I confirm, not sure how much Chad knew since he had been gone.

"He give you problems like that often?" Ford asks, his focus solely on me. There's something in his voice that surprises me. It's a touch of danger mixed with concern. I'd expect that response from Chad, but not from his friend. The one I've known for approximately four hours.

I shrug. "I can handle Connor."

Ford sits up straight in his Adirondack chair and meets my gaze. "There's not a doubt in my mind that you could handle him, but the point is, you shouldn't have to."

Again, I lift my shoulders. "He may be a dick, but he's harmless."

"No one should put their hands on you without your consent, Shayne." His words are soft yet sharp, as if it truly bothers him that Connor did what he did.

I give him a nod, suddenly unable to form words. There's something so powerful in the intensity of his eyes and the way he captivates my attention that leaves me a little speechless, which is crazy talk, because I'm *never* speechless.

"If you want, I can show you a few self-defense moves while I'm home," Chad chimes in, his stance relaxed in the chair, but I can see the tightness around his mouth from over here.

"I'll be fine, Chad, but thanks for the offer. Jet isn't going to allow anything to happen to me at work. Did I tell you he upgraded the security at the back of the building when I moved in?"

When I moved into the apartment above the bar that Jet once lived in, he made sure everything was in tip-top working order, and that included video security monitoring and an alarm system on the doors. He spared no expense in making sure I was safe and that no one could access the apartment without my permission.

"I know Jet's got your back, Shay. That's one of the main reasons I didn't pitch a fit when you started working there," Chad adds, earning an eye roll. Like he would have had any say over what job I took. The fact was I needed money, and bartending made that happen. The tips are good, and no one bothers me most of the time.

While Chad starts telling Ford all about getting up early in the morning and taking care of the farm, I lean back and just gaze at the stars. I've always loved watching the night sky, the clouds rolling in, the jet airstreams, the occasional falling star. There's something so peaceful and serene about it that has always called to me. Often as a child, I'd slip outside to escape the fighting between my mom and whatever boyfriend she brought home for the night. I'd go lie in the middle of the yard and just stare up at the stars, hoping and praying I'd see a falling one so I could make a wish.

I'd dream about freshly mowed green grass and carpet that wasn't covered in mold, pet, and food stains. In those dreams, there'd be a father and mother, both who would ask me about my day as we sat around the dinner table together. They'd tuck me into bed every night and occasionally steal a kiss or two before they left me to fall asleep under those glow-in-the-dark plastic stars. Never in my dreams would a drunk man stumble into my bedroom in the middle of the night and want to "lie with me" for a while. Mom would never beg me to ask for money from my aunt and uncle, making me promise it was "the last time" I had to tell a lie about what it was for. I'd never have to mow lawns for my neighbors and squirrel away the money just so I could make sure the gas was kept on so we had heat in the winter. In those dreams, I never fell in love with the charming man who promised me the world, only to find out it wasn't his to promise.

"Shay?"

I'm pulled from my thoughts and find two sets of eyes on me. "What?"

"I just asked if you needed anything from the house. I'm gonna run inside and grab us another round of beers," Chad says, watching me closely.

"Oh, no, I'm good. I'm done drinking. Thanks."

He nods but hesitates to move just a bit. I can tell he wants to interrogate me, but he thinks better of it. I'm grateful, because talking about my fucked-up past is the last thing I want to do right now, especially with Ford staring at me from across the fire.

When the screen door slams shut behind Chad, I gaze back up at the bright, starry night sky. "Don't you just love them?" I whisper to no one in particular.

"What's that?" Ford replies softly, and even though I don't look his way, I can feel his eyes on me like a caress.

"The stars. There's something so magical and soothing about them."

He doesn't reply right away, and I start to feel a little self-conscious. Probably because I sound like a silly girl talking about magic and all that bullshit. We all know magic doesn't exist. It's an illusion, a façade to hide behind.

"When we were overseas, I used to sit on the ground and watch the stars. It was the one thing connecting me to home halfway around the world. Even though I was sweating my balls off or was occasionally getting shot at, the stars kept me grounded. They linked me to the people thousands of miles away that I missed like crazy."

I glance his way, expecting to find him looking up too, but that's not where his gaze is locked. It's on me. "I'm sure it was hard to be so far away for so long."

Ford nods. "In the beginning, even though there was a hint of excitement at being in a new place, new orders, new job, it evaporated quickly when reality settled in. It helped I had guys like Chad to help pass the time. We worked together, but we became close, you know?"

My throat tightens with emotion. "I'm glad he had friends like you there. We all missed him like crazy, even though he drives us nuts most of the time," I reply with a grin.

He chuckles and sets his empty bottle down on the ground. "He drove me bonkers more times than not, but he helped keep me sane too."

"And I'm glad you had him as well. It helps to have friends."

He gives me a slow nod, his eyes dancing down my body like a touch. "Speaking of friends, how about we talk about those plans I don't have while I'm here?" He gives me a lazy smile, which feels like little shocks of electricity are coursing through my veins. What is it about his grin that's completely my undoing?

Before I can reply, Chad returns without beer. "Apparently, that last round was all we have. Probably for the best though, considering we're up before the sun tomorrow morning."

I glance at my phone and notice it's almost midnight. "Four a.m. is gonna suck," I tease, knowing I'll be sleeping in my own bed still while they're up making coffee and getting ready to muck stalls.

"Where do you think you're going? You've been drinking too," Chad states, nodding to the two empty beer bottles at my feet.

"That last one was more than an hour ago. I'm fine to drive home, Chad. I haven't had that much," I insist, gathering up my empties and placing them in the outdoor trash bin.

"Ain't happening, Shay. Don't make me wake up my mom."

My eyes narrow. "You wouldn't."

"Oh, I would if it meant you were safe and not out driving while buzzed."

I roll my eyes dramatically. "Fine, loser. I'll crash on the couch, even though I'm not buzzed."

"Not happening." This from Ford.

"But you're using Cassie's room." It's an assumption, but I know it's accurate. Where else would Ford be staying while he was here?

"I'll take the couch," Ford states pointedly, crossing his arms over his expansive chest.

"That's silly. Your stuff is already in her room," I insist.

"I'm not sleeping in a bed while you are on the couch, Shayne. Not happening," he stresses.

I glance at Chad, hoping he'll chime in and tell his friend he's being ridiculous, but all I get is a smirk. Throwing my hands up in the air, I move around them and head for the house. I make sure to be extra quiet as I slip inside. Even though my aunt and uncle are sleeping upstairs, I don't want to wake them.

The moment we're inside, Chad makes sure the door is secure and heads for the stairs. "I'll let you two fight it out," he adds with a huge grin before disappearing to the second floor.

"The couch is fine by me, really."

Ford's already shaking his head in disagreement. "Where do you normally sleep when you're here?" he asks, clearly looking to make a point.

"Well, usually with Cassie. She has a full-size bed," I answer with a shrug.

Another one of those panty-melting grins spreads across his handsome face. "Well, if you're used to sleeping with someone in that bed, who am I to argue with that."

That comment earns him an eye roll.

"Right, since we're not to that point in our relationship yet, we'll just have to go with my original idea. You take the bed and I'll take the couch."

First off, I ignore the way my heart kicked up a few beats by the use of the word *relationship* and focus on the facts. "You're way too tall for that couch, Ford. You'll be uncomfortable and miserable all night."

"I've slept in worse places," he mumbles softly, and something tells me he's not exaggerating. Ford sighs and steps forward, just touching the edge of my personal space. "Listen, Shayne, I won't be able to sleep upstairs in that bed knowing you're down here on the couch. Please. Just do this for me, okay? Besides, if I don't get a good night's sleep because I'm fretting about you down here, then I'm liable to hurt myself tomorrow milking a cow or something. I don't want to disappoint your uncle tomorrow with less-than-stellar cow milking skills."

I snicker, only because he's being completely ridiculous, and it's a little cute. Okay, really cute. "Fine, but when you wake up and need a chiropractor because of that couch, I don't want to hear one peep out of you."

He awards me the biggest grin like he just won the ultimate prize. "Come on, let me grab a few things from the room."

I follow him up to Cassie's childhood room and giggle as we step across the threshold. "What?" he asks.

"I'm just sorry I'm going to miss seeing you snuggled up under that pink and blue quilt," I tease.

Ford takes in the room. The yellow walls, the boy band posters, and the pink draped over everything. "Yeah, your cousin got a big chuckle when he brought me up here." And then his eyes darken just a little under the low lighting. "You know, if you're worried about not seeing me in that bed, the offer still stands to share."

I chuckle but shake my head. "You're impossible."

"Impossibly gorgeous, maybe? Sexy?"

"Arrogant?"

He snorts. "That too."

I watch as he heads to a duffle bag sitting on the floor. Ford digs in and pulls a folded T-shirt and pair of shorts out. "Here." He hands them to me. When I give him a questioning look, he adds, "So you have something to sleep in."

"Oh, I can just see what Cassie left here. If there are no pajamas, I can just sleep in my jeans and shirt. It's no problem."

He's not having it. "No way. That sounds uncomfortable as hell. Here," he insists, shoving the change of clothes into my hands.

"Fine."

He returns to his bag and grabs a small shaving bag, another shirt, and shorts. "You take the bathroom first."

I slip down the hallway, thankful Chad is done by the time I get there. "You all set?" he asks when I meet my cousin.

"Yeah, Ford let me borrow some clothes to sleep in," I state, holding up the items in my hand like a loser.

He gives me a big smirk. "Oh, I bet he did. I'm surprised he didn't volunteer to help you change into them… or out of 'em."

"Shut it," I mumble, stepping around him and flipping on the light switch.

"Hey, Shay?" When I turn around, he continues. "For what it's worth, Ford's a really good guy. Had some shit luck with women in the past—or one in particular—but he's a damn good guy. I'd trust him with my life. And yours."

"Why did you tell me that?" I ask, my throat suddenly Sahara-dry.

He shrugs. "Just thought you'd want to hear it from someone who spends hours upon hours with the guy in not-so-favorable circumstances."

I nod and close the door, not wanting to think too much about his statement. Yet, as I change into the too-big sleep shorts and the army T-shirt that smells like his now-familiar musk and sandalwood soap, I can't stop thinking about what he said. I also can't help but wonder what he meant by shit luck with a woman from his past. Ex-girlfriend, most likely.

I'm sure Ford is a great guy, but he's only here a week. The last thing I need to do is let myself get caught up in something that's only meant to be temporary. Yet, as I bring the soft material of the shirt to my nose and inhale, I can't help the sliver of anticipation and excitement that sneaks in like a thief in the night.

Maybe if the circumstances were different, I'd be more at liberty to explore this weird chemistry, the wild spark I feel when he's near. Unfortunately, that's not in the deck of cards for us. He's only here a week. No more. So it makes no sense getting caught up in something that has no future.

I grab one of the spare toothbrushes from the vanity drawer and a cloth to wash the makeup off my face. When I'm ready for bed, I take my clothes and quietly slip out the door, only to find Ford waiting, leaning against the wall. I open my mouth, but it shuts quickly when his eyes slowly peruse my body. Glancing down, I take in the oversized shirt and shorts and my bare legs. Thank God, I shaved this morning. I mean, not that he's going to feel them or anything, but at least I don't look like Sasquatch standing in my aunt and uncle's hallway, right in front of a gorgeous guy.

"That T-shirt's never looked so good," he whispers softly, his eyes burning with intensity as he finally draws them up to meet my gaze.

"Uh, thanks?"

He chuckles low at my weird comment turned question.

"Well, good night," I murmur, slipping by him and heading for Cassie's bedroom.

"Shayne?"

I stop and turn around, anticipation washing over me like a warm summer rain.

"I'll never forget the image of you wearing my shirt. Good night," he croons, his words as smooth as honey.

I bolt for the safety of my cousin's bedroom and quietly shut the door, cutting off the hottie and his charming words. The last time someone said all the right things to me, I wound up in a whole mess of trouble and was labeled the town whore.

Don't think about him *right now, Shayne.*

Instead, I slip into the safety of the bed, pulling the homemade quilt all the way up to my chin. Warmth spreads through my body, but it's not because of the blanket. No, it has everything to do with the softness wrapped around my abdomen. Ford's shirt. I can practically feel his body pulling me close and holding me tight.

I turn on my side, trying to get comfortable, but all I can think about is Ford. Maybe I should have invited him to sleep on the other half of the bed. It would be a hell of a lot more comfortable than the couch downstairs. But something tells me, if I did, it would be trouble. Trouble because I'd never have been able to keep my hands to myself, and I'd be praying his control was nonexistent, like mine.

I hear the door in the bathroom open and can picture him walking toward my doorway to head down to the living room. I glance at the crack at the bottom of the door just as the shadow falls on the hardwood floor and stops. Holding my breath, I wait to see what he does, my body humming with hope.

But as quickly as that shadow falls, it disappears, followed by the sound of Ford's heavy footfalls descending the stairs. A mix of sadness and relief sweeps in. Ford climbing into this bed has bad idea written all over it. I know it. It would never work, not past a handful of days.

I know that too.

Yet, he's the only one I think about as I slowly drift off to sleep.

Chapter 5

Ford

PULLING OPEN THE BATHROOM DOOR, I TAKE A FEW STEPS AND stop. I want to reach for the handle to see if it's locked, but I know I can't do that. Quickly, I force myself to keep moving as my feet carry me downstairs to the couch. Plopping down, I lean my head back and close my eyes. What is it about Shayne that has me all twisted in knots? She's beautiful, the most beautiful woman I've ever laid eyes on, but that still doesn't explain this…need I have to be around her. I was thinking about barging in on her while she was sleeping, for fuck's sake.

I wouldn't have done it. I would never invade a woman's privacy like that, but it took willpower to descend those stairs, knowing she was behind that closed door. It's not just the fact that she was in that room all alone. She's wearing my clothes. My. Clothes.

I will never, as long as I live, forget that image. It's burned into my mind, a memory to cherish.

Knowing I need to try and get some sleep, I stretch out on the couch. It's not uncomfortable, although I do wish it was a foot or so longer. Doesn't matter, though. It beats the cots and the sand I'm used to. Pulling the blanket over me, I shut my eyes, and all I see is her.

Shayne.

Damn. I've known her a matter of hours, and she's already causing me to lose sleep. Pushing her to the back of my mind, I let myself go into deployment mode. I frequently have trouble sleeping when deployed. I have to think about home, my parents, my sister, Faith, and the reason I'm there fighting, fighting for the freedoms of my family. My country. Thankfully, it works when on American soil as well, as I quickly drift off to sleep, dreaming of beautiful blue-green eyes.

I'm jolted awake by a loud clanking sound. Sitting up, I'm on high alert until I remember I'm not in the desert. I'm in Kentucky, at Chad's parents' place.

"I'm sorry," a feminine voice says softly from behind me. Turning to look over my shoulder, I see Shayne. She holds up a glass. "I was thirsty," she says, placing the glass back on the counter and turning the lid on the gallon of milk before putting it back in the refrigerator. "Wait, did you want some?" she asks.

Of you? Yes. "No thanks," I say instead.

"I'm sorry I woke you."

"You all right?" I ask.

"Yep," she says, popping the *p*.

Moving over to one side of the couch, I pile the blanket I was using on my lap and pat the cushion next to me. "Wanna sit?"

"I should let you get back to sleep."

"I'm up. You're up. Come sit." I pat the cushion again. I watch as she grabs her glass and heads my way.

"You sure?"

"Positive." That's all the reassurance she needs to take a seat. She doesn't sit on the cushion next to me. Instead, she sits with her back against the armrest, and her legs pulled up underneath of her. "What time is it?" I ask her.

"A little after two."

I've barely been asleep an hour. "Tell me something. Anything."

"What do you want to know?"

"You. I want to know you." The lighting is dim here in the living room. Just the small light over the stove from the kitchen is on. Thankfully this house has an open-floor plan, or we would be in complete darkness. Not that I mind the dark, but I'd prefer to be able to see her.

"Me?" she asks, surprised. "There's not much to tell."

"I find that hard to believe." Reaching over, I tap her knee, feeling her soft skin beneath my fingertips. "Come on, give me something."

"Fine, but you have to give me the same as I give you."

"Trust me, sweetheart, I'm a giver," I assure her.

"Fine. Favorite color is pink. And before you say something about me not being a girly girl, I know that, but it's feminine and soft, and I just love it." She shrugs.

"Pink is a good color." My mind instantly goes to parts of her body that I'm sure are a pretty pink that I'd like to explore.

"Your turn."

"I don't know, black or gray, I guess."

"Really?"

"Yeah. Black is slimming." I rub on my flat abs over my shirt, making her laugh.

"For real?"

"Yes." I chuckle softly. "Is that morbid?"

"No. Not at all." She shakes her head. "Okay, next, let's see…" She taps her index finger against her chin as she thinks. "Oh, I hate onions. Bleh." She pretends to gag.

"I'll pretty much eat anything," I tell her. And again, my mind detours to how much I'd like to eat her and all her pink sweetness.

"Your turn. You tell me something." She takes a sip of her milk.

"I'm twenty-one. Enlisted in the army right after graduation."

"A baby." She laughs. "I'm twenty-three, and I worked at the grocery store in town up until two years ago when I turned twenty-one and started at Jet's. I worked at the store all through high school, and it just made sense to stay. That is until life happened, and well, the tips at the bar help my bank account."

"I used to think I wanted to make a career out of the army. Now I'm not so sure."

"No? What changed?"

You. "I don't know, really. I've just been thinking a lot lately. When I enlisted, I signed-up for four-year active duty. I've been thinking about signing up for two more. However, I'll still have two years after that in the reserves. My overall contract was six years regardless."

"Yeah, Joan mentioned that Chad was thinking about the same."

I nod. "Yeah, we both talked a lot about it and we're both thinking two years sounds better than four."

"Having regrets?"

"No, but if I'm honest, I'm not sure I want to at all now having met you." I can see the shock written all over her pretty face.

"You barely know me."

"Yeah, but I want to know you, and that's going to be hard as hell to do when I'm living in the desert six to nine months out of the year."

"You chose the desert, right? Didn't y'all have to list three places you were willing to go or wanted to be stationed or whatever it's called?"

"Yeah, we did, and Chad and I had all three of the same locations listed. We've been lucky the last three years—from basic to our assignments, we've been together."

"You two are close." It's not a question as much as her making an observation.

"I trust him with my life."

"I'm glad he has you. I'm glad that you have each other," she says softly. "So you're stationed at Fort Campbell too?"

"Yeah. Luckily, it's not too far from home. My family can come and visit often when we're not deployed."

"I'm sure you miss them."

"I do. But they're used to it. My grandpa and my dad both served."

"A military family," she muses. "Wait, am I supposed to refer to you as a military brat?" she teases.

"Nah, not me. However, I have met more than my fair share. I get it, though. It's hard being away from your mom or dad and sometimes both. It's tough on a kid."

"You turned out okay," she observes.

"Yeah, I did. I had my twin sister Faith. We were best friends growing up. We had each other so moving around wasn't so bad. Sure it sucked, but it's all we knew."

"You have a twin?" There's awe in her voice.

"Yeah, she and I are close. Well, we used to be before I enlisted. I'd like to think that we still are."

"She didn't want to follow in the family footsteps?"

"She did, but she followed my mom. She's going to college to be a kindergarten teacher. She has one more year of college before she graduates."

"Bless her. I don't know if I could do that. Hell, I don't know if I could do what either of you do in your careers."

"You don't like kids?"

Why does the thought of her not liking and potentially wanting kids of her own bother me?

"I love them, but I don't know if I could handle a room full." She laughs.

"So, kids, you want them someday?"

"Yeah, I do. If I ever find that special someone."

"You been looking?"

"No." Her answer is flat. "No. I've not been looking. I've kind of sworn off relationships."

"Kinda hard to have a baby when you've done that," I tease.

"Yeah, well, I need to be stable, and working at a bar isn't really what I would call stable. Not really. Sure, I'm gainfully employed, but I don't want to be working nights when my family is at home without me. The same goes for weekends. I want to be an active parent. I don't plan to have kids until I know that I can do just that." There's conviction in her voice that tells me there's a story there. A story I want to hear, but I don't want to pry either. "I'm working on me."

You're perfect. "Makes sense. However, if you wait for everything to be perfect, life might pass you by." I grew up hearing my mom tell me that very thing.

"Maybe."

She's starting to close up on me, and I don't want that. "I like all genres of music." I go back to our tit-for-tat discussion that we seemed to have gotten away from.

"Me too." She smiles. I wish the room had more light so I could see those eyes of hers sparkle. Then again, this is intimate, and I like that we're sitting here in pretty much a dark living room, swapping facts about one another.

I watch her as she opens her mouth to say something else but quickly closes it. "I should be getting back to bed. Unless you want me to take the couch?" she offers.

"I'm good here," I tell her. I try hard not to let disappointment show in my voice. I could sit and talk to her for hours.

"Okay. Well, I'm sorry I woke you. I know you're getting up early with Chad to work the farm."

"I'll be fine. I've gone with less sleep. Besides, I would have gone without any at all to talk to you."

She stands and takes her glass to the kitchen. I hear the faucet turn on and off and then her soft footfalls. "Goodnight, Ford."

"Night, Shayne." I keep my eyes on her until I can no longer see her. Then I stare a little longer, wishing, hoping, willing her to change her mind and come back downstairs to spend time with me. It doesn't happen, not that I really thought it would. What also doesn't happen is sleep.

Lying back down on the couch, I pull the cover over me and close my eyes. I can't think of anything but Shayne as I replay our conversation and commit it to memory. I try my deployment trick, but it's useless. She's all I can think about. She's what I'm still thinking about at four thirty when Chad makes his way groggily down the stairs.

"Morning, sunshine," I say, scaring the shit out of him. He jumps a good two feet in the air before cursing.

"What the fuck, Ford? Why are you awake?"

"Something about cows that need milking." He shakes his head and drags his tired ass to the kitchen. Standing, I fold the blanket and place it neatly over the pillow that I used and place them on the center of the couch.

"Seriously, how are you this alert?"

"How are you not?" I counter. With our jobs, we're used to lack of sleep and being up at odd hours.

"I might have drunk more than I thought," he admits, as he starts the coffee pot.

"Morning, boys," Joan says, entering the kitchen. "How's bacon and eggs for breakfast?"

"Perfect," I tell her. "Can I help?"

"No, I've got it."

"So, when is Cass coming home?" Chad asks his mom.

"She had a final yesterday. She's leaving this morning and will be home later today."

"How is she?" he asks.

"Good. She loves her classes. She's living her best life. Isn't that what you kids say these days?"

Chad and I both chuckle. "Yeah, something like that," he says, placing his coffee cup under the stream unable, or maybe unwilling to wait until the machine is finished doing its thing.

"She's going to be a teacher, right? My mom and sister both teach kindergarten," I add to the conversation.

"She is. An art teacher. She's not sure what grade, but I think she's leaning toward elementary and middle school." Joan starts cracking what looks like fresh eggs into a large glass bowl. "She was disappointed that she couldn't make it home yesterday."

"That's all right, Shayne entertained us," Chad replies.

"Wait, is there anything else you're not telling? Cassie is a girl, right?" I ask him. I'm teasing. I've seen pictures of Cassie, she's beautiful too, but her cousin, Shayne, she takes my breath away.

"No." Chad laughs.

"What did I miss?" Joan asks, placing bacon in the pan.

"Oh, you know. Nothing much. Ford, here, assumed that Shayne was a guy."

"How was I supposed to know. It was my cousin Shayne this, my cousin Shayne that. You never mentioned a gender, and I'd never seen any pictures," I defend myself. Joan is grinning wide, so I know my lack of knowledge about her niece is amusing her.

"What's so funny?" Henry asks, entering the room.

"Tell him," Joan sputters with laughter.

Chad explains, and Henry's smile tells me he's also amused. "So, you were shocked?" Joan asks.

"He was more than shocked. He was knocked on his ass, Mom. I swear my boy here got cartoon eyes when he saw her."

"Chad," Joan chides him. "Leave him alone."

"He's not wrong." I shrug.

"She's not had it easy," Henry tells me. It almost seems like a warning.

I nod. "That's what I've heard."

"Enough about Shayne. Ford, grab yourself a cup of coffee. We have juice and milk in the fridge."

"Glasses are in the cabinet next to the fridge." Chad points to the cabinet.

"Thanks."

The next twenty minutes are spent talking about the farm and how things are going. I sit back and listen, chiming in where I can. I don't know much about farming. I grew up in the country, but milking cows is not something I can say I'm proficient in.

"You ready?" Henry asks.

"As I'll ever be," I tell him. I take my plate to the sink with the intention of washing it.

"I've got that. You go on. Thanks for your help today." Joan pats me on the shoulder.

"Thank you for having me. I'm happy to help." It's the truth. Going home to an empty house after being deployed for nine months didn't sound like a good time. My parents offered to change their trip, but I told them not to. Chad offered me to come home with him, and Mom and Dad have talked about coming to base for a week after we settle back in.

"You're welcome here anytime," she assures me.

With a smile and a nod, I rush out the back door to get this day started.

Four hours later, after having violated the herd of cattle, fed the chickens, collected the eggs, fed the cows, and mucked the horse stalls, I'm exhausted. It has nothing to do with the work. Although challenging at times, it's my lack of sleep that has my ass dragging back into the house.

"How did it go?" Joan asks.

"He did good," Henry says, slapping me on the shoulder as he goes to kiss his wife.

"Ford, honey, you look exhausted. Why don't you go shower and lie down before lunch?"

"I'm good. I won't sleep tonight," I tell her.

"Well, tonight, you'll be in Cassie's room. I didn't realize Shayne stayed over until she came down this morning, not long after you all went out to work."

"Where is Cass going to be?" Chad asks.

"She's going to stay with Shayne. She usually splits her time between here and there when she's home from school."

"I don't want to put her out. The couch is fine." *Or I can stay at Shayne's.*

"Oh, you're not." Joan waves a hand in the air. "This is what they do. Those two are close."

"She doing okay? Shayne, I mean?" Chad asks. "Connor was at the bar last night. He was giving her a hard time, that is until Ford stepped in."

"Yeah, she's good. That boy." Joan shakes her head.

"He's caused her enough trouble. Thanks for stepping in, Ford." Henry turns his gaze to Chad. "Where were you?"

"I was right beside him, but this guy"—he points at me—"was on his feet and taking care of the situation before I had the chance to. I knew he had it under control."

"What's the deal with him anyway?" I ask.

Henry shakes his head. "Her story to tell, son. Connor, though, he's always coming into the bar and harassing her."

"I'll talk to him," I blurt without thinking.

"You do know that if you get busted fighting, shit's going to hit the fan, right?" Chad asks.

I run my hand over my buzzcut and sigh. I know he's right, but the thought of this guy constantly giving her shit pisses me the hell off. "What about when we're not here?"

"Jet looks out for her," Henry assures me. "I made sure he knew."

"Thought it was her story to tell?" I mouth off before I can think better of it. "I'm sorry. I just…" My voice trails off.

"He's all up in his feelings for Shay." Chad laughs.

"It is her story, Ford. However, I needed to know that she was going to be okay working there. Jet lives in this town. Jet knew the gist of it. I just filled in a few blanks, clarified a few things."

"My sister, Shayne's mom, she wasn't a good mother. We've tried to take care of Shayne as much as we could. She spent a lot of time here when growing up. Now, she's determined to make it on her own. To build a better life for herself," Joan says softly.

Our conversation last night comes to mind. She's not sure she's ready for a family. She's working on her. That must be what she meant. I'm glad Henry and Joan are there for her. It sounds like they're all she has.

That knowledge sits in my stomach like sour milk. I can't explain it, but I want to be there for her. Only, I'm leaving in a few days and then going back to base. I'm not who she needs, no matter how badly I want to be.

Chapter 6

Shayne

I JUST GOT OUT OF THE SHOWER AND WRAPPED A TOWEL AROUND my body when I hear the knock on the door. I grin from ear to ear and race to answer, not even caring I'm dripping water from my hair, and my feet are still wet. The moment I throw the lock and pull open the door, my cousin flies through the entrance and slams against my body.

"Shay!" Cassie squeals in my ear, all arms and legs as she plasters herself against me, and I struggle to hold up my towel.

"Let me shut the door," I say, reaching around her and securing the lock. "I'm so glad you're here."

"Me too," she beams. At nineteen, Cassie is a younger, more feminine version of her brother. Her long, dark hair is pulled up in a messy bun, and her hazel eyes shine with a youthful excitement I never experienced. The world is her oyster, ripe for the taking.

By her age, I was jaded, working full-time at the local grocery store and trying to avoid my mom. She'd beg to borrow money, insisting she'd

BENEATH THE FALLEN STARS

pay me back the next week. Only, I knew that'd never happen. She never paid me back and didn't seem to care. The money was already spent before it even changed hands, most likely on something I didn't want to know about. I'd blissfully tell myself it was for rent or the electric bill, but I was naïve like that at times.

"Let me run and throw on some clothes," I tell her, leaving her standing in the kitchen-and living-room combination.

I move to the only bedroom in the apartment. Basically, this place is three rooms, the third being a small bathroom. But it's home and works for me.

After throwing on a pair of skinny jeans and a fitted tee with Jet's logo on the chest, I head back to where I left my cousin.

"So, rumor has it, you have a thing for the hottie sleeping in my bed," Cass sings the moment I step into the room.

"What? Who told you that?" I ask, trying to divert attention.

"Chad. You know he's like a teenage girl when it comes to gossip," she replies, her laser-focused eyes zeroed in on me. "So? Tell me about him," she adds with a grin.

I roll my eyes and plop down on the old striped couch beside her, finger-combing my wet hair. "What's to tell? He's a friend of Chad's, and he's visiting for a week. End of story." I make sure to keep my focus elsewhere, so she can't see the lies. Cassie, while four years younger than me, has always been able to read me like a book.

"Right," she hums, clearly not believing my story for a second. "I heard he wants to ask you out."

After a few long seconds, I turn in my seat and face my cousin. "He did say that, but I don't know, Cass. He doesn't live here. It would be, like, six days, and he'd be gone."

She studies me for a few moments. "Okay, I see your point, but that really doesn't mean anything. The way I see it, you have two options. You can go on a date, maybe even steal a goodnight kiss. Have some fun with him while he's here, and then say goodbye at the end of the week. Or, if you really like him, you can date long distance. I know it's not ideal, but you could make it work," she suggests.

I snort out a laugh. "You make it sound so easy."

She shrugs. "Well, it doesn't have to be hard. I mean, he's leaving next Wednesday to go home for a week, right? Chad's going with him. Then they're returning to base. Hang out with him while he's here. Get to know him. Let him buy you a few dinners, maybe even get naked once or twice, and then bid him goodbye with the memory of how amazing he was in bed."

My eyes are as wide as hubcaps. "Cassie!" I giggle.

"What?" she asks. "I met him earlier at the house. Something tells me that boy would kill it between the sheets."

"Oh my God," I mumble through my laughter.

"I'm serious. He was helping toss hay bales from the loft. Shirtless."

That catches my attention.

This morning I saw him from the stairs before he left to help with chores, and he was very much still clothed from the waist up. Even then, Ford was looking edible. I'm kinda glad I ran off before I caught sight of the shirt coming off. No way would I have been able to form coherent sentences with him not wearing one, the hot sun glistening off his sweaty abs.

"You're picturing it, aren't you? You just licked your lips like a hussy in heat."

"Cassie!" I bellow, once again, laughing. "God, I missed you," I add, throwing my arm over her shoulder.

"Me too," she replies, hugging me close. "But in all seriousness, I think he really likes you. He wouldn't stop asking questions about you."

I sigh and lean my head back against the couch. "We don't even know each other though."

"Well, I'm no expert, but I think this is how you get to know each other. It's this brand-new thing called *dating*."

"You're such a smartass," I grumble.

"So I've heard. Anyway, my point is, maybe let him take you to dinner. You know, Sunday night, when you're off work. You guys can go to that little Mexican joint you love so much."

I slowly turn to face her. "What did you do?"

She shrugs. "Nothing!" she insists, her eyes dancing with all the lies she's telling. "Okay, so maybe I mentioned to him that you're off on Sundays."

Groaning, I slam my head back against the cushion. "Seriously, Cass? You're meddling?"

She smiles. "Of course I am. I'm worried about your vagina. It hasn't come face-to-face with a penis since you-know-who, and we don't talk about him."

My wide eyes just stare at her. "How do you even know anything about the state of my vagina? Wait, don't answer that," I state, getting up and moving to the kitchen for a glass of water.

"*Because* you locked up the vajayjay with that chastity belt the moment Douche Canoe left town, and it's not fair to you or your vag. You've given him too much control, even after it happened a year ago."

I greedily suck in a deep breath, which comes out shallow and slightly labored. It always does when I think about Rodney and what he did.

"All I'm saying is it wouldn't hurt you to go out with Ford. He's cute, built like a tank, and makes ice cream melt when he smiles. And, he's only here for a little bit. How much harm could it cause?" she asks, standing across from me at the counter.

A lot, actually.

Unless I go into this knowing exactly what it is. A temporary fling. A way to pass time. I'm sure that's all I'll be to him anyway. It's not like we could form a lasting bond or relationship in just a few days, right?

"I see your point, Cass, and I promise I'll think about it. Now, what's going on with you? Are you still seeing what's-his-name?" I ask, finishing my water.

"Palmer? Ugh," she grumbles, shaking her head. "What a dick. Turns out, he was just trying to get close to my roommate, Pepper."

"Seriously?"

"Yep. When I found him going through her panty drawer, I called him on his bullshit. He told me he was more interested in her than me," she informs, a flash of sadness crossing her features.

"I'm sorry, sweetie."

Cassie shrugs. "It's fine. I left him with a little something to remember me by anyway, so it's not likely he'll be forgetting about me anytime soon." The smile she gives is victorious.

Grinning, I can't help but ask, "What did you do?"

"You mean after I kicked him in the balls? He made the mistake of telling me where his spare key was hidden, so I snuck in and put laundry detergent down his pipes. Every time he flushes or takes a shower, he gets a nice sudsy surprise."

I bark out a laugh. "You're evil. I love it."

"And I love you," she replies before sobering. "I want you to be happy. You know that, right?"

I nod, a golf ball of emotion suddenly forming in my throat.

"Then, I think you should go out with him. Maybe you find out he's a pretty picture but doesn't play with a full deck of cards, if you know what I mean, or maybe you guys really click. Anything's possible, but I think you owe it to yourself to find out. Your dusty ol' vagina will thank you."

The bark of laughter spilling from my mouth is light and easy, and I pull her into a hug. "I've missed you."

"I've missed you too. Now, go dry your hair and get ready for work. I'm gonna hang out downstairs for a while tonight."

Cassie has come to the bar several times, but Jet always makes her leave before ten. That's when the place gets busier and slightly rowdier too, and he doesn't want to worry about someone messing with her. She'll hang out at the end of the bar, have dinner, and keep me company until she comes upstairs and waits for me to get off work. Even though we close at one on Friday and Saturday nights, I know she'll be wide awake and waiting on me.

She always does.

That's what best friends are for, even if they come in the form of nineteen-year-old cousins. She's got my back, and I hers.

"Hey, Shayne!" someone hollers from the opposite end of the bar. "Can I get two Bud Lights when you get a moment?"

"Sure thing!" I yell back over the George Strait song pumping through the speakers. As soon as I finish the screwdriver and collect the customer's four bucks, I grab two bottles of beer from the cooler, pop the tops, and slide them across the bar. "Six dollars."

Jet checks on me before heading over to shoot a game of pool with one of his regulars, and I make a quick trip to the opposite end of the bar to where Cassie sits, eating a half-dozen honey barbecue wings and fries. "I've missed these," she coos, licking sauce from her fingers. "Those national wing places have nothing on these puppies."

I give her a smile as the front door opens. Goose bumps prickle my skin as awareness courses through my body.

"Hey, little sis," Chad greets, sliding onto the stool beside Cassie and reaching for one of her fries.

"Hey! Get your own!" she hollers, moving her plate farther away from his greedy fingers.

"We just ate dinner with Mom and Dad," he states, leaning over her and snatching a few fries, quickly shoving them in his mouth before she can stop him.

"Hi."

I turn away from my bickering relatives, my gaze slamming into soulful green eyes. "Hi," I squeak, my throat dry.

Ford gives me a small smile as he slides onto the third stool. I have a few seconds to take in his appearance. Tonight, he's wearing dark jeans and a snug black T-shirt with an American flag on the front. Underneath it, the words *I'll defend with my last breath* is printed, along with the website for veteran's awareness. His hair is cut short, and even from across the bar, I can smell fresh shampoo and soap. The combination of appearance and scent makes my lady parts stand up and take notice.

"What can I get you?" I ask, leaning forward just slightly to catch another whiff.

"I'll take a Bud Light," he answers, pulling his wallet out of his jeans and grabbing a few bills.

"Miller Lite," Chad chimes in, though I already have his beer out of the cooler and opened.

They visit at one end of the bar while I continually make my way from one end to the other. We're not super busy yet, but I know it's coming. It's only eight, which means this is the calm before the storm.

"Come on, Ford, let's go shoot a game. Cassie, you can play the winner," Chad says the moment she finishes her dinner and pushes her plate away.

I grab the dirty dish and slip it into the bin before refilling her Pepsi and getting two cold beers.

"Let's go," Chad says, hitting Ford in the arm before heading over to where the billiard tables sit.

Ford doesn't make a move to follow, and after a few minutes, he leans forward and catches my gaze. "So, I was thinking..."

I position my forearms on the bar and get closer so I can hear. "About?"

"You. I heard you have Sundays off and was thinking you might want to have dinner with me."

I try to fight the grin from spreading across my lips. I know this has bad idea written all over it with a Sharpie marker, but that doesn't stop me from smiling. "Yeah? Cassie told you I like Mexican, right?" I ask, watching as a blush creeps up his neck, confirming her earlier comment about them talking about me.

He shrugs and takes a drink of his beer. "She might have mentioned it."

"Did she also mention I don't date?"

He sobers and leans forward even more, the warmth of his breath kissing my cheek as he whispers, "She did mention that, yes, but I thought maybe you'd take pity on me, since I've been overseas for the last nine months, fighting for our country."

I bark out a laugh, ignoring everyone and everything around me. All I can see, all I can hear, is him. Everything else is just... nothing. "Pulling out all the big guns, I see."

He shrugs and gives me a panty-melting smirk. "What can I say? I'm desperate to spend time with you."

"Hey, Shayne, can I get a round of drinks?" someone yells, catching my attention.

I nod but keep my focus on sexy green eyes.

"Come on, Shayne. One date."

This is where I should let him down gently, tell him I'm just not interested, but that would be a nose-grower, and to be honest, that lie isn't very easy to get out. The truth is, I really want to go. I'm attracted to him, yes, but it's more than that. He's as easy to chat with as he is on the eyes. Plus, I just feel this giddy exhilaration every time I'm near him.

That's why I end up answering with "One date."

I'm rewarded with a delighted grin, one that causes my heart to do a happy little jig and warmth to pool between my legs.

"Ford, come on! You're up!" Chad bellows from the doorway, catching my attention.

"I'll let you get back to work," Ford says, grabbing his beer from the bar. "I'll be back later so we can plan our date."

With a wink, he slides off the stool and heads over to where my cousin is standing and smirking. My eyes automatically drop to take in the way his ass fills out those dark jeans. Hard and mouthwatering, that's the only way to describe his backside. I bet you could bounce quarters off that thing all night long.

When he stops, I glance up, straight into dancing green eyes. My heart hammers in my chest as embarrassment creeps up my neck. I was totally just busted ogling his ass.

Kill me now.

Ford winks and turns, disappearing into the other room.

"Jesus, girl. Get a grip," I mumble to myself as I push off the bar and make my way down to fill orders.

I don't know if I made the right decision accepting his invite or not, but I'm surprisingly very excited about Sunday. Even if it doesn't go well with Ford, I know Cassie's correct. It's time to stop giving Rodney any more power over me. He might have fucked me over, but that doesn't mean everyone will do the same, right?

I glance up and catch Ford walking around one of the tables, cue in hand. He gauges the table, takes his position, and lines up his shot, jeans stretched across his firm ass. My mouth goes dry once more as images I have no business thinking about parade through my mind like the opening scene of an adult movie.

Just as he pulls back to shoot, he glances over his shoulder, meeting my gaze. I can feel the electricity all the way through the room. It's full of desire and promises of naughty things behind closed doors. I watch as he gently swings forward, his stick hitting the cue ball, sending it flying into the stripe across the table. He doesn't even watch his shot. No, those green eyes are on me.

Chad steps over and slaps him on the shoulder, finally grabbing his attention. It's then he turns, noticing he sunk the nine ball as easily as if he were actually watching his shot. He turns back my way and gives me a smile. It's cocky, but do you know what?

I like it.

I'm in way over my head with this one.

Chapter 7

Ford

I'M NERVOUS. I'M NEVER NERVOUS. I'M IN THE ARMY. I FIGHT THE bad guys. I've been on three deployments in three years and have seen things that I never want to remember. However, as I pull Joan's Toyota Camry into the back of the bar Shayne lives above, I feel like I'm going to be sick. Parking, I turn off the engine and wipe my sweaty palms on my jeans.

What is it about Shayne that has me reacting this way?

When she agreed to tonight's date on Friday, I wanted to lean over the bar and kiss her. I wanted every man, hell, every woman in that bar to know she was mine. But she's not mine. Not really. Sure, she agreed to a date. One date, as she specifically stated. I'm leaving next week. In just a matter of days, I'll be back in Ohio with my family, and she'll be here.

Without me.

The thought has kept me up for the past two nights. I've barely slept, but I'm not tired. Oddly, I'm wide awake and more excited than any man should be to be spending time with a woman. I don't understand this side of me, it's new, and I have to admit, when her mesmerizing eyes are locked on mine, I can't find it in me to care. Instead, I just want more of her. She's all I can think about, hence the past two nights without sleep.

Pulling in a deep breath, I grab the keys and the flowers lying on the passenger seat and climb out of Joan's car. I feel like a giant driving this thing, but that's okay. It brought me to Shayne and is giving me time with her, just the two of us. It could have been the tiniest car on the planet, and I would have driven it with glee.

Approaching the building, I notice that it's clean, although run-down. When I go to open the door, it's locked. There is a speaker on the side with only one button. I press it, waiting for her to answer. "Hello," her sweet voice comes over the speaker.

"Hey, Shayne. It's me. Ford."

"I'll be right down."

"I can come up," I offer. I stare down at the flowers. Call me crazy, but I feel like I need to knock on her door and hand her these flowers.

"It's okay."

"I have something for you," I confess into the speaker.

"Uh, okay." The door buzzes, and when I reach for it, I find it un-locked. Her apartment is on the second floor, and the stairs to lead me there is the first thing I see when I enter. There is another door that has *private* spelled out in all capital letters. From the sound coming from there, it's the kitchen of the bar. Needing to see Shayne, I take the stairs two at a time. My intent is that the exertion will help calm my nerves.

It doesn't.

Standing outside her door, I wipe one hand on my jeans, trans-fer the flowers and wipe the other the same way. Then I raise my hand to knock. The door immediately pulls open, and I can't fight the smile that crosses my face. One, her quick answer to the door tells me she was waiting for me. The second reason, that's all Shayne and her beauty. She stands before me in a flowing top that has one shoulder bare. She's in a pair of tight jeans, ripped at the knee, and her feet are in these black boots that stop at her ankles. They look uncomfortable as fuck with that heel, but they're sexy. My eyes roam back over her, and I reach her face. She's biting on her bottom lip. Reaching out, I tug it free with my thumb.

"You're gorgeous."

A blush coats her cheeks. "Thank you. You said Mexican, and it's casual, so…" Her voice trails off.

"You're perfect." My words hold double meaning. Her outfit is perfect, but she's also perfect for me. Don't ask me how I know. It's this feeling deep in my gut.

"Nice flowers." She nods toward my hands.

"These?" I hold them up, and she nods again. "I thought so too, but now that I'm standing before you, they pale in comparison." She swallows hard. "These are for you." I hand them to her.

She takes them eagerly, pulling them to her face and breathing them in. "I need to put them in some water." She backs up and waits, which tells me I'm being invited inside.

Her apartment is small but clean. Her furniture has seen better days, and that makes me think of how Chad told me that she's had a rough life. The thought of her being hurt or upset bothers me.

"It's not much, but it's home," she says, wrapping her arms around herself. Glancing up at her, I see that the flowers now sit on her small kitchen table.

"It's cozy."

"Maybe this was a bad idea," she starts.

"What are you talking about?"

"Obviously, my place isn't good enough for you." The set of her chin is defiant.

"Shayne, what are you talking about?" I don't move even though I want to pull her into my arms and tell her she's lost her damn mind. What happened from the time she went to the kitchen to place the flowers in water and now?

"The look on your face. You're scowling. I knew this was a bad idea." I cannot only see but feel her walls going up.

Not happening, gorgeous.

In three long strides, I'm standing toe-to-toe with her. My hands cradle either side of her face, and her eyes close. "Look at me." My voice is soft and soothing. When her eyes don't open, I try again. "Let me see those beautiful eyes," I whisper. Slowly, her eyes flutter open, and they're swimming with tears. "The look on my face has nothing to do with where you live. I was thinking about you, though."

"See." She tries to pull away. I drop my hands and crush her to my chest. My hug is fierce, and eventually, she gives in, relaxing into my hold. "I was thinking about how you've not had the best breaks in life. The mere thought of you being hurt or upset guts me."

"You don't even know me."

"I know that." I rest my chin on top of her head. "I feel like I do, though. I know it sounds crazy, even to me." We stand in silence as I hold her. I would be content to stand here just like this the rest of the night. However, I promised her dinner at her favorite place, and I don't want to be another let down in her life. So, reluctantly, I loosen my hold and peer down at her. "You ready for some Mexican?"

"You still want to go?"

"Do I still want to spend the evening with the most gorgeous woman I've ever laid eyes on? Yes."

She smiles. "You don't have to suck up to me. I already agreed to the date."

"I'm not sucking up. I'm telling you the truth. I've been looking forward to tonight. No way are we not going."

"Me too," she agrees, a soft smile playing on her lips.

"Do you have what you need?"

She pulls out of my arms, and moves around the kitchen placing her flowers in water. She then grabs her purse, and opens it. "Phone, keys, wallet," she says softly to herself. "Ready." She looks up at me.

I offer her my hand, and she hesitates but places hers in mine. I lead her out of her apartment, stopping so she can ensure the door is locked before we descend the stairs.

"Have you lived here long?" I ask, making small talk.

"About two years." She pauses. "It was all I could afford at the time, and I slept on an air mattress for over a year." We reach Joan's car, and I open the door for her. "Thank you," she says, ducking into the car. I wait until she's buckled in to close the door and rush to the other side. "It was the better alternative to where I was living."

"Your mom?"

"More like egg donor," she mumbles.

"I'm sorry. I can't even imagine what that was like for you."

She shrugs. "I got out. I worked as many shifts as I could at the grocery store. The minute I turned twenty-one, I knocked on Jet's door, and he took a chance on me. I make more money per hour slinging drinks, and the tips are good. They're almost double my income some nights."

"That's awesome." I glance over to see her nod.

"I'm saving it. You never know what could happen. I never want to be dependent on someone else to take care of me ever again."

There is conviction in her voice that not only tells me she's determined, but she's strong as hell. She could have let her upbringing pull her down. She could follow in her mother's footsteps, but she wants more out of life. I admire her for that. It couldn't have been easy.

"Joan and Henry did what they could. Mom would clean her act up long enough for me to not get taken away. She needed the check that state sent her."

"You're lucky to have them."

"Yeah. Chad and Cassie are more like my siblings. I spent a lot of time there growing up. Mom would disappear with her latest fling, and Aunt Joan would find out and have me stay with them. I'm sorry I'm dumping all of this on you. I'm sure this isn't first-date material."

"Honestly, you could be talking about the weather, and I'd gladly listen. I like the sound of your voice." I glance over to find her watching me.

"You're unlike anyone I've ever met."

"Is that a good thing or a bad thing?" I keep my eyes on the road, but I would love nothing more than to be able to watch her as she answers me.

"I'm not sure yet."

"You let me know when you do," I say as I pull into the parking lot of the Mexican restaurant. I turn to smile at her. "Ready?"

"Definitely." She reaches for the handle and is out of the car before I can tell her to wait so that I can open the door for her. "I hope you're not one of those guys who is grossed out when their dates actually eat."

"Why's that?" I ask, reaching around her to pull open the door.

"Because this is my favorite place. I don't indulge in it much, and I intend to do that tonight."

Her words have my cock swelling behind my zipper. She's confident yet guarded, and I want to tear down those walls. "I'd be disappointed if you didn't," I say softly, my lips next to her ear. "Two, please," I tell the hostess. With my hand on the small of her back, I follow them both to our table.

"I don't think I can walk. You're going to have to carry me." Shayne's head is resting against the seat as she turns to look at me.

We spent almost three hours in the restaurant, just talking and laughing. Just like she assured me that she would, she ate everything on her plate, and I enjoyed every minute of watching her. Now we're sitting in the parking lot of her building. I'm not ready for our night to end, but I don't know this town well enough to offer her something else we could do. Obviously, I suck at planning dates. I was so excited she said yes, and was determined to take Shayne to her favorite place. Everything else just fell to the wayside.

"I can carry you."

"What? I was kidding. You'd break your back."

"You are aware that I'm in the army, right? The pack I have to carry probably weighs more than you do."

"Really?" she asks, eyes wide.

"Yes." Grabbing the keys, I climb out of the car and make it to her door before she has a chance to climb out. Pulling open the door, I offer her my hand. As soon as she closes the door, I scoop her up in my arms.

"Ford!" she shrieks. "What are you doing? Put me down." She laughs.

I pretend to lose my grip, and she tightens her arms around my neck. "You smell good," I say once we're inside and making our way upstairs.

"I can walk." She makes no move to release her hold on me. Good, because I like the feel of her in my arms.

"I can carry you."

When we reach the top of the stairs, I stop in front of her door. Reluctantly, I place her on her feet.

"Thank you."

"For what?"

"Dinner, the company, the lift to my apartment." Her eyes are bright, and they appear to be more blue than green at the moment.

"You're welcome."

Her head is tilted back, looking at me, and I only have eyes for her. I'm not ready for this night to end, but I can't force myself on her either. I can't just invite myself into her apartment.

"You want to come in? Or not, I mean if you need to get back…" She lets the offer hang between us.

"I'd like that. I'm going to call Chad and let him know, so Joan doesn't worry about her car."

"Oh." Her cheeks flush. "Okay." She fumbles with her keys and finally gets the door unlocked. "Come on in." She stands back, letting me pass.

Pulling my phone out of my pocket, I dial Chad. "She kick your ass to the curb?" he asks in greeting.

"Nope."

"Well, all right then. What's up?"

"I'm hanging out with Shayne at her place. Are you at home? I want to make sure your mom doesn't need her car, and she's not worrying."

"I'm home, and she doesn't need it. You staying the night?" he asks.

"I'm...I don't know."

"Be good to her."

"That goes without saying."

"I'll let Mom know."

"Thanks." I end the call, sliding my phone back into my pocket.

"You want something to drink?" she asks.

"No, thanks. I feel like I could explode."

"You and me both." She plops down on the couch and pats the cushion next to her. "Take a load off."

I take the offered seat. I leave a little space between us, not because I want to but because I don't want to scare her away. "No TV?" I regret it as soon as I ask. She didn't have a bed for a fucking year. I doubt she has a TV either. I know money is tight for her.

"Oh, yeah, it's in the bedroom. It's just me, and my bed is a hell of a lot more comfortable than this old couch." She rubs her hands on her thighs. "We could... I mean, do you want to watch a movie?"

"Are you okay with me being in your space? You willing to share that comfortable bed with me?"

"You promise to behave?"

No. "Yes."

"Come on. Let's see what we can find." She stands from the couch and makes her way to the front door. I watch as she tests the lock and then turns to face me. "You coming?"

"Lead the way." I stand and follow her down the short hallway and into her room.

"It's small, but I promise the bed is the best." She turns on the small bedside lamp, giving the room a soft intimate glow.

She's right. The room is small. The bed is pressed up against one wall. There is a dresser that holds the TV and a nightstand, and what I assume is a closet door. She kicks off her shoes, grabs the remote, and climbs up on the mattress.

Doing the same, I bend down to unlace my boots and set them to the side before taking my spot next to her. "Wow, you're right," I say, rolling to my side to stare at her.

"About what?"

"The bed. I'm used to cots or worse, most recently sand."

"It's a good thing, what you all are doing." She rolls to her side as well. "Tell me something I don't know."

"Let's see. I've only ever had one serious girlfriend."

"So you're the player type," she teases, although something I can't describe flashes in her eyes.

"No. I'm definitely a relationship kind of guy."

"Then why the lack of relationships?"

"I had a bad breakup, and well, living in the desert isn't exactly a great place to find love."

"Are you looking for love?" she asks.

"Aren't we all? Are you?"

"One day," she says wistfully. "I need to get my life in order."

"You seem to be doing a pretty good job of that."

"I—I don't trust easily. So it's going to be hard to be able to open up to someone to reach that point."

Reaching out, I place the palm of my hand against her cheek. "Who hurt you?"

"I—I just don't want to be like my mom. I never met my dad. He found out about me and told Mom to take care of the problem, and bolted. My life was hard growing up, and I want more. I want better."

My heart cracks wide open for her. "Thank you for tonight. For agreeing to have dinner with me." I drop my hand because touching her soft skin makes me think about touching her everywhere, and I'm not a one-night stand kind of guy. No matter how fucking tempting she is.

"You look tired," she observes as I cover a yawn.

"I didn't sleep well the last couple of nights."

"You want to talk about it?"

"You like talking about yourself?"

"What?" Her eyebrows furrow as she tries to figure out what I mean.

"All I could think about was you and tonight."

"Really?" There's both surprise and awe in her voice.

"Really," I say over another yawn.

"You want to take a nap?" she asks.

"No, I'll be okay."

"Ford, you're dead on your feet."

"I don't want to miss my time with you. I'm not ready to leave you," I confess.

"I didn't ask you to leave. I asked you if you wanted to take a nap."

"With you?"

"If that's what you want."

"It's late."

"Are you going to turn into a pumpkin?" she teases.

"No." I reach out and tickle her side.

"Then stay."

"One condition."

"What's that?"

"You let me hold you." Her eyes widen at my request. "I promise I'll be good, I just… I really want to know what it's like to hold you in my arms."

"I'm not... I mean, we can't—" She stumbles over her words.

"Hey." I move in closer to her, wrapping my arms around her. "I just want to hold you. I promise. If anytime you are uncomfortable, I'll leave. Chad knows I'm here. Do you really think if he thought I would hurt you, he would let me be here with you?"

"No."

"Call him."

"What?"

"Call him. Ask him what you should do."

"No. That's crazy."

Digging my phone out of my pocket, I dial his number, placing him on speaker. "She finally kick your ass out?" Chad chuckles.

"Nah. I'm actually going to stay awhile."

"Yeah? You really like her, huh?" he asks.

My eyes lock on hers. "I do." She gives me a curious look, and I don't dare take my eyes off hers.

"She's a hard nut to crack," he warns me.

"I can be patient."

"All right, well, I'll tell Mom not to expect her car home tonight. Keep her safe."

"Always." Ending the call, I roll over and place my phone on the nightstand before facing her again. "Let me hold you." I hold up my arm, and she gives me a subtle nod before moving in close, rolling over, pressing her back to my front. I wrap my arms around her and bury my face in her neck. My eyes are heavy as I relax into the mattress. There is only one thought as I drift off to sleep.

How am I going to leave her?

Chapter 8

Shayne

'M WRAPPED IN THE WARMEST BLANKET. SOFT, YET FIRM, WITH the most comfortable cotton pressed against my cheek. I can feel the early morning sunshine bleeding through the old blinds, and I can smell rich musk and sandalwood. I want to bury my nose in it and revel in the absolute perfection of this sleep. It's heaven, basically, and I never want to leave this bed.

My pillow moves, mumbling follows, catching me by complete surprise. Suddenly, I'm not sleeping, not dreaming. I'm very much awake, and so is the one I'm pressed firmly against.

Images of last night flood my mind. Our dinner date, followed by coming back here. We moved to my bedroom so we could watch a movie, but I don't remember much after the opening credits. Ford was exhausted, passing out pretty much the moment he laid down on my bed. Normally, I might be insulted by his lack of interest, but I know that's not what it was about. There was no pressure to take our night further, not even when we lay down beside each other on top of my bed.

I hold my breath, trying not to move a single muscle. Will he go back to sleep, or is Ford an early riser? Something tells me it's the latter more than the former. I imagine in the army, there isn't a lot of mornings for sleeping in.

Speaking of rising, I can now confirm he has...*risen*. Oh my God, his erection is pressed against my leg, hard and long and begging to be played with. I, of course, hold completely still, waiting for the moment he finally fully wakes. I can tell the moment he does, because he jerks, his entire body rigid with surprise.

I have no time to figure out how I'm going to play this. His deep, husky-with-sleep voice whispers, "Shayne?"

My reply comes out as a nervous squeak. "Yes?"

He relaxes finally, pulling me into his chest even closer, his arm wrapping around my shoulders and holding me tight. "Morning," he murmurs, getting all snuggly comfortable against my tense body.

"Hi," I croak, my throat Sahara-dry.

Just as I start to feel my tight muscles relax once more, he jumps, pulling his arm out from under my neck. "Shit, your cousin. Cassie," he states, his green eyes wide as he searches the room.

I can't help but chuckle. "I don't think she's hiding in here, so no worries."

Ford turns his worried gaze to me. "Oh, yeah. I meant, you know, she was supposed to stay here last night. With you."

I shrug and stretch. With the action, his eyes drop to where my jean-covered leg slides along the quilt. "After you talked to Chad, she sent a text saying she was staying at her parents' house."

"Oh," he replies, sagging with relief. "That's good, though probably not for her since most of her stuff is here, right?"

"She has things there too," I insist, a blush creeping up my neck at the way he's watching me.

Ford lies back down, turning on his side to face me. "So, what are your plans today?"

"I work four to nine."

"Hmm, Chad mentioned there's a bonfire tonight somewhere close by, someone's farm? Why don't you come after you get off work?" he asks, a glint of hope in those green orbs.

But I'm unable to enjoy that glimmer in his eyes, not when he mentions the Stetson farm. "Oh, uh..." I start, unable to come up with an excuse. I don't want to tell him I'm not a fan of hanging out with those my own age.

"I mean, you don't have to if you don't want. I just thought it might be a great way to hang out a little more. I'm only here for two more nights," he says, sadness creeping into his words and hanging between us like a heavy cloak.

I swallow hard. The thought of him leaving on Wednesday makes me sadder than I ever thought possible, but why? I barely know him. We've been on exactly one date. Granted, he spent the night, but it wasn't like that. There was cuddling, and that's it. I mean, we haven't even kissed.

Yet.

"I have an idea," he says, sitting back up and stretching his arms over his head. The hem of his shirt creeps up, exposing a little sliver of bare stomach. That tiny peek of skin is enough to heat up my body like I stepped into a sauna on a July afternoon. "I need to take your aunt's car back to her, and I'm sure there's somewhere to grab some food on the way. Why don't we go eat some breakfast before I take the car back?" He leans forward and swipes a strand of hair off my forehead, letting his fingers linger just a touch.

"Okay," I reply, touching the back of my head. "Though, I should probably shower. I'm sure I resemble a raccoon right now," I add, realizing I didn't wash the eye makeup off my face before I fell asleep.

Ford blows out a puff of air. His eyes dance across my face, taking in my appearance. I'm sure I look a fright. No way can black smudgy eyes and morning breath be sexy this early. "You look beautiful."

I want to argue, to insist I'm the exact opposite of beautiful, but the honesty and sincerity in his gaze has my mouth wired shut. "Do I have time to throw my hair up in a ponytail and hat?"

"Of course," he says, tossing his legs over the edge of the bed and turning to extend his hand. I don't need his help to get up, but I'm not about to miss the opportunity to touch him, even if it's just with our hands and only for a few seconds.

"Do you mind if I use a touch of your toothpaste?" he asks, running a hand through his short hair.

"Actually, I can do you one better." I move across the hall to the small bathroom. I open up the bottom drawer, pull a spare toothbrush out, and hand it over. "I keep a few in here in case Cass shows up on a weekend and doesn't have one."

"Does that happen often?" he asks, slipping around me and reaching for the toothpaste.

I shrug. "Mostly in the summer when she's not at school."

While I leave Ford in my bathroom to brush his teeth, I return to my bedroom and rip off last night's shirt and jeans. I hear the door close and the water turn on, so I move to my closet to grab a pair of cutoff shorts. I know the apartment is small and not very soundproof, but I feel like he deserves a little more privacy than me standing outside the door, listening to him gurgle mouthwash.

Throwing on the shorts, I grab my brush and rip it through the tangles. Once it's somewhat tamed, I pull it into a ponytail and grab the ballcap I wear when I'm helping my aunt and uncle on the farm. It may not be pretty, but at least it'll help hide my greasy bedhead. Just as I'm slipping my feet in a pair of flip-flops, the bathroom door opens, and Ford's heavy footfalls echo through the room.

"Bathroom's all yours if—"

I glance up and find him staring at me with an intensity that steals my breath. "What?" I ask, my hands going up to finger-comb my long ponytail. "I promise I'll wash the makeup off before we go."

He smiles and shakes his head. "No," he insists, walking toward me. "This—" he starts, adjusting the hat on my head, "—looks adorable on you."

"Oh," I reply, blushing. "Give me a few minutes, and I'll be ready."

Slipping into the bathroom across the hall, I notice the toothbrush he used sitting on the side of the sink. Something warm and bubbly tickles my chest as I picture that very item having its own spot next to mine.

Stop it, silly girl. You're getting way ahead of yourself.

I brush my own teeth and use a clean cloth to wipe the remnants of makeup off my face. I take a hard look in the mirror, trying to see what Ford sees. My hair is a weird shade of blonde. Not pretty, really. Plain. That's how I'd describe it. It's also a touch on the thin side, and when it's down, it lies limply against my neck.

My eyes are probably my best feature, a shade of blue-green that reminds me of the ocean. I was once told I had beautiful eyes. Of course, that was before I found out what a lying, cheating sack of crap the compliment-giver was. My face is narrow, and my nose curls upward, but not in that "cute" way it's described in fashion magazines and blogs. I think it gives people a gross view straight up my nose, but maybe that's just me.

Sighing, I realize I don't see what Ford does. At all. Unless he's already heard all the rumors and is just hoping to get lucky while he's on leave. Though, that thought doesn't strike me as holding an ounce of truth. Admittedly, I've been bamboozled by a gorgeous guy before, so what do I know?

After quickly using the restroom and washing my hands, I head out to find my breakfast date. Locating Ford isn't difficult, considering how small the apartment is. He's waiting in the kitchen, his hands stuffed in the pockets of his blue jeans and boots on his feet. The shirt he wore last night is wrinkled, having slept in it, but he still looks positively edible.

"Ready?" he asks, rocking back on his heels.

"Yep." I grab my small purse and keys and move to the door. I lock the deadbolt and make my way down the stairs, Ford making sure the apartment is secure before he descends after me. When we reach the base of the stairs, there are two doorways. One leads to the back of the bar, while the other to the back parking lot. That one we keep locked since it's happened more than once that drunken patrons have stumbled up the stairs.

"So, am I going to follow you? There's a little diner on the way that makes the best homemade French toast," I suggest as we step outside.

"I have an idea. How about we grab breakfast, return the car to your aunt, and then hang out until you have to go to work? Or is that too much? I'd understand if you wanted to just be alone before work," he says, a hopeful glint in his eyes as he awaits my response.

"You want to hang out more? What about Chad?"

He shrugs and steps closer. "Ehh, I just spent nine months with him in the desert. I think spending a few hours with you today will be okay. Besides, we've got that bonfire tonight. I'll hang out with him then. Unless I can convince you to come for a bit. Then I'll get to spend more time with you."

My heart skips around in my chest like a young girl playing hopscotch, and I can't help but grin. "All right."

His lips break out in a breathtaking smile. "Great. I'll follow you to the diner."

Ford makes sure I'm secured in my own car before slipping into my aunt's vehicle and following me out of the lot. It only takes a few minutes to get to our destination, but my eyes repeatedly cast a glance in the rearview mirror, and my mind is focused on one man the entire time. I don't even know how I make it to the diner in one piece.

As soon as I pull into a parking spot, Ford follows suit, jumps out, and practically races to my door. Once it's opened, he extends a hand, helping me out. He did that last night too, and I love the way his warm, rough fingers feel against my skin.

The moment we step through the entrance, I'm surrounded in the familiar sights and sounds of Foreman's Place. It's been here for decades, first opened by Darwin Foreman and his wife, Peggy. Their daughter, Suzanne, owns it now. While she's implemented new specials, the core comfort foods that put this place on the map all those years ago can still be found on the menu.

"Have a seat anywhere!" Doris hollers as she pours a cup of coffee at one of the tables. Doris Hankey has worked here almost as long as the restaurant has been open. She's a staple, just like the faded white-and-red checkered tablecloths, the sticky plastic menus, and the ripped black vinyl booth seats.

Recognizing everyone, I head for the farthest booth from the door and slide in the side with my back to the room. I always prefer keeping a low profile. It's a familiar habit when I return to the place it all went down. Actually, I've only been here a few times in the last year, mostly with Cassie or my aunt and uncle.

"This place is great," Ford says, sliding into the booth across from me and reaching for the menus behind the napkin dispenser.

Just as he slips one across the table for me, our server arrives. "Good morning."

Shit.

No.

"Morning," Ford replies happily, while my heart tries to claw from my chest.

"Can I get you some coffee? Oh. Hi, Shayne."

I slowly glance up to see Daphne Jones giving me the exact same look she's given me for the last year. Even though I did nothing to her, she still despises me.

Disdain.

"Daphne. Hi." I try to keep my tone even, but even I can hear the clip in my voice. "No coffee for me, thanks. I'll just have an orange juice."

"I'll have a coffee and ice water," Ford replies, oblivious to the sudden tension surrounding me and our server or the disgusted face she gives me as she turns and walks away.

"Everything okay?" he asks, worry marring his gorgeous features.

Okay, maybe not so oblivious.

"Yeah, sure, fine," I state too quickly, studying the menu as if it holds state secrets.

Before he can ask further questions, Daphne returns with our drinks, setting mine down on the table with a little too much force. "Are you ready to order?"

Ford indicates for me to go first, so I steel my spine and pretend everything is all right, that one of the girls who made my life hell a year ago isn't staring at me with judgmental eyes and waiting for me to order food. Food that will no doubt sit in my stomach like a lead balloon, if I even get any down my throat.

God, I'm going to throw up.

"I'll have French toast," I reply, my throat as dry as cotton as I return my menu to the holder behind the napkins.

Daphne writes on her little pad of paper. "Any side piece? I mean side dish," she adds quickly, giving me a condescending smirk. "Hash browns, bacon, fruit?"

I swallow the hurt and paste on my best I-don't-give-a-crap-about- your-pettiness smile, letting her know her childish comment doesn't affect me. "No, thank you."

Daphne turns, taking in Ford for the first time. I can see the moment his hotness registers with her. "What would you like, sir?"

"I'll have the same, but with a side of hash browns and gravy," he replies, not even giving her a second glance as he slips the menu into the holder and reaches for my hands.

"Your food will be out shortly," Daphne states, flipping her hair over her shoulder and scurrying toward the kitchen.

"So… what was that about?" Ford asks, gently squeezing my hands.

"Daphne? Oh, nothing."

His eyes bore into me, studying me in a way I'm not accustomed to. I wonder if he's going to call me on my lie. I'm sure he can feel the tension and discomfort. It's thick and hangs over me like a heavy fog. But if he senses it, he doesn't dig for more information. Instead, he asks, "So what do you want to do after we return the car?"

I relax instantly and realize he has a way of making me do that whenever he's near. It happened at the bar that first night, sitting around the bonfire, and now this morning. Hell, I even felt incredibly comfortable last night. I mean, I let this man sleep in my bed at my side. Who does that following a first date?

"Well…" I start, clearing my throat and leaning in a little closer. "How do you feel about fishing?"

His emerald eyes light up with delight. "Love it. Haven't been in a few years, but when I was a kid, my dad and I used to fish at a local pond every chance we could."

"Well, we can return the car and grab my gear from the barn. I'm sure Chad would let you use one of his poles. There's a small pond at the back corner of the farm where we used to swim as kids. It's not big, but Uncle Henry stocks it every few years. We might catch a few catfish or maybe bass."

Ford gives me the biggest smile, making me feel like I won some sort of award or something. Not many would get all excited about worms and dirt, but I'm quickly discovering, Ford isn't like most men. Hell, he's not like any man I've ever met.

That thought's both exhilarating and terrifying.

"You have yourself a date, Shayne."

"I can't wait."

And I can't. I'm excited to spend a little more time with Ford. We're on the clock, and I'm not just talking about the fact I have to work at four. I'm talking about after today. The fact he leaves to head home on Wednesday. Then, back to base. Who knows when the next time I'll see him again will be?

And why does that thought make me incredibly sad?

Chapter 9

Ford

BREAKFAST WAS AWKWARD. WELL, NOT ENTIRELY, ONLY WHEN the waitress was present. I could visibly see the difference in Shayne. Her shoulders would stiffen, and her eyes would stay downcast to her lap. There's a story there, one that I want to hear, but I won't force her to tell me. I can only hope she tells me in her own time. The only problem is that if it's not in the next two days, who knows when it will be. In a letter? Over the phone? Maybe I can convince her to come to base and visit?

Regardless, whoever that chick is at the diner, she dimmed the light in Shayne's eyes, and I'm determined to get it back. To see her blue-green orbs sparkle with happiness. That is today's mission.

"Are you sure you know where you're going?" I glance over at Shayne, who is driving us along the edge of a huge wheat field in Chad's parents' UTV.

"You wound me," she says, placing her hand over her heart.

"I'm just saying we've been driving on the edge of this field for a while now." I should know. I've spent the entire drive staring at her and the wisps of her dirty-blonde hair falling from underneath her hat. She's effortlessly beautiful.

"I told you the pond was at the edge of the property."

"And how much property do they own?" It's a rude question and is none of my business, but for real, we've been driving for at least fifteen minutes. We could have already been to town by now.

"About four hundred acres. Give or take." She shrugs.

"Damn," I mutter under my breath.

"Are you not enjoying the drive? The scenery?" she asks, glancing over at me.

"Nothing wrong with the scenery," I reply, my eyes still drinking her in.

"How would you know?"

"Trust me, I know."

"You haven't taken your eyes off me." She grips the steering wheel, and her eyes are straight ahead, but I see the slight pink that coats her cheeks and the way she bites down on her bottom lip. She's worried about what I'll say, and she shouldn't be.

"That's how I know." Reaching across the seat, I tap the bill of her hat. She turns to me and smiles, lighting up my world. The sparkle is back, and it's directed at me. It's a heady feeling, one I want to hold onto. I've never regretted joining the army, and I still don't, but fuck if it's not inconvenient when I just found the most fascinating woman I've ever met.

"We're here," she says, gradually bringing the UTV to a stop. She turns to look at me. "Ready to catch some fish?"

"Wow," I say, nodding. "This place is unreal. I can't believe you and Chad got to grow up here."

"Yeah. We had some good times, fishing, swimming, and just roaming these fields when we were kids."

"I can see it. You with pigtails running wild." I smile at the thought.

"You make me sound like Pippi Longstocking." There's a playful pout on those pretty pink lips.

Leaning in close so that my lips are just a breath from hers, I whisper, "You're so much sexier." To give my words a punch they deserve, I close the distance and press my lips to her cheek. Her intake of breath tells me I've shocked her. I know without a shadow of a doubt it's both my words and my lips pressed against her skin that's caused the reaction.

I want to kiss the breath from her lungs. I want to lay her out on the grass and worship her. The list of things we could do, that we could share, is endless as they flash through my mind, but I don't act on any of them. If anything, I'm a gentleman. That's how I was raised. It's also a little bit of self-preservation. I'm leaving, and I don't know if I'll ever see her again. Sure, Chad and I are friends and will remain so, but life gets in the way. She could be long gone from this small town by the time I'm able to give her all my time and attention.

I'm a soldier.

My life is not my own.

It's what I signed up for. I knew what I was getting into. Eyes wide open and all that, but sitting here next to her, I can't help but wonder if I would have met her first, would I have made the same choices?

A vision of Sara pops in my head. She wanted me to choose her, and I wanted to choose the army. It's harsh, but so is life. However, if it had been the beauty sitting next to me asking me to stay, I don't think I could have ever walked away from her. The thought of doing so just after knowing her for days is already twisting and turning with unease in my gut.

"You ready to be schooled?" she asks, stepping out of the UTV.

"You know they call me the fish whisperer," I tease. I step out of the UTV and meet her at the back. I grab the cooler, and tackle box, and the other bag she tossed in the back while she grabs the poles. "I'll come back for the chairs," I tell her.

"Nah, we're staying right here." She points over her shoulder. "It's only a few feet."

"So all of this?" I look down at the bags I'm carrying.

"Snacks."

"Can you be any more perfect?" I ask. I didn't really mean to say the words aloud, but I'm not going to take them back. "Fishing, no-frills, and snacks. Next thing you're going to tell me is you've got cold beer inside this cooler."

"Am I that obvious?"

"Obvious? No. Not at all. Every man's dream girl? Most definitely."

"You're a sweet talker, Ford Gregory."

"Only for you, Shayne Danner." I toss her a wink and get busy pulling the small container of worms out of the tackle box so that we can bait our hooks.

"I'm not one of those girls who's afraid to touch a worm," she says, placing a chair beside me before setting one up for herself.

"I'm being chivalrous."

"Oh, is that what you're going with?" She chuckles.

"I'm trying to woo you."

"Woo me?" Surprise dances across her face.

"I guess I need to step up my game." I laugh.

"You're trying to woo me?" Her voice is soft, and the laughter is gone.

"Abso-fucking-lutely."

"You barely know me."

"That's all a part of the wooing process."

"Ford—" She quickly snaps her mouth shut.

"Look." I step toward her, cupping her jaw with my hand. Her skin is so damn soft. "I know I don't know you, Shayne. I don't know you, but I want to. I want to know what brings this sparkle to your eyes, and I want to know what dims it." I think about the girl at the restaurant. "I want to know your hopes, your dreams, and your fears."

"You're leaving."

Swallowing hard, I nod. "I am. I might not be here with you, fishing at the pond, hanging out where you work, or grabbing breakfast with you, but I'll be here with you." My eyes bore into hers, willing her to believe me.

"This is crazy," she whispers.

"So you'll do it? You'll keep in touch. You'll let me get to know you? I know it's a lot to ask, and it's unconventional, but something in here"—I place my hand that's not cradling her cheek against my chest—"tells me that not knowing you would be the worst decision I ever made."

"Where will you go next?"

"I'm not sure." I drop my hand from her face and take a step back. "We never know until we get our orders. I'll spend a few days at home with my family, and then it's back to base. We can write, talk on the phone, and if you think you can get a weekend away, you could come to visit me."

"What makes you think I'd want to use my free weekend to come and visit you?"

"Hoped is more like it." I chuckle. "Look, this sounds certifiable even to me. I'm aware that we just met, but in my line of work, you learn to trust your gut."

"And what is your gut telling you?"

"That we can't let this opportunity pass us by."

Those blue-green eyes watch me intently. Finally, she breaks her silence. "You know what my gut is telling me?"

"What's that?" I ask, leaning in close. It's like she's a magnetic force that I can't seem to pull away from.

"That we have fish to catch." Her hands press against my chest, and her lips connect with my cheek. "Bet I can catch more than you," she whispers huskily.

"Game on, beautiful."

Her smile is bright, and that sparkle is back. I hope I can keep it there the rest of the day. "So, about tonight. You think you can find someone to cover for you?" I'm not ready to be away from her. Funny thing is, I'm not sure I ever will be. She's cast her spell on me, that's for sure.

"About that," she says cautiously. "I'm actually off."

"Shayne Danner, did you call in sick for me?" I'm only teasing. She told me this morning she had to work from four to nine.

"No." She looks down at her feet and wrings her hands together, and my hackles raise.

"What's going on?"

Placing her pole on the ground beside her chair, she buries her face in her hands. "I'm sorry." She lifts her head to look at me, and there's sorrow written all over her face.

"What are you sorry for?" My voice is soft, but my guard is up. She looks as though she's on the verge of tears.

"I lied to you. I'm off tonight."

I take a minute to let my mind wrap around her words. *She lied to me.* "Why?" That single word feels heavy as it leaves my lips.

"I told you, you don't know me."

"How am I supposed to get to know you if you're not honest with me? Why did you lie to me, Shayne?"

"I have a past."

"We all have a past."

"Mine is ugly."

"I'm sure that's not the case."

"Trust me. You don't want someone like me in your life. You're too... good."

"Do I get a say in this?"

I watch as she closes her eyes and focuses on pulling in slow breaths. When her eyes finally open, they are swimming with tears. "I didn't know how to tell you that I can't go to the bonfire."

"Why?"

"History." She shrugs.

"Do you care to share that history with me?"

"Maybe one day?" It comes off as a question.

"So you don't have to work tonight, and your history makes you think you can't go to the bonfire."

"I don't think. I know I can't go."

I feel as though this is a turning point for us. Here sits this gorgeous, intriguing woman who has a past I know nothing about. I have bits and pieces from Chad, but there's more than that. I have a feeling it might be even more than Chad knows. She lied to me but came clean, not even twelve hours later. It's obvious that she was scared to tell me. We all make mistakes, right? My gut tells me she needs an olive branch. It's also telling me that other than Chad and his family, and maybe her boss, she's not been given many in her lifetime. Until now.

"So, what are we going to do?"

"Wh-What do you mean?"

"Tonight. You and me. What are we going to do?"

"You're going to go with Chad, and I'm going to go home and relax." Her tone says that's the end of the discussion, but I've got news for her. Wherever she is, that's where I'm going to be too. At least for the next two days. Instead of arguing with her and spoiling our day, I reach down, grab her pole, and hand it to her. She gives me a watery smile, and we leave it at that.

We spend a few hours at the pond, and just as she predicted, Shayne caught more fish than me. However, I was distracted, only half-assing the task. I couldn't seem to take my eyes off her, and more times than I care to admit, I was too slow to react, and the fish got away. That's fine. I'll take an empty hook for memories of her any day.

The sun is starting to set beyond the trees by the time we call it a day. "I guess you need to get back and get ready," she says, placing our gear in the bed of the UTV.

There is something in her voice that tells me she's not happy about it. There is a hint of sadness in her tone, and after the day we had together, the thought of her being upset tears me up. "I told you I'm not going. We're going to hang out. Just you and me." It's not a suggestion; it's a statement. I know Chad won't mind, and truthfully, I don't care if he does. I've never met any of those people, and I get it. He wants to introduce me. Not to mention, they were mean to her, or someone who is going to be there was mean to her, and I don't trust myself not to dig and defend her. That's the effect she has on me. I don't need to be hauled off to jail, and my time is better spent with her anyway.

When I leave here, it's not going to be his friends that I met keeping me up at night. No, it's going to be the beauty standing in front of me. The memories of my time with her, and besides, how can I ask her to take a chance to get to know me if I'm not putting in the effort as well?

"You don't have to do that. I think I'm just going to go home and shower and chill."

"Perfect. Do you mind waiting for me to shower before we go back to yours?"

Her head tilts to the side as she studies me. "Chad might be mad you ditched him."

She said *might* because we both know he won't care. In fact, I can see him being happy that I put her first. He's protective of her and told me not to start something if I was going to just leave her. Well, the thought of leaving her causes an ache in my chest.

"We both know he's not going to care. Come on, spend the evening with me?" I stick my lip out in a pout, making her laugh.

"You're impossible."

"Is that a yes?"

"That's a yes." Her smile is bright as she nods her head at me.

"One more thing." I hold my hand out to her.

"What?" Her eyes flash to my hand and then back to me.

"I get to drive."

"You don't know where we're going," she counters.

"Trust me?"

"Fine, but if I tell you to turn, you have to turn. I'm not getting lost out here in the dark with you."

"I'd protect you," I say with a wink. I'm being silly, but there is truth to my words. I'd never let anything happen to her. Not if it was within my power. It's not just because I'm a soldier, and it's ingrained in me. No, it's something that's uniquely Shayne.

She drops the keys in my hand and points a finger at me. "I'm watching you." She mock glares.

"Let's do this," I say, sliding behind the wheel. "Thanks for today." Reaching over, I entwine my fingers with hers.

"I should be thanking you. You have limited time, and you spent the entire night and day with me."

"I wish I could stay, but I miss my family. I also know my mom would be crushed if I didn't come home to see her."

"Are they home yet?"

"Nah, they're getting home the same day I leave here."

"I'm sure they miss you. I know we all miss Chad like crazy."

"Yeah," I say, not able to contain my smile when thinking about my family. "My sister went with them as well. She's on summer break from her third year of college."

"And you're twins, right?"

"Yep. She's my little sister, though. I made it out five minutes before she did." Shayne giggles. Which is a new sound coming from her. "She hates it that I call her my little sister. Even if she would have been born first, I'd still call her that. She's about a foot shorter than me."

"Hey!" She turns to look at me, blue-green eyes narrowed. "I'm a foot shorter than you. Are you calling me little?"

"If the shoe fits," I tease her.

"I changed my mind. I don't want you and your negativity in my space." She barely has the words out of her mouth before she's biting down on her lip, trying not to laugh. "And what's with the granny speed?" She points to the dash where we're barely going ten miles per hour.

"I can't keep my eyes on the road safely and watch you if I go any faster. Not without wrecking, and I have to keep you safe."

"It's the pedal on the right, and keep your eyes ahead," she says it like she's a driver's ed instructor.

"No can do. It physically pains me to pull my eyes from you."

She rolls her eyes, but her smile tells me she's not as annoyed as she would like me to believe. "Do you sit around practicing these cheesy lines?"

"Hey." I release her hand and pinch her side. She wiggles away from me, laughing freely. "I'm a gentleman."

"Sweet talker," she counters.

"Only for you." I flash her an exaggerated grin.

"You know shit's starting to get deep. You might want to be careful where you step."

"Ha ha. Funny girl." I grab her hand in mine. "I'm driving, woman. I need to concentrate." She makes a show of zipping her lips and tossing the key over her shoulder. "Much better," I tease. Then I do exactly what she told me to do. I push the pedal on the right. The sooner we put away this gear, and I get showered, the sooner we can get to her place. Where I plan to cuddle the hell out of her. In two days, I'm going to have to walk away from the first woman to ever make me want more than the life I've built for myself. That only deserves some cuddles. My hope is that my time with her will be enough. That the memory of her laughter and the feel of her in my arms will get me through until I can see her again. She might not know it yet, but I wasn't kidding when I said I was wooing her. Even if I have to do it from thousands of miles away, I'll make it happen. I'm determined to keep her in my life.

When we reach the barn, I rush to help her put the gear away. "I'm going to run to the house and shower. You're going to wait on me, right?" I ask her.

"You sure you don't want to go to the party?"

"I want to be where you are." Unable to resist the pull she has over me, I lean in and press my lips to her temple. "I'll be quick." Turning, I take off in a run to the house.

The house is empty, so I use the key the Anthonys gave me to use while I'm here. Grateful for their hospitality, I feel guilty that I'm glad they're not home. I don't want to stop and make small talk. All I want to do is wash my rank ass and get back to Shayne. Grabbing some clothes, I toss them on the vanity and send Chad a message.

> **Me: Hanging with Shayne tonight.**
>
> **Chad: Loser.**
>
> **Me: She's prettier than you are.**
>
> **Chad: I'll give you that.**

Setting my phone on the counter, I turn on the water and strip out of my clothes. The water is barely warm before I step under the spray. Every moment of today replays in my mind. Who would have thought sitting in the hot sun, fishing would end up being the best date I've ever been on? Today was definitely good for this country boy's heart. The weather, the scenery, and the company. I just hope that in the next two days, I can convince her to give this a go. Distance be damned, I want to see where this crazy ride takes us.

Chapter 10

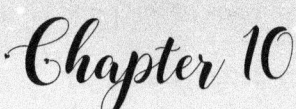

Me: I need help. Ford wants to hang out tonight. What should we do?

Cassie: Grab a box of condoms since the ones you have probably expired a year ago and get freaky with him! *insert eggplant emoji*

Me: STOP! I'm not sleeping with him. He's leaving in less than 48 hours.

Cassie: You're so boring in your old age, Shay. All I heard when I read that was he's leaving in less than 2 days. 2 days of getting freaky.

Me: There's something wrong with you.

Cassie: I'm staying at the house tonight. Make sure he stays with you.

Me: UGH! You're such a brat.

Cassie: So I've been told. But… if you're really looking for something to do, you can take him to the bonfire. I'm sure everyone we know will be there.

I groan out loud, wishing she hadn't suggested that. Even though she's underage, I know she'll be going tonight. When you're young, you don't care if it's a Monday night. Get-togethers like that happen every night of the week here. Except, I never go. I don't need to sit around, drinking cheap beer, and talking about how cool I am to everyone else.

Me: You know that's not my thing.

Cassie: I do know. What about camping? Rumor has it you guys have been back at the pond all day.

Me: It's already getting dark.

Cassie: Fine, then what about roller skating or bowling? Since everyone's headed to the bonfire, you know Finnegan's will be dead.

She has a point. Finnegan's is the local "hangout," offering a twelve-lane bowling alley, arcade room, pizzeria, and skating rink. If it were a weekend, that place would be packed, but since it's only a Monday night, I'm sure there's not a lot of activity, outside the men's bowling league.

Me: Good idea.

Cassie: Have fun. We're just finishing up dinner and are getting ready to head back home. Chad said Ford just texted him and told him he's hanging out with you. I think that boy has it bad!!

Me: I don't know about that, but he was pretty insistent. I feel bad he's not even spending much time with Chad this week.

Cassie: They're in the service together and have been overseas for months. I think they've spent enough time together. Plus, it's been great having Chad here and catching up with him.

A pang of sadness sweeps through me as I think about Chad and the time I'm missing with him. Sure I've seen him, but I feel guilty he's been home for a few days, and we've spent such a small amount of time together. He's leaving at the same time Ford is, heading to his friend's hometown before returning to his life in the military.

I make a mental note to spend tomorrow with my cousin.

> **Me:** I want to hang out with Chad tomorrow. Maybe we can all go bowling in the afternoon before I go to work at five?

> **Cassie:** I just ran it by Chad. It's a plan. All four of us can go and hang out. We'll meet you at the bowling alley at one.

> **Me:** See you then!

I slip my phone into my pocket just as Ford comes out of the house, making sure the door is locked behind him. He's carrying a duffle bag with him, his hair still wet and glistening as he approaches.

"I talked to Chad and told him I was hanging with you tonight," he says. "I hope you don't mind me being presumptuous. I grabbed my bag in case I stay again. This way, my stuff isn't in Cassie's way."

We move toward my car, his large body radiating heat like a furnace and the scent of rich soap wrapping around me like a comforting blanket. "I talked to Cassie too. We're going to all go bowling tomorrow afternoon before I have to work, if that's okay with you," I state, reaching my vehicle.

"That sounds great," he replies, tossing his bag in the back seat. "Do you mind if I drive?"

I roll my eyes but shake my head. "I suppose it's probably been a while since you've driven."

He holds open the passenger door and closes it once I'm inside. As soon as he slips into the driver seat, he replies, "It has been. Chad drove here in our rental, and since we arrived, he refuses to let me drive his baby."

I chuckle a laugh. "You mean Big Bertha?" I ask, referring to Chad's 2010 Ford F-350. That thing is a beast, but he loves it.

Ford chuckles as he starts up the car, pointing to the big truck parked over by the barn. "Last night, he asked his mom to let me drive her car instead of letting me drive his because, and I quote, 'no one drives my baby girl.'"

"It's sad, really, his love for his truck, but to be honest, everyone around here's the same way. Country boys and their big trucks."

He turns my car around and heads up the driveway to the road. He's familiar enough with the farm to know how to get to town and to the bar, so I just sit back and let him drive. "I've got a truck back home, parked in my family's shed. I can't wait to take her for a spin. My dad says he starts it every weekend and drives it for me, but I've been chomping at the bit to get behind the wheel."

"Let me guess, she has a name too?" I ask, leaning against the door and watching him drive.

"Oh, she does," he confirms, shooting me a panty-melting grin before his eyes return to the road.

"Is it Sally? Susie? Stella?"

He throws me a quick wounded look. "You think I'd name my girl something cheesy like that?"

"Well, then, enlighten me."

He smiles as he drives. "Her name happens to be Margaret, not Maggie. She's a classy lady. A 1979 Chevy 2500 with a four-inch lift kit. She's a square body, which I've loved ever since my dad had one when I was little, black with a silver rally strip down the hood. She's crazy fast and sexy, in a sophisticated way. Not trashy and flashy like Big Bertha."

I feel wetness gather in my lashes I'm laughing so hard. "Oh my God, that's the funniest thing I've ever heard."

He shakes his head. "You wound me, beautiful Shayne. I'll send you a picture of my girl when I get home, okay? Then you can see how stylish she is. You'll feel bad for laughing at her the way you have been," he replies, the teasing tone so effortless, I can't help but smile.

"I can't wait," I reply, realizing how true that statement is. I can't wait for him to send me that picture of his truck, even if that means he'll be gone, and I probably won't ever see him again.

We're silent as we pull into town. Ford drives into the back lot behind Jet's and parks in the space beside the back door. He's out and grabbing his bag before I even have my belt off. Smiling, I slip from my seat just as he comes around and hands me the keys. I open the back door, making sure it's locked behind me, and lead us up the stairs.

As soon as we're inside and the kitchen light is on, I say, "Make yourself at home. I'll be quick," and toss my keys on the counter and glance around uncertainly. Ford has been here before. Hell, he spent the night here, but suddenly, now that we're back in my space, I'm a bit nervous again.

Ford kicks off his shoes and sets them by the entry before grabbing his bag and moving to the living room. "Take your time," he says, getting comfy on the couch.

I nod, retreat to my bedroom to grab a change of clothes, and then step across the hall to the bathroom. I strip out of my shirt and turn the water on, eager to wash the scent of fish and mud off my skin. I can feel the low pulse of music coming from downstairs, but I'm so used to it, I barely notice anymore.

I try to hustle through a shower but end up spending extra time scrubbing under my fingernails and washing my hair twice to get the smell of worms off me. When I'm finally squeaky clean, I wrap a towel around me and step out. As I approach the sink, I can't help but press an ear against the door, trying to catch any noise coming from the living room. I hear nothing but the faint sound of Alabama from the jukebox below us.

I slip into a pair of cotton shorts and an oversized T-shirt before reaching for my toothbrush. I may not be getting freaky with Ford, like Cassie suggested, but I wouldn't discount a little kissing, even though that's probably not the wisest decision either. But it's not like I'm the poster child for good, solid decision-making skills.

After running a brush through my hair, I leave it down to dry and return to the living room. Ford is exactly where I left him, sitting on the couch with his bare feet up on the coffee table. His eyes roam my body, starting with my wet hair and slowly working their way down. They linger on my chest, no doubt noticing the way my nipples pebble against the soft material.

When our eyes finally meet, there's hunger written in the darkness of his irises. He slowly gets up and takes long, methodical steps toward me. As he stops, his right hand comes up and cups my cheek before brushing wet strands of hair off my forehead. I lick my lips. "I know I'm casual, but I was afraid we'd fall asleep again like last night."

"I want you comfortable, Shayne. This is your home, and you can trust me with you in it." He slides his thumb over my bottom lip. "I would never hurt you."

It's hard to swallow over the thickness in my throat, so I just nod. "I know you wouldn't."

Those four little words. They seem simple enough yet mean everything. It means I trust him. Not only to be here, in my space, but with my deepest, darkest secrets. Funny thing is, they're not even really secrets. Everyone knows about my past, about what I did. Ford could ask anyone in town and find out what he needs to know.

Or at least their version of the story.

But he hasn't.

So, yes, I trust him. It's a heady feeling to trust someone other than my aunt and uncle, cousins, and Jet. I'm still not quite ready to tell him what happened, but I do believe he'll listen to me without the judgment I see reflected in everyone else's eyes. I'm just not there yet.

"I'll be right back. I'm going to get more comfortable too," he says, heading for the bathroom. It's the first time I notice him holding something in his hands.

I make myself busy in the kitchen, grabbing some chips and salsa from the cabinet, as well as two bottles of beer. If we drink, that pretty much ensures he's staying here tonight.

With me.

The door opens as I turn around, and when he rejoins me in the living room, I stop in my tracks. My tongue falls out of my mouth. My eyes feel like they're on fire, since I'm staring, wide-eyed and unable to blink. Ford is wearing a pair of green sweatpants that hang dangerously low on his hips, and a tight-fitting US Army tee.

I've never understood the obsession with sweatpants. Women everywhere freak out about a fit man in gray ones. Cassie practically drools on herself whenever she talks about a guy in college wearing them, but I've never seen the appeal.

Until now.

Ford in a pair of sweatpants might be the greatest vision I've ever witnessed. They leave little to the imagination—if you know what I mean—and fit so perfectly, entire romance novels could be written about the way he looks right now.

"You okay?" he asks, breaking through the fog in my brain and wearing a smirk.

"Oh, uh, yeah. Great. Perfect. You?"

He grins, taking a seat on the couch and kicking up his bare feet. "I'm good."

"I brought snacks," I rush out, dropping down on the couch beside him in a very unladylike plop.

"Perfect," he replies, reaching for a chip and dipping it in the hot salsa. I wait to see if he's going to freak out and chug water like I expect but am surprised when he chews and swallows without so much as a blink of spicy discomfort. "This is good."

"Aunt Joan cans her own every summer with ingredients from the garden. She always makes me about a dozen jars of super spicy," I tell him, dipping my own chip in the tomatoey goodness.

"So, what do you want to do tonight? I'd suggest a movie, but you see how well that turned out last night. Though, I'm not nearly as tired as I was then," he says, dipping another chip.

"Well, how about we order some food. I'm getting hungry again," I start, noting it's several hours after my aunt had my uncle deliver a basket of fried chicken to the fishing hole. "And then we can play cards. Do you know how to play rummy?"

"Rummy?" he asks, sitting up straight, his eyes sparkling with excitement. "I'm the rummy king!"

I dramatically roll my eyes. "You mean like you were the fishing whisperer earlier?" I tease, jumping up and heading for the junk drawer, where I keep a deck of cards.

"You got lucky. Besides, I was sidetracked."

"By what?" I ask, returning with the cards and my phone.

"You."

I blush. Ford Gregory is as smooth a talker as they come, but for some reason, it doesn't feel like a line when he says things like that.

We end up ordering dozens of wings from the bar downstairs, along with a variety of fried sides, and while the food is being made, he deals the cards. I learn quickly Ford is a much better rummy player than he was a fisherman.

By the time Jet knocks on the door with containers of food, my sides hurt from laughing, and for the next few hours, we eat, we laugh, and play cards.

It's one of the best nights of my life.

"Strike!" I holler, throwing my arms up victoriously before adding a little shimmy and a shake.

"Yes!" Cassie bellows, joining me in our celebratory dance. "We win again! Girls rule!"

"I think we were hustled," Ford grumbles to Chad as they watch us rejoice in our latest victory.

"Uh, yeah. Either that or you're just really bad at bowling," Chad teases.

"Me? You barely hit a one hundred. Maybe next time we play with bumpers?" Ford asks, standing up and stretching. When he does, his T-shirt moves up, exposing a little sliver of tanned, toned skin with a light dusting of dark hair. The same skin my hand was resting on this morning when I woke.

Chad glances at his wrist. "It's probably time to go. Shayne, you have an hour until you start work."

I sigh, my excitement now crushed into a deep sadness I try to hide behind a grin. "Yeah, you're right. What are your big plans tonight?" I ask, sitting down and removing my ugly bowling shoes.

"Mom's making me my favorite, pot roast, for dinner. I wish you didn't have to work so you could join us," he replies, slipping his own shoes off and replacing them with work boots.

"Maybe next time," I whisper, trying to keep my focus on replacing the socks on my feet with flip-flops and not on the fact my cousin leaves early tomorrow afternoon.

And with him, Ford.

"But we thought we'd come up and hang with you afterward since you're closing," he adds, standing up and grabbing his shoes.

When I look up, I see Ford already has his own shoes on, as does Cassie, and all eyes are on me. I feel mine well up with tears, but I quickly blink them away and pick up my shoes, shoving my no-show socks in my bag. "Tuesdays are usually slow, so I should be able to visit with you all," I reply, bypassing where they stand and returning the well-used shoes to the counter.

"Great," Chad boasts, tossing his own footwear on the counter and heading for the exit.

As we walk, I feel a warm hand graze against my own. I know who it is. Even if I were blind, I'd know his touch anywhere. I don't pull away, just let his large hand wrap around mine in comfort.

When we reach my car, which is parked beside Big Bertha, I feel Ford tug on my hand. "You're okay with us stopping by later, right?"

"Yes, absolutely."

He gives me an easy smile, one I've seen on his handsome face many times over the last few days. "Good. We can discuss sleeping arrangements later," he adds, opening my car door for me and stepping back.

"Presumptuous, aren't we?"

Ford shrugs as Chad fires up his massive truck. "I don't expect it, but I will state, for the record, I've slept better the last two nights, holding you in my arms, than I have in years. I'd gladly go back to your aunt's and sleep there, but it wouldn't be the same. Plus, I can hear Chad snoring from across the hall. It's horrible."

Smiling at the man who's quickly chiseled through the stone wall surrounding my heart, I go up on my tiptoes, press my lips against his scruffy cheek, and whisper, "I'd like for you to join me. One last night."

When I meet his eyes, I see the pain flash through them before he masks it with something else. "It's a deal, beautiful. I'll see you at Jet's later."

As soon as I slide into my seat and turn over my car, cranking up the air conditioning, he pushes my door shut and steps back. Ford doesn't move as I back out of the parking space and head for the exit. It's hard to focus on what's in front of me when my eyes keep flying back to my rearview mirror.

To the man who doesn't move until I'm completely out of sight.

To the one I feel myself falling for, even though it's a bad idea.

Chapter 11

Ford

"GIVE ME A FEW TO CLOCK OUT, AND I'M ALL YOURS." SHAYNE gives me a bright smile. The one that, no matter what I'm doing, has my heart flipping over in my chest.

"Should I go around back?" I don't know what the protocol is for going home with an employee who lives above the bar. I don't want to get her in trouble.

"Nah. Give me a few, and I'll take you through the kitchen with me."

I nod, holding up my bottle of water, letting her know I'll be right here. I don't plan to leave this stool that I've been holding down since Chad and I arrived a couple of hours ago. He's long since gone. Some buddies of his came in, and they went to a party. They invited me to go along, and I felt kind of bad for declining, but it would take a literal war to pull me away from Shayne tonight.

Chad and I are leaving in less than thirteen hours for my home in Ohio. Don't get me wrong, I'm excited to see my family, but leaving Shayne, even though I've only known her a week, is tearing me up inside.

I want to spend every minute I can with her. I want to soak up every single moment, every memory of our time together. We also need to talk about what happens next. I know that she's incredible and sexy, and everything I never knew I wanted. Just because I'm going back to base doesn't mean we can't do this. There are countless military families that make it work.

I want to make it work.

Although I want to nail down what our future might hold, I'm not going to bring it up tonight. If she decides she can't do it, or hell, if she's not interested, then that's going to ruin the night. I want this last night with her to hold her close and just… be.

"All set," Shayne says, appearing next to me.

"Lead the way." I place my hand on the small of her back and let her guide us through the kitchen and to the door that will lead us to her apartment. "I'm glad that door stays locked," I say when she has to pull out her keys to unlock the door.

"Me too. Jet and I are the only two who have access. He even goes out of his way to threaten the staff that if they ever were to find it unlocked, they are to notify him immediately and never go inside, or he will prosecute them for trespassing."

"Really?" I ask, closing the door behind us and making sure the lock is engaged.

"Yep. He's good to me. He's helped me so much."

"I'm glad that you have him in your life."

"Yeah," she says softly. "Me too."

We reach her apartment and she unlocks the door, stepping back to let me inside. My eyes scan the room for my bag, but I don't see it. "My stuff?" I ask her.

"Oh, I put it in my room." Her cheeks flush a light pink.

I want to kiss her.

Up to this point, it's not something we've done, but I want to. No, I need to more than my next breath. Stepping close to her, I cradle her face in the palm of my hands. Her beautiful eyes tell me she knows what I'm thinking, but I refuse to take from her in any capacity without asking her permission first. I don't know everything that happened to her in her past, but I know it's not good. My mind can create some pretty terrible scenarios, and I never want her to feel as though she doesn't have a choice. Not with me.

"You're beautiful." My words are barely a whisper.

"You're here. I don't need flattery."

"Shayne—" I stop and pull back. Lacing my fingers with hers, I lead us to the couch and tug her into my lap. "Tell me," I urge gently, "what happened to make you think that the only reason I would tell the most beautiful woman I've ever laid eyes on that she is, in fact, beautiful, would be to get your time or your body?"

"I can't." Tears well in her eyes, and that emotion grips my heart like an iron fist. I hate seeing her upset.

"Can't or won't?" I keep my voice gentle. I don't want her to think I'm upset with her. I just need to understand.

"Maybe a little of both. If that's truly how you see me, then I don't want anything I have to tell you about my past to ruin that." She bites down on her bottom lip and blinks hard.

"There is nothing that you could tell me that would make me think any differently."

"You don't know that."

"Try me?" It's a challenge. I hate to throw it down, but I want her to open up to me. If I want us to be able to have something lasting and long-distance, at least for the next year, we need to be able to be open and honest with each other. I wasn't going to do this tonight, but here we are.

"I'll tell you, just…not tonight. I just want to be with you."

I can't very well fault her for that. I said the same thing about the talk I want to have with her. "Deal." I smile, letting her know I'm not angry or upset. However, I do know that in order for us to take this further, she's going to have to tell me. "Now, I have a serious question for you."

"O-Okay," she says hesitantly.

"It's actually more like a favor."

"Anything," she says, her mood a little brighter.

"You see, there's this woman, she's beautiful, kind, smart, and a blast to hang out with. I've been spending a lot of time with her this week, and well, I want to kiss her, but I don't know how she'd feel about that. What do you think? I need your advice. Do you think she would let me?"

A slow, sexy grin pulls at her lips. "You know, I think she just might. However, are you any good at it? Kissing, I mean? You might need some practice."

"Maybe, it's been a while for me. But there's another problem."

"What's that?" she asks, playing along.

"I don't want to kiss anyone but her. So, how am I going to get practice?"

She giggles. "Ford?"

"Yeah, baby?"

"Kiss me."

"My pleasure." My hand slips behind her neck, and I fuse my lips to hers. I take my time savoring her. Her taste explodes on my tongue. I could kiss her just like this for the rest of the night.

I lose track of time as my lips mold with hers. Her hands are in my hair, and my arms hold her as close as I can get her at this angle. When she slows the kiss and pulls away, I groan. I'm not ready to stop kissing her. I never want to stop kissing her.

"Come with me." She stands from my lap and offers me her hand. She doesn't comment about my hard cock that's clearly visible through my sweats. No, her eyes stay locked on mine. Knowing I would follow her anywhere, I place my hand in hers and let her guide me to her bedroom.

She doesn't bother to turn on the light as she moves us through her room and to the bed. My pulse is thundering loudly, and I swear she can hear it. My palms are sweaty, but I refuse to let go of her hand to wipe them on my sweats. Instead, I will myself to be patient and follow her lead.

"Lay with me?" Her softly spoken request greets my ears.

From the light of the moon, I can see her silhouette as she climbs onto the bed. I waste no time kicking off my shoes and climbing in beside her. Snaking my arm around her shoulders, I pull her into me, holding her close.

"Ford?"

"Yeah?"

"You don't need practice," she says, making me laugh.

"No?"

"You passed with flying colors."

"Good to know," I say, giving her a soft squeeze.

"Ford?"

"Yeah?"

"Can we do it again?"

"You want to kiss me, beautiful? You don't have to ask. I'm all yours." She has no idea how true that statement is. It's baffling to me that those words left my mouth, but it's the truth all the same. In the span of less than a week, I've fallen hard and fast for this girl. Almost like a shooting star, if you blink, you might miss it, and that's exactly how I feel about this moment with her. I don't want to miss a single second. I'll need the memories to get me through until I can see her again.

I really hope she lets me see her again.

She surprises me when she moves to straddle my lap, leaning in and pressing her lips to mine. My hands land on her hips, holding her to me as I let her control the pace. Her lips are soft and hesitant, but that's fine with me. My hands and my mouth are on her. What more could I ask for?

A few hours later, we're lying in her bed, both of us in a lot less clothing, our lips are swollen from kissing, and our bodies entwined. Every part of me is touching every part of her. This night with her has been more intimate than sex. I feel connected to her in a way that I've never felt with another person.

"Next question," I say, pulling myself back to our conversation. We've been lying here for the past hour, in the dark, wrapped up in one another and answering random questions about each other.

"It's my turn." She playfully swats at my arm.

"Fine," I say dramatically. "It's your turn. Ask away."

"Kids. Do you like them?"

"Yeah, I mean, who doesn't?"

"Do you—"

I cut her off. "It's my turn," I chastise her playfully.

"Ugh. We're terrible at this game." She chuckles, and I feel that sound in my soul. I wish I could bottle it up and take it with me. I can just see myself sitting under the desert stars listening to that sound. I know without a doubt it could bring me home to her.

"Hey, speak for yourself." I pretend to be offended. "Now, it's my turn. Do you want kids?"

"Question stealer."

"Is that your answer?" I ask, tickling her side.

"Stop. No, th-that's not my answer," she says, sputtering with laughter. I ease up, letting her catch her breath. "I don't have a good answer to that question."

"Now I'm intrigued." I don't push her to tell me. If she wants to, she will.

"I didn't have the best life growing up. The only role models I have that were good to their children are my aunt and uncle."

"I'd say you've got parenting in the bag then."

"I don't know. I mean, they're not my parents. What if I turn out like my mom?"

"Close your eyes." I wait a few seconds. "Are they closed?" I can't tell from the way that we're lying together.

"Yes."

"I want you to picture your life as a mother. It's five, hell, even ten years from now. You're married to a man who cherishes you, and you're happy. Your marriage is solid. Sure, there are hard times, but that's life. Hard times are not conducive to just marriage. Anyway, you have a little girl who looks just like you." I take another pause, letting her set the scene up in her mind. "Do you see it?"

"Yes."

"What do you see, Shayne?"

"We're in the backyard. Me and my husband and my daughter. We're having a picnic under a big tree."

"How do you feel?" I have no idea what I'm doing. All I know is that I want her to picture her life in a way I'm sure she's never allowed herself to see. She has so much love to give. She could never be like the woman who raised her. I don't know much about her life then, but I know without a shadow of a doubt that Shayne's heart is too big to not smother those she loves with emotion.

"I feel… happy."

"Shayne, you would be a fantastic mother. The mistakes of others are not your own. You can't live in the shadows of how they lived their lives. You have to live for you. Forge your own path."

"I've made mistakes," she whispers.

"We've all made mistakes. Tell me, did you learn from that mistake?"

"Yes." Her voice is strong and filled with conviction.

"That's all that matters. You made a mistake, life knocked you down, and now you're better because of it. The mistakes of our pasts shape our future."

"That sounds like a Hallmark card," she teases.

"More like a mom card. My mom is always spouting off words of wisdom. She writes to me when I'm deployed, and almost always, there's something in her letters that gives me a dose of her mom wisdom."

"I love how close you are to your family. I want that," she confesses. "If I ever find a man who accepts me for my past and my present, and we have children, I want us to be close. I want to be everything that my mother never was."

"Then that's what you'll be. You have the control, Shayne. Don't let this town, or a snotty waitress, or even your mother tell you any different." I hope I'm not overstepping. I don't know her past. I don't know her secrets, but I do know that we are all human. It's in our DNA to make mistakes. How we learn and grow from them is what defines us as a person.

"I'm going to miss you."

I place a kiss on her forehead. "I'm going to miss you too."

"It's weird, right? How can I feel as though I have this...connection to you when I barely know you?"

"I feel it too. Maybe it was fate." I've never really been one to believe much in fate, but I don't know of any other explanation for Shayne coming into my life. All the stars aligned for my parents to be on vacation my first week home from leave. When Chad offered me to come home with him, I jumped at the chance. I could have gone home and just chilled for a week, but my best friend offered for me to visit with his family, so I, in turn, offered him to visit with mine."

He talked about Shayne so much, I feel like I've known her much longer than a week. I can't believe I didn't realize she wasn't a guy cousin, but a beautiful female cousin who, with one look, captivated me.

That has to be fate.

"I'm leaving soon, Shayne," I whisper into the quiet of the room. In mere hours I'll be driving away from her.

"Yeah."

"I want us to stay in touch." I want more than that, but I still don't know if she's ready. I don't know if I'm ready to put myself out there with her if I don't know what she's hiding from me. I can't be stuck on base or, worse, deployed with secrets between us. All I can do is hope that she will eventually confide in me.

"I can write to you."

"And maybe come visit me on base? I don't know if you ever get long weekends or more time than that off work, but it's only about a three-hour drive from here."

"Are you able to leave?"

"We can, but we have days we're on duty, and we're only allowed to travel so many miles from base, and we have to be back at a certain time. I wish I would be able to come and see you, but unless I'm granted another leave, a long weekend maybe, I won't be able to."

"I'm sure we can figure it out."

"We can," I agree.

"I really want to keep you as a part of my life, Ford."

"How big of a role are we talking here? Pen pal? An old friend? Boyfriend?" I go ahead and toss the suggestion out to see what she says.

"All of the above."

"Pen pal and old friend. We've got that in the bag. I want us to be more. I would be honored to be able to call you my girlfriend, but we're not there yet. I need to know that you trust me. I'm going to be gone a lot over the next year, and more than likely deployed at least half if not more of that time." I curse myself inwardly for even bringing this up tonight. I told myself I wasn't going to.

"I'll tell you. I promise. I just… I don't want anything to ruin our time together. I want to let you in. I'm just so damn scared that you're going to see me differently, and I'm going to lose you. It's only been a week, but you are already so important to me."

"I'm all yours. We leave at one tomorrow afternoon. The only thing we have to do is pick up the rental car. This way, Chad doesn't have to worry about how to get his truck back home. He doesn't want his baby on base. He says leaving it in the deployed lot is a risk he's not willing to take." I chuckle, remembering that conversation with Chad. "Until then, I'm all yours."

"That sounds like Chad." She snuggles in close. "I don't want you to hate me."

"I could never hate you, Shayne."

"The town does."

"I find that hard to believe."

"It wasn't my fault, but I still hate myself for it."

"Hey now, none of that. Tonight, pretend that whatever it was that happened was just a bad dream. Tonight, for the next few hours until I have to climb out of this bed, let's just… be," I say over a yawn. "Let's try to get some sleep."

"I like sleeping with you."

"Me too, beautiful. Me too."

I pull her a little tighter and fight off sleep. I'm used to going long stretches without rest, and tonight is going to be one of those nights. I want to memorize what it feels like to hold her all night long. I still can't believe I found her, someone who I'm willing to risk my heart with again, but I know without a shadow of a doubt that my Shayne is worth it. I just need these memories to get me through until the next time I can see her.

Chapter 12

Shayne

I'M EXHAUSTED, BUT I REFUSE TO NAP. WE'RE DOWN TO HOURS. Hours of time is all I have left with Ford. One o'clock draws closer and closer with each passing second, the tick growing louder with every movement. I've never hated time as much as I do right now.

We're headed to my aunt and uncle's. Chad and Cassie went to pick up a rental car that the guys will use to drive to Ford's hometown and should be back by now. Aunt Joan is making lunch for us, and if I know her at all, probably doing everything she can to keep the tears at bay. I wonder what her trick is? What is she thinking about to take her mind off the fact her only son is getting ready to leave again for an undetermined amount of time? I'd really like to know. I may need to implement some of her techniques to keep myself from going crazy with worry.

Sure, we've been here before, but for me, this time is different. This time, there's Ford. I've come to truly care about him in such a short amount of time that I can't even comprehend what it's going to be like tomorrow when I wake up alone. I've gotten used to seeing him, touching his warm skin, and being the recipient of his amazing kisses.

What's next?

The answer is daunting.

Emails and stolen phone calls whenever we can squeeze them in, if that's what I choose. He made it clear in the early morning that he wants to keep in touch, wants to see where this crazy connection takes us. I'm not against it. Oh no. In fact, it's the exact opposite. I crave him, the deep timbre of his voice and the softness in his touch. There's no way I'd be able to say goodbye today and never speak to him again.

I'm just terrified the distance will be too much.

What happens then?

Heartache.

That's what happens.

But I refuse to think about that. I can't. Instead, I focus on getting through the next two hours. What happens after that will just have to wait.

We pull down the long driveway in my Honda, Ford behind the wheel, and our fingers entwined on my thigh. Neither of us have said much since we started to get ready for the day. It's as if neither knows what more to say. We have, however, said plenty with touch. There have been dozens of lingering traces and stolen kisses. It's as if we're saying more with our hands than we are with our mouths.

"Ready?" he asks, shutting off the car and turning to face me.

"Yep." The word comes out in a high pitch, as if I didn't speak it.

He gives me a small smile and squeezes my hand before slipping out of the car. Ford meets me at the passenger door, places his warm hand at the base of my back, and escorts me to the front door. As we approach, I'm wrapped in the familiarity and comforts of this farmhouse. The cows in the pasture, the delicious scents floating through the doorway, and the deep boisterous sounds of my uncle telling a joke to whoever is in the kitchen.

And now, I'll always associate this entrance with the final time I walked in with Ford.

The sadness makes it hard to breathe.

"Hey!" I holler chipperly as we push through the doorway.

"Hey!" a chorus of voices replies from the kitchen.

Kicking off my shoes, I follow the laughter and smile as I step over the threshold. "Chad was just telling us about the time he and Ford sang karaoke their first night off base," Aunt Joan says, wiping a tear from her cheek.

"Ugh," Ford groans behind me. "Why?" he asks his friend, the humor evident in his question.

Chad just laughs. "Because it was horrible. And funny."

I take a seat as a glass of freshly squeezed lemonade is placed in front of me, anxious to hear more.

"That was the tequila talking," Ford states, taking a quick sip of his own drink.

Chad nods. "And the dare."

"Dare?" I ask, my eyes completely focused on the man sitting beside me.

"One of the other recruits dared us to sing."

"One hundred bucks each," Chad replies.

"What did you have to sing?" I ask, catching the glance between Chad and Ford.

"Nothing," Ford mutters, casting his eyes downward.

"You have to tell her," Cassie adds through her fit of laughter.

"No, I don't. I have to maintain some sort of dignity on this trip," Ford argues, though there's a hint of a grin on the corner of his lips.

"Tell her or I will," my cousin demands, her hair pulled up high on her head and a humorous glint in her eyes.

"Nope."

"It's okay," I state, reaching over and squeezing his hand. "You don't have to tell me if you don't want to."

He sags into the chair and sighs. "Good. Thank you. If I told you, then there's a good chance you'd think less of me, and I don't think I could handle that today."

Something inside me cracks. My heart. It bleeds with affection for this amazing man. How he thinks I could think anything less of him is beyond me. He's perfect.

Everyone is silent for a minute before Cassie blurts, "'It's Raining Men!'"

And the room bursts into fits of giggles.

I can't hold it in, and I follow suit. Even after I glance at Ford and see the color drain from his face. Clearing my throat, I whisper, "That's what you had to sing?"

He nods, mortification clearly written across his handsome features. "I needed those hundred bucks. There was also a lot of liquor involved. I'm just glad you weren't there to see it."

I give him a reassuring grin and place my hand on top of his. "It's okay. I don't think any less of you."

Ford lets out a long sigh of relief as Aunt Joan places bowls of food on the table between us. Everyone digs in, filling their plates with homemade macaroni and cheese, asparagus from the garden, and grilled beef tips. A delicious homecooked meal for their last one in Kentucky. We all dive in, my mouth full of creamy mac and cheese, when Chad drops the bomb on the lunch table.

"I have it all on video."

"Wanna go for a quick walk?"

I finish loading the dishwasher for Aunt Joan, trying to ignore the time on the clock above the stove. Thirty minutes. They're leaving in thirty short minutes, and I am not okay.

"All right," I whisper, my throat dry and my heart trying to rip out of my chest like the Hulk. I take another quick glance at the clock on my way to the back door.

Twenty-eight minutes.

The sun is bright in the sky, the complete opposite of my mood. It should be gray and dreary out here. Then it would be just like my mood.

Ford leads me to a two-seater swing under the big oak tree and waits for me to take a seat. He sits beside me, his long legs moving the swing effortlessly, and pulls me against his side. "Here," he says, reaching down and grabbing a gift box sitting on the ground.

"What's this?" I whisper over the hammer pounding in my own chest.

"Open it and see."

I lift the lid off the white box and find a folded sheet of paper. When I lift it from the box, I realize it's sitting on top of a book. No, not just a book. A notebook. I lift it up, my hand sliding across the smooth, hard cover, the image of a sunset staring back at me.

"I thought, maybe we could add old-fashioned letter writing to our modes of communication," he says, pointing to the envelopes in the bottom of the box.

My fingers hold a slight tremble as I open the notebook and reveal a note on the first page.

My beautiful Shayne,

This week has been one of the best of my life. I'll never forget my time in KY, but most importantly, I'll never forget my time with you. I hate leaving you behind, but knowing I'll be able to continue communicating with you makes the distance not seem so empty. The thought of not waking up beside you tomorrow morning is grim, so is the realization I won't be able to kiss you goodnight. I'll just have to stock up on plenty of kisses now before I go. But know this, beautiful. Know that wherever I am, whatever I'm doing, you'll be on my mind. Meeting you was a gift I plan to cherish for the rest of my life.

Every day apart is one closer to being together.

Thinking of you always,

Ford

I'm not sure when the tears started to fall, but they did. Big fat drops of wetness soak into the paper and cause the blue ink to spread. When I look up, those amazing green eyes hold so many emotions, it's almost overwhelming.

"I picked that up yesterday at the gift shop in town. I think the lady thought I was crazy, asking to buy some of her envelopes too, but she found a box in a drawer and sold them to me," he states, a sexy little grin on his lips.

I try to hold the box and the items in my hand but feel them fall away as I throw myself against his hard chest and grip his shirt. Ford holds me close, his large hand running down my hair right before his lips press against the crown of my head.

"I'm going to miss you," I whisper, wishing I was as tough as I pretend to be. But sitting here right now, just minutes away from watching him leave, I realize I'm nowhere near the badass I portray. I may come off gruff, with a take-no-shit attitude at work, but that's not who I am. I'm a woman whose heart is weeping with loss—a woman who found herself falling more every day for a man who makes her giddy with excitement.

"I'm going to miss you too. But we're going to write, text, email, and call all the time, right?" he asks, moving to meet my eyes.

I nod, sniffling. "Yes. Every day."

He smiles and relaxes, pulling me back against his chest. I can feel his heart pounding a steady beat against my cheek. It's a reminder and a reassurance to his vitality. I commit that sound to memory.

We sit here, slowly swinging under the faint breeze, until the back door opens. It's Chad, and he's carrying bags. My aunt, uncle, and cousin follow him and slowly make their way to the Toyota rental car sitting by the barn.

Ford sighs. "Well, I guess it's time."

I swallow over the lump in my throat and vow not to cry. I will *not* cry anymore, not until I'm alone at home. Ford needs to feel my strength right now, not witness my weakness. It's that strength I want to send him home with, back to his base.

Standing, he scoops up the notebook and box I dropped when I threw myself at him. He places everything back inside and closes the lid before depositing it on the seat beside me.

I scoop up the box, anxious to hold it, needing to feel the slight weight in my arms. Only then do I stand. Our eyes meet once more, the sadness ebbing from our physical beings so thick you could cut it with a knife.

With legs made of lead, we make our way to the rental car, me cradling my box as if it were more precious than gold or fine gems. Ford moves his hand, removing it from my lower back, and heads to my car to retrieve his bag. Everything is in there, ready to go.

There's nothing left but goodbye.

Ford goes to Uncle Henry and shakes his hand. Words are exchanged, but I can't hear them over the blood swooshing in my own ears. I watch as he moves to my aunt next. She pulls him into a warm hug, the same ones she used to give me before I had to return home to my mom when I was younger. He even gives Cassie a hug and kisses her on the cheek. They exchange a few words, and whatever he says makes her giggle. Cass hits him in the chest playfully before they turn to glance my way. If it weren't for the affection clearly directed toward me, I'd be a little jealous.

Then, he's moving my way. I try to take a step forward, ready to meet him halfway, but my legs don't seem to work right. Instead, I stay where I am and remind myself to breathe. Ford slowly lifts a hand and touches my arm, sliding it up and around my back before pulling me into a hug. I inhale the familiar scent of his soap and deodorant, committing it to memory, as I rest my head against his chest. "I promise to call you later."

I swallow hard. "I have to work until nine."

He pulls back and meets my gaze. "Then I'll call you after nine," he replies, the softest grin on his lips.

"Okay," I whisper.

Ford places both hands on my neck, his thumbs gently caressing my jaw, as he lowers his lips to mine. The kiss is tender. Sweet. Final. Absolute, because neither of us knows when we'll share our next one.

"Thank you for saying yes, Shayne," he whispers, his warm breath tickling my lips.

Before I can reply, he releases me and steps back. The warm air suddenly feels cold against my skin. Ford gives me a reassuring smile, one that tells me it's going to be all right. He walks backward, heading toward the car and away from where I stand. Each step he takes feels like a knife cutting at my chest.

"I'll talk to you soon," he assures as best as he can, but even I can see the uncertainty in his eyes.

I nod, unable to form words.

Then, he's there, standing at the passenger side door and ready to climb in. Chad comes over and gives me a quick hug goodbye, but my eyes remain on his friend. I'm terrified to break eye contact.

My cousin climbs into the driver's seat and shuts the door, starting the rental and cranking the air conditioning. Ford remains standing at the passenger side, a mix of sorrow and comfort in those amazing green eyes. He lifts his hand, giving me a wave, and then slips into the vehicle. I hear the door shut and the horn honk as it moves forward, heading for the roadway.

Heading away from me.

I watch as they reach the end of the driveway and turn left. I watch as the car picks up speed and eventually disappears from my sight. I watch as the man I'm falling for leaves, return ticket unknown.

Only then do I allow the tears to fall.

I had hoped I'd be able to wait until I was home, but there's no stopping them. They fall in earnest, the warm river of wetness a steady reminder of the pain I feel.

The pain of losing Ford.

Sure, there will be letters. There will be phone calls and emails.

But it won't be the same.

It'll never be the same again.

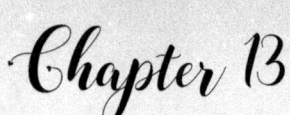

Chapter 13

Ford

MY FISTS ARE CLENCHED TIGHT WHERE THEY REST ON MY thighs. My heart is beating erratically in my chest, my eyes burn, and there is a lump the size of the entire state of Kentucky in my throat. I knew I had to leave her. I knew I was only here for a matter of days, but I pursued her anyway. Never in my wildest dreams did I think it would feel like this when I drove away from her.

Broken.

It's on the tip of my tongue to tell Chad to turn the car around and go back. I need one more hug. One more taste of her lips, but I know that one more of anything when it comes to Shayne will never be enough.

"You all right over there?" Chad asks from his seat behind the wheel.

"Yep." One-word answers are really all I'm capable of right now.

"You two planning on staying in touch?"

"Yep."

"She's different with you," he says casually.

This pulls my attention as I turn to face him. His eyes remain on the road, but I know he can feel my gaze. I swallow hard, willing my emotions to stay at bay and ask, "What do you mean?"

He shrugs, never taking his hands off the wheel or his eyes off the road. "I've never seen her be taken with someone so fast. Shayne's lived a hard life, and what happened..." He lets his voice trail off. "She's usually more reserved, doesn't let anyone get close." Finally, he glances over at me. I can see the surprise in his features. "She let you in."

"This isn't one-sided," I bite back defensively.

"That's not what I'm saying, Ford," he sighs. "She's had a rough go of it, and then when she did finally feel like she might be moving on with life, forging her own path, she got knocked down again. If you want to be with her, she's going to need your patience."

"She has all of me." Five small words, insignificant on their own but phrased together, they mean so much. They were out of my mouth before I could even process what I was saying, but I find that it's true. How it happened in a week, I have no idea, but I'm not going to question it. I know that life is short and that you have to take each day, every encounter as an opportunity.

Meeting Shayne was my opportunity.

"That's a pretty bold statement, brother," Chad comments.

"Yep," I reply, and he throws his head back in laughter.

"Back to one-word answers, I see."

My lips twitch. "Fuck me. I didn't think it would feel like this to walk away from her."

"You can't think of it like that. You're going to work. Doing your job. If you both want this to work, you're going to have to remember that."

"When did you get so wise?"

"Just telling it as I see it. You're not leaving her to just go travel the world because you feel like it. You're doing the job you were trained to do, to defend our country. That's a big deal."

"Are you fishing for compliments?" I joke.

"Nah, I know we're badass at what we do. Shayne knows it too. She's not going to be Sara."

And there it is. Mic drop. The route of the storm raging inside me. How can I expect her to wait for me?

"Did you?"

"Did I what?"

"Ask her to wait for you?"

Shit. I must have said that out loud. "No."

"Exactly. Shayne is a big girl, and she can think for herself if she wants this. If she wants to be with you, she's going to have to be understanding that being in the army is your job. And you don't want to be with someone who you have to ask them to wait for you. You want someone who will wait for you because they think you're worth it. Because the thought of doing anything but waiting for you just isn't possible in their mind."

"And Shayne?" I hold my breath, waiting to hear his answer. I feel as though I know her, and she said she wanted this. That we were going to try and make this work, whatever it is that that looks like.

"Shayne is loyal and trustworthy. If you two are in this, if you decide to take this thing the distance, she's going to be there when you come home."

I don't know why but hearing him say that has some of the tension leaving my body. I've fallen hard and fast, and admittedly, there is still so much we don't know about one another. She still hasn't shared with me the story of her past. She's so terrified of me thinking differently of her. Whatever it is, is a huge part of who she is today. I could never look at her any other way than filled with adoration. It's hard to trust without knowing what she's holding back. However, at the same time, my gut tells me that with Shayne, what you see is what you get. I don't see her writing me nasty letters telling me that I ruined her life and that waiting was never an option.

Chad's right. She's not Sara.

She's everything.

We're about ten minutes away from my parents' place. Chad's still driving, refusing to let me take a turn, which is fine. I don't mind occupying the passenger seat. It's given me more time to daydream about Shayne. Speaking of Shayne, opening up the message icon on my phone, I send her a message.

Me: Almost home. About ten minutes out.

Shayne: You made good time.

Me: Chad has a lead foot.

Shayne: This I know.

Me: Have a good night at work.

Shayne: I'll try.

Me: I miss you already.

Shayne: I miss you too.

Me: Call me when you get home?

Shayne: Yes.

Satisfied that I'm going to talk to her in a few hours, I slide my phone back into my pocket. "Turn right up ahead," I instruct Chad. Not that he needs it. The GPS had guided us this far. As soon as we pull into the driveway, the front door opens, and out steps my family. My parents, my twin sister, Faith, and my grandparents. The car is barely stopped before I'm pushing open the door and racing toward them.

Faith is the closest, so I wrap her in my arms, lifting her off her feet. We might be twins, but she's still tiny at five-foot five compared to my six-two. "Ford!" she screeches in my ear, but I don't stop spinning.

"I missed you, little sister."

"Five minutes, Ford Gregory." She laughs. "You're five minutes older," she says, as I'm placing her back on her feet.

"Five minutes is five minutes, little sister." I kiss her on the cheek and then move to my mother, lifting her in the air, minus the spinning.

"It's good to have you home," Mom says. I can hear the emotion in her voice. I don't know if it's the rawness of my feelings for Shayne and having to leave her, or if it's just that I missed my family that much, but I'm fighting with emotion yet again.

"It's good to be home," I say, releasing her.

"Son." My dad's deep timbre greets me as he pulls me into a tight hug. "Good to have you home." He passes me off to my grandparents, and somehow, I end up with my arms around my mom and my sister by the time it's all said and done.

"Chad, good to see you," my dad says.

"You too, sir," Chad says politely.

"Hey now, none of that. You're on leave, relax." Chad nods.

"I've got dinner ready. I made homemade pulled pork barbecue and all the fixings," Mom explains as we all file back into the house.

Chad and I tell them stories about the guys and us while deployed, and my family catches me up on everything I've missed while I've been gone. While I still miss Shayne, it's really fucking good to be home.

"What kind of mischief did the two of you get into this last week?" my sister asks.

"Nothing much," I say before Chad can answer.

"Come on now. You can do better than that." My sister Faith gives me a pointed look.

"We went to the bar where Chad's cousin Shayne works and had a few drinks. It was pretty low-key," I admit.

"Oh, Shayne." Faith looks at Chad then back to me. "Is he cute?" she asks just as I'm taking a drink of my sweet tea. My mom makes *the best* sweet tea.

"Yeah, *she's* cute," I admit, not even trying to hide my smile.

"She?" Mom and Faith ask at the same time.

I nod. "Shayne is a she."

"I love that name." Faith smiles. "And by that grin you're sporting, I'd say you and Shayne are…special friends?" My sister winks.

"She's incredible. I really think that all of you would like her."

"Wow." Faith sits back in her chair. "I wasn't expecting that."

I shrug. "She and I spent a lot of time together this last week."

"What? Did he leave you high and dry?" my sister asks Chad.

"Nah, I was catching up with family and friends. We all hung out as a group a lot, and my little sister, Cassie, too."

"Well, don't worry." Faith gives Chad a saucy look. "I can keep you company while the two of you are here."

"Faith!" my mom scolds her, but there's no heat in her tone. Faith has always made it a point to flirt with my friends. Not that I blame her. I started it by hitting on her best friend when we were in high school. She's never let me live it down. Although, from the look in Chad's eye right now, I'd say that he's not the least bit put off by my sister's flirting.

After Mom and Faith wave us away when we offer to help clean up, Chad and I grab our things from the rental and carry them inside. He's sleeping in the guest room while I take my old childhood room. It feels weird to be sitting here on this queen-size bed staring at my childhood. It seems like a thousand years ago when it's been three. It's funny how time away from home changes you. I feel like a different person, but somehow this place still feels like home to me.

It's just after eight when my phone rings. The ringer is up as high as it will go, and my phone is clutched tightly in my hand. I've been waiting on this call. I wasn't expecting her call until after her shift at nine, but I'm not going to complain that I get to talk to her sooner rather than later.

"I've gotta take this," I tell my sister and Chad. We're sitting out back around the firepit, much like the first night home at Chad's place. We're both just small-town boys at heart.

"Is that her?" Faith asks excitedly.

I hold my hand up, waving her off as I swipe at the screen, placing the phone to my ear. "Hey, you."

"Ford!" Faith says much louder than she needs to.

"Hi," Shayne replies, and my body relaxes into the Adirondack chair I've been holding down the last hour or so at the sound of her voice.

"Let me say hi." Faith stands and tries to take the phone from me.

"Stop it, brat." I laugh, turning away from my sister.

"Do you want me to let you go?" Shayne asks.

"No. My sister is a menace and wants to talk to you." The words are barely out of my mouth before my sister manages to wrangle the phone from my hands and run to the other side of the fire to stand beside Chad.

"You got my six?" she asks him, making us both laugh.

"I've got you," Chad says, patting the arm of his chair for her to sit.

"Shayne, hi, I'm Faith. Ford's twin sister." The two of them carry on a conversation, and I'm only privy to one side. Not that it matters. I've been open and honest with Shayne. I have nothing to hide. *Unlike her.* I can't help the thought that crosses my mind.

"Give me back my phone," I call out over the fire, and Faith just sticks her tongue out at me. Needing to talk to Shayne, to hear her voice, to tell her how much I miss her already, I stand and stalk toward my sister.

"Uh-oh, Shayne, he's coming after me. I can't wait to meet you. I gotta go." Faith thrusts the phone at me, losing her balance in the process, falling into Chad's lap. He tickles her side, making her squeal. I block them out as my feet carry me away from their antics. I need some quiet to talk to my girl.

"Hey, babe, sorry about that. My sister, she can be a little much."

"She sounds so much like you. You have similar personalities."

"I'd say it's the twin thing, but she and I are close. We always have been. Well, I guess that's because we're the same age, so yeah, it's a twin thing," I ramble. Her soft laughter fills my lungs with air. "How was your night?"

"Good."

There's something off in the sound of her voice. I was too busy fighting off my sister to notice at first. There is definitely something wrong. "Shayne, what's going on?"

"Nothing," she says, her voice cracking.

I stop walking and focus everything on her, on the tone of her voice. "Baby, you can talk to me."

"Just had a bad night."

"It's just me. I left Faith and Chad back at the fire. I'm sitting on a bench outside the barn. Tell me what's going on." I keep my voice gentle, but what I want to do is insist that she tell me. I just left there hours ago. What could have happened between now and then?

"Shayne, if this is going to work, you have to talk to me. Communication is important for every relationship, but ours demands it. Honesty, trust, and communication are what's going to keep us going strong when I'm not there to hold you." I hear her sniff, and it's killing me that she's so upset.

"Where are you?" I ask her. I hate to think of her out driving when she's upset. I tilt my head back and look up at the stars. The night sky is bright, and I'd give anything to have her with me right now. That's when an idea hits me.

"My apartment."

"Go to the window."

"What?"

"You heard me. Go to the window. Turn off all the lights in your apartment, and open the window."

"Ford?"

"Trust me," I whisper.

"I do trust you."

"Then, please, for me, turn off the lights and open your window." I hear her walking through her apartment as she does as I ask.

"What now?"

"Look up at the sky. What do you see?"

"Stars. The moon."

"You know what I'm doing right now?"

"What?"

"I'm looking up at the very same sky. The very same moon and the very same stars. I might not be there to hold you or to kiss you, but I am with you, Shayne."

Her voice breaks into a sob.

"Please, talk to me. Tell me what's going on."

"I didn't want to do this over the phone."

"Didn't want to do what over the phone?" Is she breaking this off already?

"Tell you about my past."

"Did someone from your past hurt you?" My senses are on high alert. Not that I could do shit about it when I'm here, and she's there.

"No. Just… this town, and my history. It was a rough night."

"Look at the stars, Shayne. Pretend I'm there with you. Pretend that my arms are wrapped around you. You're safe with me. Your body and your heart. Please, I'm begging you to let me in. That's the only way this is going to work." I hate to drop that on her, but I don't know what else I can say to get through to her.

"Can you let me get it all out before you say anything? Please? I just… I need to get it all out, and then we can go from there."

"That's fine. I'll stay quiet, but, Shayne, you need to know that I'm going to still feel the same way about you once you tell me whatever it is you have to say."

"How do you feel about me?"

"I'm falling fast and hard, and I'm not scared. I'm not afraid of what you have to tell me, and I'm not afraid of how strongly I feel about you.

What scares me is the thought that you don't trust me with your past. With your heart."

"You have my heart," she whispers, causing mine to trip over in my chest.

"Then give me your past. I'm right here, looking at the same night sky. You can tell me anything."

She's quiet for a few moments before she speaks again. "There was this guy—" She pauses, and I know that whatever it is that happened hurt her deeply, and without knowing the story, I know that if I ever run into the bastard, he's going to meet my fist.

Chapter 14

Shayne

ALL I CAN DO IS STARE OUT AT THE NIGHT SKY. MY HEART IS beating in my chest with dread. With fear. But not at Ford. I could never be afraid of him. I'm about to say words I've barely spoken to anyone. My aunt and uncle know the basics. Cassie too. After everything went down last year, it was their house I ran to when I needed to bury my head in the sand and hide from the world for a few hours. Then Chad called home a few days later, and Cassie filled him in. They're the only ones I confided in with the real story. Everyone else took what they saw or heard from someone there, and the story was twisted from there.

Sighing, I close my eyes and take a seat on the floor. When I open them, I can still see the stars, the bright white specks of light in the sky. The same stars and sky Ford is looking at right now, even though he's in another state. That thought is soothing to my frazzled mind.

"I met Rodney more than a year ago. He showed up at the bar one night for a drink with another man and stayed until we closed. He was an architect, in town making a pitch to the hospital board for the new surgical wing they're building. Rodney was young, the youngest at the firm he worked for, smart, and driven. What I think drew me to him right away was the fact he didn't openly hit on me, like everyone else seemed to do."

Ford is quiet, so I keep going.

"He didn't live in town but often returned for work. When he was finished with meetings, he'd always show up at Jet's. We… well, we hit it off right away. He was twenty-eight, which seemed a lot older, but we didn't care. It was just nice to talk to someone who had their life together, you know? For a few weeks, he was in town a lot. His firm was overseeing the project, meeting with town and hospital officials, and answering any and all questions regarding the expansion.

"It was about three weeks after he first arrived in town that he asked me to dinner. We went to the expensive Italian place on Main Street, the one with the warm bread and fancy cloth napkins. Afterward, we walked through the park and he kissed me for the first time. It felt nice, like I was being put first for once in my life."

I take a deep breath, hating reliving this point in my life. I felt stupid, gullible, and ashamed. Worse, I felt used and alone, much like I did as a child, begging for any sliver of attention I could get from my mom, knowing deep down it was never going to happen.

"We worked around his schedule and mine, stealing away any free time we could get when he was in town. Instead of staying at the hotel, he stayed with me above the bar. Within a month, he had a drawer in my bedroom and a suit in my closet since it was easier that way with him coming and going. We made plans. Even though it felt a little rushed, there was this exhilaration I couldn't explain, and frankly, didn't want to. We'd stay up into the wee hours of the morning, talking about what the future might hold. I felt content, happy, for the first time in my life."

"What happened next?" he asks, his voice even and calm.

"His wife showed up at the bar."

I hear his intake of breath and the scuff of his shoes against gravel. "Jesus, Shayne."

I find myself standing and starting to pace my apartment as well, the familiar sense of doom and embarrassment taking over. "And before you ask, no I didn't know he was married. I'd never date a married man, Ford, I swear."

"I know you wouldn't," he replies gently, though I can hear the hint of aggravation in his voice. "Keep going."

I sigh and close my eyes, reliving that moment as if it happened only yesterday. "It was a Tuesday. Rodney had returned home the Friday before and was expected back in Jefferson on Wednesday to meet with hospital officials for the final approval of the design. It was busy for a Tuesday night. Jet was gone, but it was nothing I couldn't handle."

"This pretty woman walked in. I remember glancing up but not recognizing her. Our eyes met briefly, and I recall how hers turned venomous at that very moment. It was like someone flipped a switch. She made a beeline for the bar and started yelling at me, accusing me of sleeping with her husband. I was so shocked, all I could do was stand there at first because I thought she had the wrong woman. I wasn't sleeping with a married man. I wouldn't."

The words start pouring from my lips faster now, as if they couldn't be contained, even if I tried. "She threw a bunch of papers all over the place, at the patrons in the bar. I glanced down at one that landed in front of me and realized it was one of my text conversations with Rodney. I was so confused. Why did she have those?

"And then it hit me. I knew why. Her husband was Rodney, the man I'd been seeing. The one who was so easygoing and casual when he convinced me to go out with him. The one who slept in my bed. He told me he was single, a few months out of a long-term relationship, and I believed him. I *believed* everything he said." The past comes out in a hushed cry.

"It's not your fault, Shayne. That's on him, not you. He's the one who told you a load of bullshit, knowing full well he was married." Ford practically growls through the phone, and while the sound is menacing, I know it's not aimed at me.

"She called me a homewrecker, Ford," I whisper, recalling exactly how it felt to have Rodney's wife wield those words at me like an axe, hitting me square in the chest. "Because it was true. I was one."

"No, you weren't. Not like that," he argues, but it's useless. I know the truth.

"But I was. I ruined that woman's life. Can't you see? And the worst part was, because the bar was so busy, everyone saw. Everyone heard. And those who weren't there that night saw the videos and pictures snapped from two dozen cell phones in the building. I was the homewrecker. The woman who stood there and couldn't even come up with a single word to defend herself."

"Because you were blindsided, not because you were guilty."

"But I was guilty, Ford. Even if I had no clue he was married, my actions destroyed her. They destroyed her marriage. She was pregnant—"

"And that's on him!" he bellows, interrupting me. "Not you, sweetheart. All you did wrong was trust the wrong guy. I know you feel guilty and responsible, but you were a victim, like his wife."

I blink hard, not even realizing I'm crying.

"Do you know one of the first things I noticed about you?" he asks, breaking the silence.

Shaking my head, I sniffle and dab at my eyes with my shirt sleeve. "No."

"I noticed your brilliant blue-green eyes. Eyes so gorgeous, they reminded me of the Pacific the first time I returned home from overseas. Home. That's what the ocean signified, and that's what I felt when I first saw your eyes. It hit me like a fucking sucker punch to the gut. But after I got over the initial shock of seeing the most beautiful woman in the world, I felt drawn to your strength. It was in the way you carried yourself, as if you've been knocked down repeatedly but kept getting back up."

"What if I'm too tired to keep getting back up, Ford? What if I just don't have the strength to fight these people anymore?" I ask, my voice barely audible.

"Then you let me help you. I'll help you get back up, Shayne, and help you fight. Fuck those people. I don't even know what happened tonight but fuck them. You're better than all of them."

"I feel like I've been fighting my whole life. First, fighting against my mom, fighting hunger and tiredness, and the whispers that trailed wherever I went. Even as a young girl, I could hear them. Now, they continue. I can't even go to the grocery store without hearing someone's hushed warning to anyone who'll listen about keeping your husbands close so I don't steal them. I just… I just wish it didn't bother me so much, but…"

"But it does. I get it." Ford exhales deeply. "What happened tonight?"

"That waitress from the other morning, Daphne, well, she came in with another girl we went to school with, Brenna. They started talking loudly with Connor—"

"Connor, the asshole I had to put in his place for touching you?" I can feel the venom through the phone line.

"Uh, yeah, that Connor. He's a regular in there. They were all talking about the wife coming in, and as much as I tried to ignore it, I just… couldn't anymore. I was sad because you were gone, and then everyone was throwing it in my face about sleeping with a married guy. I've been called a whore more times than I can count, but tonight, each time they said it, the word carried extra weight. To make it worse, they had pictures of the texts and started reading them aloud. I was humiliated and angry and—"

"What did you do?"

Shame sweeps through my veins. I hate that I reacted at all, let alone how I did. "Brenna went over to the jukebox and started playing that

Gretchen Wilson song 'Homewrecker' and, well, when she came back up to the bar to order her drink, I threw it in her face."

I wait for Ford to be upset, to be disgusted at my childish behavior, but it doesn't happen. Instead, he starts laughing, a rich, deep sound that catches me completely by surprise. "Good."

"Good?"

"Yeah, *good*, sweetheart. She deserved a drink in the face for being such an evil bitch."

"Well, I agree, but Jet didn't. He, uh, gave me some time off."

He's silent on the other end of the line, and I pull my phone back to see if we were disconnected. "Time off?"

I sigh with embarrassment. "Yeah. He called the other bartender and sent me home to get away for a bit. She's taking my hours this weekend."

"This weekend?"

"Yes. She's working for me Friday and Saturday night."

"What about tomorrow and Sunday?" he asks.

"I was already off those nights."

"Come here."

His words give me pause. "What?"

"Come to Ohio. He gave you time off because he knew you needed a break. So get out of town for a few days. You can drive here tomorrow; hell, I'll even rent you a car. Stay until I have to return to base Monday morning."

"I can't," I argue, almost as a reflex, even though the idea is intriguing.

"Why not? Chad's here. You can visit with us and see my hometown. It's not too long of a drive. Just a few hours, Shayne." There's hope in his words and excitement in his voice that has my heartbeat kicking up with anticipation.

"I don't know," I reply, but in my mind, I'm already packing my bags. Why can't I go? My usual excuse is work, but that's not a problem right now. I have the four days off and don't have to return to Jet's until Monday at four. That gives me plenty of time to go there, visit, and come back.

Except going there means... what? We're in a relationship? In a way, we are, even though we haven't put a name to it. We decided to stay in touch as much as possible, to get to know each other, and see where it goes. Going to Ohio would definitely be doing that, right?

But is meeting his family too much? I barely know him, and suddenly, I'd be meeting his parents and twin sister. She sounded super nice earlier on the phone, but that was before I just showed up at their house uninvited to see her brother.

Only... I have been invited.

"Come. Don't say no. Come see where I'm from and spend a little more time with me. I've been missing you like crazy, and it's only been a handful of hours. Give us a few more days before I have to report," he pleads, an urgency very evident in his deep voice.

"Okay."

"Okay?"

"I don't need you to rent me a car though. Mine should be fine. My uncle taught me to change my own oil when I was a teenager, and I just put new tires on her last winter." Relief rushes through me. I'm going to Ohio. To see Ford.

"I'm so fucking happy you're coming here, Shayne. So damn happy you don't even know."

"Me too," I reply with a smile, realizing I am. I can't wait to see him again. Watching him drive away earlier this afternoon about killed me. Sure, this next time he leaves will probably be ten times worse, but I don't care.

It's a risk I'm willing to take.

I have to.

It's as if it's out of my control, like the sun rising in the east and setting in the west. It just... is.

"How about I text you my address in the morning and you can let me know when you get on the road? It'll take you about three and a half hours to get here, give or take. If you leave in the morning, traffic shouldn't be too bad," he rambles, making me smile.

I gaze back out the window and sigh.

"What's wrong?"

"Nothing," I answer honestly. "I was just looking up and saw the Big Dipper."

"Me too. It's bright tonight."

"It is." Deep breath. "I'll see you tomorrow?"

"Yeah, sweetheart, you will. And about all that other shit that happened tonight? Let it go. I know it's easier said than done, but I have faith in you. You're an amazing person with a heart of gold, and I'm lucky as hell to have caught your eye."

"Pfff, I don't know about all of that."

"I do," he insists. "I knew it from the first moment I laid eyes on you."

I'm grinning again, something I seem to be doing a lot of where Ford is concerned.

"I'm sorry you've been hurt in the past, Shayne, but know I'll never do that to you. I'll never lie to you or use you the way he did. In fact, I've made it my life's mission to never see anything but a smile on your face for the rest of my life. It hurts me to hear the pain in your voice or see it in your eyes. I'll never be like them. I promise."

A few tears fall as I turn and relax against the wall. "Thank you."

"You don't need to thank me for protecting and caring for you, Shayne. Never. Now, as much as I'd love to stay up all night, talking to you on the phone, you have a big morning. I'm going to let you go so you can pack and get yourself organized."

"'Kay."

"Good night, sweetheart. See you soon."

"Night, Ford. I can't wait."

And then he's gone, leaving me alone in my small apartment with the sound of laughter and country music humming through the floorboards.

Except, I don't really feel alone. Not in the same sense that I always did.

Ford is here, even though he's not physically in the apartment. I can smell his clean soap still clinging to the couch and see the cup he used this morning sitting by the sink. He's everywhere, surrounding me in comfort and strength, even when he's gone.

And in a matter of hours, I'll be seeing him again.

My body physically aches to feel the warmth of his arms wrapped around me.

I'm not sure how easily sleep will come tonight, but the anticipation will carry me through.

Until I see him again.

Chapter 15

Ford

I HAVEN'T SLEPT. I COULDN'T STOP THINKING ABOUT SHAYNE. About how I wanted to wrap her in my arms and tell her everything is going to be okay. I couldn't stop thinking about how she's going to be here in a matter of hours. Scratch that. Now it's a matter of minutes. She called to tell me her GPS is telling her she's five minutes away.

I'm fucking ecstatic to see her.

"Mom and Dad are going to need to replace the flooring if you don't stop pacing. At least mix it up and forge a new path," Faith jokes.

"She's almost here," I say, stopping to pull back the curtains and peek out the window.

"Is this what you had to deal with the last week?" Faith asks Chad.

"No, but it is entertaining."

"Dick," I mutter good-naturedly. "She's your cousin. Are you not happy to see her?"

"I would say yes, but I have a feeling that you're going to be monopolizing all of her time." Chad gives me a look that dares me to deny it.

"I can't help it," I say, dropping the curtain. "I—never mind." I shake my head.

"No, what were you going to say?" Faith asks.

"I don't know, really. I can't explain it. I feel this connection to her. It's unlike anything I've ever felt. It's fucking crazy. I've known her for a week, but damn if it's not that. This… vise in my chest grips tight anytime I think about her or hear her voice. Hell, if I hear her name."

"Aw, Ford, you love her," Faith says, her voice soft.

"No. No." I shake my head. "I can't love her, Faith. That's absurd. It's been a week. A handful of days." It's too soon.

"Maybe, but you know her. You said last night Chad talked about her all the time."

"Yeah, but that was when I thought she was a man. I didn't know her then as the beautiful woman with dirty-blonde hair and gorgeous blue-green eyes." The words are barely out of my mouth when I hear tires on the gravel. Pulling back the curtains, I see her car pulling into the driveway. Turning to rush out to see her, Chad beats me to it as he hops off the couch and makes a beeline for the door.

Faith is laughing hysterically as I chase after him. He reaches her first and wraps her in a hug as soon as she steps out of her car. "Hey, cousin." He grins down at her.

"Chad." She laughs, and the sound, it's fucking musical.

"Can you step away from my girl?" I ask my best friend, irritated.

"She's your girl, huh? You know about this?" He looks down at Shayne.

"I had a pretty good idea," she says, smiling up at me. "Hey, Ford."

"Come here." I hold my hand out for her, and I don't know if Chad lets her go or if it's her will to be in my arms, but she pulls away from him, and within two steps, my arms are wrapped around her. I bury my face in her neck and breathe her in—less than twenty-four hours without Shayne. I don't know how I'm going to handle being back on base without her.

"Back up, you brute!" Faith says, pulling on my arm. "I need a turn."

I chuckle and pull back from Shayne, keeping my arm around her waist. "Shayne, this is my twin sister, Faith. Faith, meet my Shayne." Shayne leans into me, but Faith isn't having it.

"I need a hug." Faith steps into Shayne's personal space and wraps her in a hug. She winks at me over Shayne's shoulder before pulling back. "It's great to meet you. This one"—she points me—"can't stop talking about you."

Shayne glances up at me. "Missed me, huh?"

"You could say that," I say, pressing my lips to her forehead.

"Shayne, you have to tell me what you did to him. I need to learn the powers of your ways." Faith links her arm with my girl and leads her into the house. "Our parents aren't home, so we have some time for you to relax before meeting them."

"O-kay." I hear Shayne reply.

"What just happened?" I ask Chad.

"I think your sister just stole your girl." He laughs.

"Fuck." I kick at the gravel beneath my feet. "You need to keep Faith occupied. I have a few more days with Shayne before we leave, and I don't need my sister monopolizing my time."

"Just so we're clear. You're asking me to spend time with your sister, who, by the way, is hot as hell? Am I getting that right?"

I glare at him. "Are you interested in my sister?"

He shrugs. "She's… yeah, I don't know."

"Well, I can't exactly warn you off her. Not that I would. You're my best friend and one of the best people I know. Just be sure. If you're not, then don't go there. She deserves that."

"You using my words against me, Gregory?"

"Yep." I grin.

"I wouldn't. Not unless I was sure."

I nod, letting him know I understand.

"How long, you know, until you knew?" he asks.

"I knew there was something about her the minute I met her, but then it just kind of grew from there. It was fast, and I know it sounds crazy, but I couldn't care less. We have our own timelines. Live our lives for us. Do what feels right, but be sure."

"Noted."

"Come on. We need to go rescue Shayne from Faith." I grab Shayne's bags from her car, and together we head into the house. Following their voices to the living room, I didn't expect to see them both curled up on the couch laughing and chatting like they've known each other for years.

"You." I point to my sister, giving her a mock glare. "She's mine." Both girls crack up laughing. "Seriously, Faith." I drop Shayne's bags and place my hands on my hips.

"Faith, why don't we take the UTV out for a ride? Give these two some time to talk," Chad suggests.

"Fine. I'll give you some time, but you're not going to hog her while you're here. We have more girl talk that needs to happen." Faith winks at Shayne, who beams a smile back at her. "I'm driving," Faith says as she stands from her spot on the couch.

"Oh, sweetheart, I'm fine with letting you drive." Chad winks at her, and my sister blushes.

"Did you see that?" I ask Shayne once they are out of the house. "She was blushing. I haven't seen her do that since we were in middle school."

"Chad's a charmer," she agrees.

"Come here you." I sit down on the couch and pull her into my lap. "Fuck, Shay, I missed you."

"I missed you too." She loops her arms around my neck.

"You feeling better?"

"Yes."

"You want to talk about it?"

"No. I don't want to think about anyone other than you for the next four days."

"Four days." I smile before kissing her softly. "Not long enough, but better than the alternative."

"Agreed. Are you sure your parents don't mind if I stay here?"

"Nope. As soon as we got off the phone last night, I told Chad and Faith that you were coming up for a few days, then told my parents. They're excited to meet you."

"Who do they think I am?"

"What do you mean?"

"To you? Who do they think that I am to you?"

"I didn't say, not really. I mean, I didn't put a label on it. I told them you were Chad's cousin and coming up for a few days. I told them that you and I got close, and we wanted to spend more time together."

"They're okay with that? I have some savings. I can go to a hotel."

"Yeah, no. That's not going to happen. I have three nights with you, and all of them, you will be in my arms."

"What if we get caught?"

"What do you mean?"

"What if your parents find me in your bed? I don't want to upset or disrespect them."

"Shayne, baby, they know you're rooming with me. I told them you would be."

"Oh." Her eyes widen. "Are you sure? I mean, I don't want them to think—" I place my finger over her lips to stop her.

"They will think that you're an amazing woman who I want to spend more time with. We're both consenting adults. Now, if you really don't want to sleep next to me, I can take the couch. It's not a big deal."

"No. I want to be with you. That's why I'm here."

"Good. Let's take your things up to my room, so you know where we'll be sleeping." With one more quick kiss, I tap her thigh, and she stands. I grab her bags and motion for her to follow me upstairs. "This is it," I say, pushing into my room.

"You have a queen-size bed?" she asks, staring at my bed that takes up most of my childhood bedroom.

"I'm a big guy," I say, holding my arms out to my sides.

"You are," she says, covering a yawn.

"Tired?" I ask, stepping close and pulling her into my arms.

"Yes. I didn't sleep well. Actually, not at all. I was too excited to sleep."

"Me either. How does a nap sound?"

"Can we?"

"Babe, we can do whatever in the hell we want." I lead her to the bed, pull back the covers, and climb in. She doesn't hesitate, and within seconds, we're cuddled up under the warmth of the blankets to ward off the chill of the air conditioning.

"Thank you," she says sleepily.

"For what?"

"Inviting me. I missed this. I missed you," she whispers.

"I missed this, and I missed you. More than you know." I kiss her shoulder and relish the feel of her in my arms. It's not long before sleep claims us both.

"Mom, no," I plead.

"What? This is a mother's right, Ford Gregory." She winks at Shayne.

"Suck it up, buttercup." Faith grins.

"Oh, you don't think I'm not bringing out your baby pictures too? That's cute." Mom laughs. "I'll be right back."

"Dad, a little help here?" I try, knowing it's not going to work.

"Son, you know there is no stopping your mother once she gets an idea in her head."

"Ugh." I lean my head back against the couch. "Why me?" I say dramatically.

I feel Shayne's hand on my thigh. "It's fine. What's the big deal?"

"I'm trying to woo you," I say, lifting my head. "I can't do that with spaghetti face and naked bath-time pictures."

"She wouldn't!" Faith exclaims.

"You know she's pulling out the scrapbooks," I tell my sister.

"Chad, how about a walk?" Faith suggests.

"Nah, I'm good here." He slings his arm over her shoulders from his seat next to her on the loveseat.

"Do you think we have time to bail?" I whisper to Shayne.

"I don't want to. I'm excited to see you as a little boy."

"Just wait. As soon as I see Joan again, she and I are going to have a chat about baby pictures."

"There aren't many," she says softly.

"That's fine. I'll take what I can get. You're about to be bombarded with my life growing up. The least you can give me is a glimpse of yours."

She smiles. "Deal."

"Here we are. Ford, why don't you sit next to Faith and let me, Shayne, and Chad have the couch."

At the suggestion, Shayne moves to the far right, and Mom plops down next to her on the middle cushion. I remain seated, refusing to give up my seat.

"Move it, Gregory." Chad laughs, looming over me.

"Fine." Begrudgingly, I stand and take the seat he vacated next to Faith.

"Why didn't we think to hide the pictures?" Faith asks.

"You know Mom. She would have found them regardless. It wouldn't surprise me if she has duplicates stashed for that very occurrence."

"Ugh, you're probably right."

"Aw, look at the two of them," Shayne coos.

"Right? Although I am biased." Mom looks up and smiles at Dad.

And so it goes. The next hour is spent with Mom, Shayne, and Chad looking at pictures of Faith and me growing up. I don't miss the soft looks that Chad gives my little sister, and I know he sees the same looks that Shayne and I are sharing. For some reason, this feels intimate. Sitting here in my parents' living room, reminiscing about old times as the girl who is quickly becoming my world, looks at the photographic evidence of our stories.

"I'm hungry. Are you hungry?" Faith stands and looks at me.

"Oh, I guess we should get dinner started," Mom concedes, closing the scrapbook. It doesn't matter. She was at the final page anyway.

"Right, Ford and I will fire up the grill." Faith grabs my hand and pulls me from the loveseat and through the kitchen out the patio door. "We need to talk."

"What's up?"

"Chad."

"What about Chad?"

"I like him."

"Okay."

"No. Like I *like* him like him."

"Okay."

"I need you to tell me what you think? If you don't want me to pursue it, I won't."

"That would make me a hypocrite. I am dating his cousin."

She points at her chest. "Sister."

"She might as well be his sister."

"Is he... I mean, is he a good guy? I know he's your best friend, but I just don't want to get my heart crushed."

"He's a good guy. Not much on relationships, from what I've heard, but that doesn't mean he's not willing to try. I know for a fact the idea of having someone to come home to appeals to him," I say, thinking about our conversation a few nights before we returned stateside. "I already told him not to start something with you if he's not serious."

"You're my priority."

"I love you, Faith. Chad's a good guy. If you're interested, see where it goes."

"And if it doesn't work out?"

I shrug. "As long as he doesn't screw you over, he's still going to be my best friend, and you're still my sister."

"I love you, big brother."

I swallow hard. It's rare moments like this that I miss the most. "I love you too." I turn her into a tight hug just as the patio door opens.

"You two all right out here?" Chad asks.

"We are," Faith assures him. "You feel like taking a walk before dinner?" she suggests.

Chad's eyes flash to me, and I give him a subtle nod. "Sure, lead the way." He motions for her to move in front of him, but she surprises him when she laces her fingers through his, gives him a shy smile, and together they walk off the porch and toward the road.

"I wondered about that," Mom says from behind me.

"Hey, I didn't hear you come out."

"It's my ninja skills." She holds up a spatula and does a goofy ninja move.

"You need any help?" I ask, laughing with a shake of my head at her antics.

"No, but you can keep me company. Your dad is showing Shayne his Mustang."

"I should save her."

"You should tell me about your sister and Chad."

"That's their story to tell."

"Figures. You two never did tell each other's secrets. How about your own? Shayne seems sweet."

"Sweet as hell, Mom."

She grins. "You're different with her."

"I'm older. I'm not a teenager with my first serious girlfriend anymore."

"I know that," she says, giving me a look that tells me she's not that blind. "What I mean is that you seem to be drawn to her. And she with you. The two of you look cute together."

"It's been a week." I feel as though that's what I need to say. I can't gush to her how I'm falling hard and fast for this girl. Or can I? If anyone would understand, it would be Mom.

Mom shrugs. "There is no timeline on love, Ford."

"Who said anything about love?"

"You didn't have to. You're my son, and I know you. I also know I've never seen you look at anyone the way you look at her."

"I haven't been home much the last three years."

"A mother knows."

"I'm not sure how we'll survive long distance." My thoughts go to Sara and the drama that surrounded us when I enlisted. I know that Shayne is not Sara. In fact, they are complete opposites. However, I've seen it with guys I'm deployed with and the distance takes its toll.

"She's a few hours from the base and from us. We'll do what we can to include her, make her feel welcome, and you do what you can from base. In the end, if it's meant to be, it will be." I send up a silent prayer that it will be. That Shayne and I can survive being separated, and in the end, it will be the two of us living our lives together.

"You're one of a kind. You know that? You and Dad both."

"If she's important to you, she's important to us. It's that simple, Ford. Life has enough drama and hardships. Love and family shouldn't be one of them."

"Hey." Dad sticks his head around the side of the house. "I'm taking Shayne for a spin in the Shelby."

"Be careful," Mom tells him.

He winks. "Always, honey."

I wave them off, and although I'm jealous that my dad is taking her for a spin and not me, I'm glad they're getting along and that they both want to go for a ride. Mom said they would include her while I was gone, and I know she doesn't mean while living on base. I'll be deployed again, and that's when it's going to hit the hardest. Shayne no longer just has Chad and his family. She has mine too. They'll make sure she's okay while I'm gone. That alone lifts some of the weight from my shoulders. She and I are going to make this thing official before she leaves, and we're going to make this relationship work.

It has to. I can't see my future without her in it.

Chapter 16

Shayne

"YOU OKAY?"

I glance to my side and give Ford a smile. "Yeah, fine. Why?"

He shrugs, bringing our linked hands up to his mouth and running his lips across my knuckles. "You've been quiet for a while now."

I sigh and relax farther into the lawn chair, feeling more relaxed than I have in… well, forever. "Just listening to everyone talk and enjoying this gorgeous night."

After dinner, Ford took me on a tour of his family grounds. They live a few miles outside Cooper on a homestead that's been in Ford's family for three generations. He explained how his great-grandpa purchased the land for a steal and built a house. Over the years, it has been added onto and updated, but the guts still remain. There are eleven acres total, six of them timbered. At one time, there was a small cattle operation, but Ford's parents weren't into raising livestock when they moved into the homestead. They eventually sold the business, continuing with their own passions in life.

I glance around the firepit. Besides Faith and Chad, Ford's parents are out here, along with their neighbors from down the road. I keep catching odd looks they give me, but I'm not sure what they mean, especially since they look away when I notice. It's as if they're curious about me, about the woman Ford brought home during his leave. And the wife has definitely taken notice of our hands linked together. She's frowned on more than one occasion, as if seeing it makes her uncomfortable.

"So, Ford, how long are you home till?" the woman, Diana, asks, sipping sweet tea.

"I report back Monday morning at six, ma'am," Ford answers politely.

"That soon? But you just got here," she replies, her tone full of sadness and question.

"I arrived home yesterday. I spent the last week in Kentucky with Chad's family," he states, his hold tightening on my hand.

"Well, I'm sure that was a nice visit." She takes another drink of her tea. "You know, Sara's off this weekend. I'm sure she'd love to catch up with you while you're on leave."

That's when I feel him tense beside me. Even though it's only our hands connected, I can sense the anxiety that sweeps through his entire body. I also see the way Chad physically blanches at her comment, which tells me he knows something I don't know.

Beth chuckles awkwardly. "I'm sure Ford would welcome a chance to say hello to Sara if they run into each other. Though, I'm sure with Shayne here, he's going to be kept awfully busy."

Is it just me, or is the entire area surrounded by a thick fog of tension? It's there, stifling the air around everyone. Even Chad looks uncomfortable. Faith looks downright murderous.

"Wanna take a quick walk?" Ford asks, already standing and gently pulling on my hand.

"Uh, yeah." I'm up, moving wherever he takes me. As we pass in front of his mom, I notice the small smile she gives her son, one laced with an apology.

"Don't wander off too far, you two," Ford's dad says, a wide grin on his face.

"We won't. I thought we'd check on my baby again. Tuck her in for bed," Ford replies to his dad, earning a bark of laughter from both older men.

We head for the barn, the one that hasn't been used in nearly two decades for anything other than storage. His dad has a huge pole building that he uses for a shop, tinkering with small engines and building rustic furniture that he sells at a local market. That's also where he stores *his* baby. His Shelby Mustang.

"How come your baby is kept in the barn, but your dad's is in the shop?" I ask as we approach the big wooden structure.

Ford laughs. "I asked the same thing when I enlisted, and he told me my truck would be kept out here. He said when I work my ass off most of my life and build the shop of my dreams, I could keep whatever I wanted in it. Until then, I get the barn." There's not even a hint of resentment in his voice as he slides the big door open just enough for us to pass through. Then, he closes it and turns on the light. "I don't mind it being out here though. Besides a few unwelcomed critters getting into the wiring, I haven't had any problems. Dad comes out and starts her up, taking her for a ride every weekend. We'll take Margaret for a spin this weekend," he says, leading me toward the truck. "Hop in."

I glance up at the big black vehicle and shake my head. "I need a stepstool."

He pops open the passenger door and gives me a wicked grin. As he places both hands on my hips and lifts, he says, "No, you don't. This is my favorite part about this big truck. I get to help the pretty ladies."

I gasp as I move through the air, my fingers gripping his hard shoulders, and am gently deposited onto the seat. "Give a lot of ladies rides in your truck, huh?" I tease, hating the tinge of jealousy that creeps up at the thought.

Ford is standing in front of me and presses forward, filling the space between my legs. His hands run up my outer thighs, warmth left in the wake. He sobers, meeting my gaze. "No. There was only one, actually. My high school girlfriend."

"You mentioned her," I say, running my hands over the muscles at his upper back.

"Her name is Sara."

It takes a second for the name to register, but when it does, I can't hide my shock. "The same Sara…"

He nods. "The same Sara." Ford takes a deep breath and leans forward, his head resting at my shoulder. His warm breath tickles my neck, and my nipples pebble against the coarse material of my bra, as desire swirls through my blood.

"We grew up neighbors, so we were always on the bus together or playing in the summer. It was the three of us, Faith, Sara, and me. Well, in high school, that's when I started to notice Sara in a different light. She wasn't my friend next door anymore, but someone I was attracted to. We didn't actually start going out until our junior year."

He splays his long fingers across my upper thighs, his index finger sliding dangerously close to the place I'm starting to ache. "What happened?" I ask, my voice all breathless, as I angle my hips to get a little closer.

"We broke up after high school when she didn't support my decision to enlist. Her mom, Diana, is great, but I think she's always held out hope that we'd get back together." He meets my gaze, something heady swirling in those deep green orbs.

"So, only one girl in the truck, huh?" I quip, trying to find the lighter side of the conversation.

His face transforms as he grins. "You're lucky number two."

I bark out a laugh. "I'm not sure that's luck or sad."

"Oh, I say it's very lucky," he replies, scooting me closer until my core is pressed against his stomach, his fingers spread wide against my lower back and ass. "I mean, you're the hottest girl I've ever kissed in my truck."

My breathing comes out in little pants. "But... you haven't kissed me... yet."

"Is that permission?" he whispers, moving his hand across my hip, as if he can't stop touching me.

"Oh, it's definitely permission," I respond, taking his lips with mine.

I might have initiated the kiss, but he takes full control instantly. His mouth owns me, claiming and possessing as if I were completely helpless to fight it. We've shared kisses before, but this is... wow. I find myself rocking against his body, seeking out sweet friction, needing to feel closer to him.

We kiss for what feels like forever. My lips are swollen and tender, but I don't care. I could kiss this man for the rest of my life, and it would probably not be long enough. It would never be enough.

When he finally pulls back, both of us gasping for oxygen, he gives me a soft smile. "Yep, definitely the hottest girl I've kissed in my truck."

Feeling a boldness come over me I wasn't expecting, I murmur, "You know, we could do *more* than just kiss."

Ford lets out a strangled groan, one that sounds like he's in physical pain. "Temptress."

I chuckle, rocking my hips again and coming in contact with his very hard, very large erection. "It's the truck," I reply with a shrug. "It's so... sexy."

His throaty laugh goes straight to my core, making my muscles clench. I never knew I could get this turned on by the sound of a voice, but here I am, ready to throw my reservations—and my panties—out the window. Ford places his hands on both sides of my jaw and lightly kisses my chin. "When I finally get you beneath me, it's not going to be in a truck, Shayne, and it's not going to be with time restrictions. I'm going to take my time with you, savoring every inch of your body and memorizing every noise that comes from these sweet lips." He brushes his across mine, making me mewl in appreciation. "Besides, it's not going to be with my parents, my sister, my cousin, and my ex's parents outside. It's going to be in a big bed when we're all alone, and no one can hear your cries of pleasure." He nips at the sensitive skin on my neck, causing goose bumps to pepper my skin.

"And there will be a lot of cries of pleasure, Shayne," he adds huskily, my body practically orgasming right then and there.

We remain where we are, our bodies entwined as our breathing begins to return to normal. He's really not going to take this further than a few amazing kisses. A big part of me is saddened, but there's also another part that's relieved.

He's right. Our first time shouldn't be in a truck. In a barn. Anywhere someone can happen upon us.

Ford wants it to be perfect, where we're completely alone, and I realize I want that too. As much as I'd love a quick romp in the truck to take the edge off, I appreciate his insistence at making our first time together special.

"We should head back out before they come looking for us," he whispers, pulling me against his chest and holding me close. It's a hug. A simple gesture, but it feels like so much more.

"Are you going to help me down? Or does your chivalry only extend to helping me into the truck?"

He smirks a wicked grin. "You think I'd only want my hands on you once?"

Then, he grabs me around the waist and helps me down. As soon as my feet are on the ground, he presses his lips to my forehead and inhales. "You smell amazing. Like fresh air and vanilla. I can't get enough of it. It's my favorite scent in the whole world."

I smile and set my cheek against his chest, the steady, strong beat of his heart speaking to my soul. "Then it's not weird that my favorite scent is your deodorant? It's rich and clean and musky, and I might have stuck my nose in your armpit the other night when you were asleep."

He chuckles, the sound vibrating against my face. "Come on, weirdo. Let's go rejoin the gathering."

Ford takes my hand, brings it to his lips, and leads me out of the barn, making sure the lights are off and the door securely locked behind us. We approach the firepit, and the first thing I notice is the fact the parents are all gone. Chad and Faith remain, and they're sitting close. In fact, very, *very* close.

"Hey," Ford says, his eyes glancing down to where Chad rests his hand on his sister's thigh.

They look up, startled, and his friend quickly pulls his hand back. "Hi. Your parents just went inside to bed."

Ford nods and leads me to the loveseat glider where his parents sat earlier this evening. Chad and Faith are directly across from us, both seeming a little more fidgety than before and unable to make eye contact. I can't help but think something happened.

Ford throws his arm over the back of the glider, his hand resting on my shoulder. "So, tell me why you both look so guilty right now."

"Come on, beautiful. We're going to town."

I jump up off the couch, eager to finally see the place Ford grew up. It's Saturday afternoon, and we have yet to leave his homestead. We've spent all our time with his parents and sister, doing everything from dinners together to pulling out their family photo albums and seeing all the naked bathtub pictures. As much as I've loved hanging out and getting to know his family, I have to admit, I'm excited to go explore Cooper.

"Let me grab a hair tie!" I holler, sprinting up the stairs to Ford's bedroom.

I really was worried about sharing a sleeping space with him under his parents' roof, but they've been super cool about it. Plus, it's not like there was any other place for me to go. With Chad using the pullout bed in the den, the only other option for me was the couch in the living room or bunking with Faith in her room.

I have to admit, snuggling against Ford's large, muscular body, nestled all comfortable-like in the crook of his arm, the scent of his deodorant escorting me to dreamland, has been the best sleep I've had in the history of forever.

When I come back down the stairs, Ford is waiting at the front door. "Where'd your sister and Chad go?"

"For a walk in the timber," he replies, holding open the door for me to exit.

His truck is already pulled out of the barn and parked at the end of the sidewalk. When we reach the passenger door, he opens it and hoists me up, much like he did in the barn Thursday night. I reach for the seat belt as he shuts my door and moves to the driver's side. "Ready?" he asks the moment he jumps up inside the cab.

"Ready," I state, practically bouncing in the seat.

"All right, Margaret, let's stretch your legs, beautiful." Then he puts the truck into gear and floors it out of the driveway, sending gravel flying across the front yard.

When we make it to the roadway, he only plays a little, wearing a happy grin on his handsome face. My hand is gripping the door panel, but not out of fear. It's actually quite fun to play around and feel the truck stretch her legs.

As we near town and he reaches over and grabs my hand, I ask, "So…beautiful?"

He gives me a look of confusion.

"You called Margaret beautiful. You call me beautiful. Is that like a *thing* for you?"

He barks out a laugh. "Are you jealous?"

"Of Margaret?" I ask, grinning widely. "Yes, yes I am. I mean, she's just a truck."

Ford gasps, releasing my hand and gingerly stroking the dash. "Don't listen to the jealous woman, Margaret. You're way more than just a truck."

I giggle, which makes him smile. "You're crazy."

He shrugs and brings my hand to his lips. "Crazy about you," he declares, waggling his eyebrows.

Pulling into town, Ford drives down the main artery through town, and I'm completely enthralled with the cute shops and green spaces. He drives to a lot and parks. "Come on, let's check it out."

We walk slowly down the sidewalk, stopping at the coffee shop for something to drink. I order an iced coffee while Ford gets a flavored iced tea, and then we stroll along window shopping. We stop in front of a flower shop and admire the garden gnomes and stepping-stones. "Someday, I'll have an area with some flowers and some star-gazing seating and lots of cute statues," I tell him, reveling in the warmth of being tucked against his body.

"That sounds nice," he replies, pointing to a stone covered in stars. "Look at that one."

"It's gorgeous," I agree, reading the perfect quote printed on the small concrete decoration. *Only in the darkness can you see the stars.*

Ford drags me inside the small store and grabs it from the window.

"What are you doing?" I ask as he tucks it under his arm.

"Buying it," he answers with a shrug.

I can't help but smile. "Uhh, you don't have a garden."

He pulls me against his broad chest, his warm breath caressing my forehead. "No, I don't, but the saying made me think of you. Of us. We're going to see a lot of darkness while I'm away, but the stars will always bring us back together."

My throat thickens with emotion as I gaze up at this amazing man. How did I get so damn lucky?

He places a tender kiss on the end of my nose and steers me toward the counter. There's someone in front of us, so I just take the opportunity to snuggle against the man who's quickly become my everything. Ford kisses the crown of my head, and I smile when I hear him inhale my hair.

"Next," the older woman behind the counter says as the one in front of us moves aside.

We step forward, my arm bumping into the lady as she juggles her purchases and her purse. "I'm sorry," I say at the exact moment she turns around and glances up.

"Ford."

"Sara."

I glance between the two before my eyes finally stop on the woman beside me. She has long blonde hair and the lightest blue eyes. She's super skinny with straight white teeth and boobs that appear a little too big for her slight frame. She's gorgeous, really. Like a real-life Barbie doll.

Perfect in every way.

Then her eyes return to me, and it's as if someone cranks up the air conditioning. I can feel the chill coming from her heart. This woman may be pretty, but I can tell she has an ugly side. It bleeds from ocean-colored eyes like a volcanic eruption.

And the way she's glaring daggers at me lets me know that particular side is aimed straight at me.

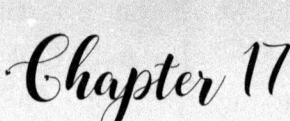

Chapter 17

Ford

"I DIDN'T TAKE YOU FOR ONE WHO WOULD BRING HOME A STRAY," Sara sneers.

Shayne stiffens beside me. "Watch yourself, Sara," I warn. My voice is cold and calculated. She's put me through enough hell, and I refuse to let her get her claws into Shayne too.

"Really, Ford, you left me for her?"

"First of all," I say, keeping my voice low. "You broke up with me. Second, it's been over between us for years." I'm trying my hardest to keep my cool. Shayne tries to pull away, but I keep my hand clasped tight around hers.

"We have history," Sara says, batting her eyelashes at me. "It was always meant to be us."

"No. It wasn't meant to be us. If that were the case, you wouldn't have dropped me like hot coals when I enlisted. It was always my plan, yet you thought you could change me. Tell me, Sara, what about that scenario says forever to you?"

"We have history."

I shrug. "We grew up in the same town, on the same road. We were friends. Then we were more. Then you ended things. Now we're over. Oh, by the way, I'd like to introduce you to my girlfriend. Babe, this is my ex, Sara."

My lips connect with Shayne's temple, and I feel her relax just a little. "It's nice to meet you." Shayne offers Sara her hand.

"He'll come back to me." Sara makes a point to look at Shayne with… pity? Disgust? I can't quite name the look, but it pisses me the fuck off.

"No. I won't," I say through gritted teeth and much louder than intended, earning us a few odd stares. "Shayne is my future." I look down at the beauty beside me. "It's like she was made for me." Her blue-green eyes sparkle at my words.

"Oh, stop with the googly-eyes bullshit. I can see through it. You're putting on a show for me."

"Yeah? You think so? Then why was Shayne the one who fell asleep in my arms last night? Why is she the first person I think about when I open my eyes and the last before closing them at night? Tell me, Sara, what do you think that means?"

"You!" Sara stomps her foot like a toddler. Casting a glare at Shayne and then me, she turns and huffs as she shows her true colors exiting the flower shop.

"I'm sorry about that," I tell Shayne, pulling her into my arms. I hold her close, just needing to feel her, to wash away the evil that is my ex. After what Shayne's already been through this week with the simple-minded fucks in her hometown, this is the last thing she needs.

"She's… awful." Her voice is soft.

"She really is. It's a shame. She didn't used to be, but when she realized I wasn't going to change my mind about enlisting, she changed." I place my arm on the small of her back and lead her away from the register.

"You broke her heart."

"That's what she tells me, but she never acted heartbroken. She just sort of went crazy. She used to write me letters all the time telling me how I ruined her life. She claimed that I stole her youth. We dated for two years, and when I enlisted, something I'd talked about since I was young, she flipped. She once told me in a letter that she thought she could change me."

"That's terrible. I'd never want to change you."

"Maybe not, but you have."

"How so?" She tilts her head to the side.

"You've settled yourself here." I place my hand over my chest. "And here." I tap my temple. "Not only that, but I'm thinking about things like the future, and even maybe not reenlisting after this next contract is up. I've always wanted the army to be my lifetime career but meeting you, it's made me look at things differently."

"We've known each other a week."

I nod. "Yep." I know without a shadow of a doubt this woman is for me. I'm ready to lay my heart on the table and I hope that she accepts it. Before I have to leave her again, we need to have our expectations defined.

"Do you think that's too fast?"

"Do you?"

She doesn't answer right away, and I love that she's taking my question seriously. I'm waiting patiently, at least that's how it appears on the outside when in reality, I'm a bundle of nerves waiting for her to tell me her answer. That's something else that's new for me since meeting her. I have this sappy shit in my head, like marriage and kids and houses in the country with white picket fences. Sure, I've never been one to play the field, but I've also never seen my future so vividly in my mind. And next to me every time is her.

"No. Not with you. I know this is going to sound ridiculous, but it feels as though I've known you for years."

"As long as you and I know the connection that we have, and we're good with the pace, I don't give a fuck what anyone else says or thinks. You're all that matters, Shayne."

"Your family?"

"I love them. They love me, and they know that you make me happy. It's as simple as that."

"I have a confession."

"I'm all ears," I say, standing. "Let me toss these empties, and pay for this sign, and we can head out." I grab her empty cup along with mine and toss them in the trash. The cashier at the register gives me a curious look but doesn't comment as I pay for the sign, and she bags it up for me. Walking back to where Shayne is waiting by the door, I offer her my hand, and she takes it with ease, allowing me to lead her out of the flower shop. "Now, this confession," I say, sliding my arm around her shoulders. She snuggles in close, and I love it. I love being close to her, holding her. I love that she's here in my hometown and that connection we have, it's stronger here. Running into Sara, I felt... nothing. She's an old acquaintance. I'm not even irritated with all her letters she assaulted me with the first two years. I'm just done with her. I don't know if that's because of the beautiful woman in my arms, but I'm pretty sure it does.

"I was jealous," she says, keeping her eyes on the sidewalk in front of us.

"Jealous?"

"Of Sara."

"What?" I stop and place my hands on her shoulders to face me. "Explain that."

"She's beautiful. She reminds me of a freaking Barbie doll. And I'm just—" She looks down at her cutoff jean shorts, tank top, and flip-flops. "I'm just me."

"Just you? Shay, baby, you're everything. I felt nothing seeing Sara again. Nothing. I don't even hate her. In fact, I was just thinking that very thing. She's someone I used to know."

"Someone you used to know," she repeats.

"And you, my beautiful, Shayne, you're… everything." Bending, I softly press my lips to hers. I'd love to do nothing more than to push her up against the storefront and devour her, but there's a time and place for that. I, for one, prefer not to have an audience when I devour her.

Pulling out of the kiss, she studies me, a small grin tilting her lips. "Well, now what are we gonna do? I've met the ex and her parents, and I feel validated." She grins.

"We're going to finish your tour of the town and head back to Mom and Dad's. Dad's grilling out again and inviting over some extended family. And we should probably check up on Chad and Faith."

"There's something there, right?" she says.

"I think so. I'm happy for them. Faith is the best, and Chad's a good guy. My best friend."

"You're a good guy, Ford Gregory."

"Yeah?" She nods. "Right back at ya, baby." Another kiss to her lips because she's here, and I have to kiss her as much as I can before I leave.

I know our time is coming to an end, and I need to savor every single minute.

This afternoon has been a blast. I love getting to catch up with extended family. What I love even more than that is that they all got to meet Shayne. I introduced her as my girlfriend. It's not something that we've talked about, but we will. Tonight. I have a surprise for her—a surprise for us.

"Thanks for coming, Mike," I say, giving my uncle a hug.

"Good to see you, Ford. Take care and be safe." He hugs me one more time before moving to Shayne. "Keep this one in line, will you?" he asks her, pointing at me.

Shayne laughs. "I'll see what I can do. It was so nice to meet you." She offers him her hand, but he pats it away and wraps his arms around her in a hug.

"You're good for him," he says, not bothering to lower his voice.

"We're good for each other." She glances at me, and something passes in her eyes that I can't name.

"That's the last of them," I tell her as Uncle Mike makes his way to his truck.

"You have a great family."

"Thank you."

"Hey, what are you two getting into tonight?" Faith asks, joining us.

"We have plans."

"Oh, okay. Chad and I were thinking about hanging out at my place. You two are welcome to join us."

"Thanks, sis, but like I said, we've got plans."

"What are we doing?" Shayne asks.

"It's a surprise."

"I'm not sure if I like surprises."

"You're not sure?" Faith asks her.

"Never really had many surprises in my life. Not good ones anyway."

"I'll be sure to change that," I say, my lips next to her ear. I kiss her neck and pull back before I lose my self-control. "So, you and Chad?" I ask Faith.

"Maybe. No. I don't know." She laughs.

"How about yes?" Chad says, stepping next to her, sliding his arm around her waist. The way he's looking at her, it's the same look I have when I look at Shayne. He glances at me and nods, and that one simple gesture tells me all I need to know. He's going all-in with my sister.

"You two kids have fun," I say, backing away from them, bringing Shayne with me. "We're going to say bye to Mom and Dad and head out. Oh, and we aren't staying here tonight," I tell them. They smile and wave. I have a feeling they won't be staying here tonight either.

"We're not staying here?" Shayne asks as I lead her into the house.

"Nope. All a part of the surprise."

"Hey, kids," Dad greets us. "Heading out?"

"Yeah. We're going to grab a few things, and then we'll be out of your hair."

"You're not in our hair," Mom assures us.

"Babe, we did go from no kids to a house full the last few days." Dad wags his eyebrows and smacks her on the ass.

"Todd Gregory." She tries to scold, but her laughter prevents it from sounding like an admonishment. That and the blush coating her cheeks.

I've grown up watching the way he loves her, and I want what they have. I know Shayne wasn't as lucky as me. I hope this works out with us, and I can show her what it's like to live in a house full of love. I can see it clearly in my mind.

I was with Sara for two years, and it didn't hurt me to walk away from her. I've known Shayne a handful of days, and the thought of not seeing her every day is tearing me up inside. If that's not telling, I don't know what is.

"On that note, you two crazy kids have fun tonight," I say, tugging on Shayne's hand to lead her upstairs to pack. "Oh, and, Dad—" I pause, looking over my shoulder. "Don't do anything I wouldn't do." I wink. Dad throws his head back in laughter, and if I'm not mistaken, I hear Mom do the same.

"I cannot believe you just said that." Shayne looks horrified as we enter my room.

"Oh, come on, how do you think Faith and I got here?"

"Ford!" She laughs.

"Pack an overnight bag."

"Where are we going?"

"It's a surprise, but I can tell you it's just going to be us. So, pack whatever you'll need for a night with just the two of us." I want to tell her not to bother with clothes and just sweep her away, but I don't want to assume. I know we've talked about more. About being together in the most intimate of ways, but I'd never pressure her for more. I just want to spend my last night home with her. I want to hold her in my arms and kiss her sweet lips. And if that leads to more, well, I'm prepared for that too.

"Don't you want to spend your last night with your family? I know you leave tomorrow to report on Monday."

I glance at the clock and see it's just after eight on Saturday night. "I've spent time with them, and now I want to spend time with you. I love my family, Shayne, but we're used to this. They're used to me being gone, but you and me, we're still new, and I need as much of your time as you're willing to give me before I head back to base."

"I'm really going to miss you." There's a mist in her eyes that she tries hard to ignore as she blinks the tears away.

"You have no idea, beautiful." I pull her into my arms and hold her close. "As much as I'd love to just stand here with you in my arms the rest of the night, we have a hotel suite with our name on it."

"A hotel suite?"

"Dammit." I shake my head. "I can't believe I said that. It's you. You're too damn distracting."

"You're taking me to a hotel?"

"Yes. And before you say anything, I want you to know I just want some uninterrupted time with you. I don't expect anything. Just your time."

"Ford?"

"Shayne?"

"Are you done talking?"

"Um... yes?"

She throws her head back and laughs. "Good. Now go pack a bag. We have places to be." She pushes on my chest, but I don't move an inch.

"Shayne, I mean it. I just want to spend time with you."

"That's great. I'm glad, but I think we need to finish what we started in the truck the other night. This day has been the longest foreplay session of my life."

"Right?" I laugh. "Running into one's ex will do that to you."

"Not that. But everything else. Every look. Every touch. I don't know that I have the words to tell you how it feels to want you like I do."

"You want me?" I ask. When I take a step toward her, she steps back. We repeat this step for step until her back hits my bedroom wall.

"Very much." She nods, her voice breathy.

"This much?" I ask. I take her hand in mine and place it over the bulge in my cargo shorts.

"More."

"Impossible."

I keep my eyes locked on hers, even when I hear her lower the zipper on her jean shorts. I hold her gaze, those blue-green eyes commanding my attention. Even when she takes my hand in hers, noticing the slight tremor, I don't look away. I stay focused on her when she slides my hand inside her tiny lace panties. My eyes are frozen on her, but my hand, well, it has a mind of its own as I trace my fingers through her folds, coating my fingers with her.

"For me?" I ask, even though I already know the answer.

"All for you."

"We need to go. Now." I say the words but make no move to pull my hand from her panties.

"We do," she agrees, as my lips collide with hers.

Her taste explodes on my tongue as I slide a finger inside her. Her tongue meets mine stroke for stroke. It's a heady feeling knowing that this need churning inside me is matched by hers for me.

"Oh," she murmurs against my lips.

"Holy fuck," I whisper. Resting my forehead on her shoulder, I try to get ahold of myself. This is not what was supposed to happen. We have a hotel suite waiting on us. I don't want my parents witnessing our first time. But, fuck, I don't know if I can stop.

"Ford?"

"Yeah, baby."

"You okay?"

With herculean effort, I pull my hand out of her panties, and bring my finger to my mouth, and taste her for the first time. *Fuck me.* "Never been better. You ready?"

"Yes."

I nod, giving myself some time to regain some control. "Before we leave, we need to be on the same page with something."

"Okay?" Her voice is a little hesitant.

"I want you to be mine. You are mine. I want us to be exclusive. Just you and me. I know it's a lot to ask, and I'm leaving, but I can't—" I swallow hard. "I can't go back not knowing that we have this settled. I can't do my job worrying about whether or not you know how I feel about you."

"How do you feel about me?"

"I'm falling hard and fast, Shayne. I want to see where we can take this connection of ours."

"Okay."

"Okay?"

"I'm yours. You're mine. We're exclusive."

"Just like that?"

"Just like that." She stands on her tiptoes and kisses the corner of my mouth. "Now, take me to this surprise."

"My pleasure."

"I'm hoping it will be our pleasure," she replies huskily. My cock takes notice of the change in her voice. I don't want to pressure her. I would be fine holding her all night, but the thought of being inside her, well, let's just say I'm down for that as well.

I don't know what I did to have this woman come into my life, but I will forever be thankful to the universe, the stars, and the moon. I don't know how our paths were destined to cross. The stars must have aligned at the right time. Whatever the reason she was brought into my life, I will forever be indebted.

Chapter 18

Shayne

I'M NOT NERVOUS.

Surprisingly.

Two weeks ago, if you had told me I would be going to a hotel with someone I knew only a short time, I would have called for a mental evaluation. No way. Instead of feeling any uncertainty, I'm excited. More than excited, actually. I'm elated.

Ready.

Are things moving too fast for Ford and me?

Quite possibly.

The last time I jumped into the deep end of a relationship, it ended with a whole heap of heartache. Worse, it wasn't just mine. I hurt an innocent woman along the way. Though I have to admit, I feel a little less guilty now that I've confessed everything to Ford. He was so understanding and kept insisting I wasn't to blame. Deep down, I always knew it was Rodney's fault and not so much mine, but try telling your-self that when everywhere you go, they look at you like a homewrecker.

Like a slut.

I had heard the whispers. Hell, sometimes they didn't even whis-per. Especially when they got a few drinks in their system, like what happened the other evening. After I threw that drink in her face, I felt a rush of guilt. I had stooped to their level. I was angry and ashamed, and then I had talked to Ford.

He helped take the guilt.

Sure, I still feel it, but the load feels a little less.

Like he's carrying it with me.

His support means more to me than anything in this world. He doesn't see me the way everyone else does. He sees past my mistakes, past the hurt I've been harboring and wearing like a coat, and he's help-ing me heal.

Something I never thought I'd be able to do.

Ford reaches over and links our fingers together as he drives into town. I'm eager to be alone with him and not in his childhood bedroom where his parents are a room away. Not in my dinky apartment above the bar with the smell of beer and music floating up the stairwell. We'll be in our own space, away from everyone.

Away from the world.

"You okay over there? You're awfully quiet," he says, breaking the silence.

I give him a smile. "I'm perfect."

"You're not changing your mind, are you? We can go back to my parents' place if you'd be more comfortable."

He barely has the words out when I declare, "No. No way. I want to go. I want this."

He grins, and the gesture lights up his entire face. Ford Gregory is the most breathtaking man I've ever seen. Better than Ryan Reynolds. Better than Chris Hemsworth. Better than Dwayne Johnson. All of whom are almost twice my age, but I don't care. That generation produced some hot as hell men.

But Ford? He's like having Ryan and Chris and Dwayne all rolled into one.

As we pull into town, I become very aware of the way he drags his thumb over the palm of my hand. It tickles a little, but with each stroke, it's like a direct line to the apex of my legs. I'm getting more turned on, wetter with each passing second. By the time we pull into the parking lot of a hotel in Cooper, I'm practically rocking in my seat, trying to find some relief from the desire pooled at my core.

Ford parks near the back of the lot, away from the main entrance, and shuts off his truck. "Ready?"

I practically sprint from my seat, eager to get inside. "Yes."

"Wait there. I'm not missing the chance to help you down," he instructs, chuckling at my enthusiasm.

Before I know it, he's at my side, placing big warm hands at my waist and hoisting me out of his truck. The second my feet hit concrete, he presses his lips to mine in a searing kiss. One that brands me as his. I welcome the burn.

He pulls away before I'm ready, which is probably a good thing. I'm sure the hotel has cameras in the parking lot. The last thing we need is to put on a show for anyone who happens to glance at the screen. "Let's go," he says, grabbing our two bags and locking his truck. With our fingers entwined once more, he adds, "I need to get you alone and naked."

A shiver slides through my body.

It only takes a few minutes to check-in at the front desk, and before I know it, we're off to the elevator. Ford carries both bags, refusing to let me take my own, as he presses the button for the third floor. It's a fairly small hotel, with only three floors total, a gym, and a pool and sauna area. A part of me feels a little disappointed I didn't bring a swimsuit on this trip. The thought of seeing Ford in trunks, water glistening off his incredible eight-pack abs, is a little overwhelming.

Until we step out of the elevator and stop in front of our room. I won't be seeing him in swim trunks. No, I'll be seeing him in less. I'll be seeing him in nothing.

My heart trips over itself with anticipation.

He pushes open the door and allows me to step inside first. The room looks to have been updated fairly recently. Instead of the standard floral bedspreads and pretty landscape portraits, this one is decorated in rich blues and grays. There are turquoise pillows on top of the deep navy and gray bedding on the biggest king-size bed I've ever seen. The truth is it's probably the same size as every other king-size bed out there, but for some reason, in the middle of the small suite, it looks massive.

In the corner of the room is a small jacuzzi tub. I've never understood why they put them in the middle of the living and sleeping space, but in this moment, I don't care about the reason. All I can think about is getting inside that tub, the hot, bubbly water soothing tired and achy muscles.

And after feeling his erection press against me, after waking up with it wedged between my ass cheeks early this morning, I'm sure to be very *achy* later this evening.

"So," he starts, dropping our bags on the floor.

"So," I mimic, turning and facing where he stands.

"What do you want to do first? Snack from the minibar? Relax in that tub?"

I step forward and run my hands up his chest. "I didn't bring my swimming suit," I whisper coyly.

He feigns shock. "You didn't? But how will we soak in that jacuzzi?"

I suggestively bat my eyelashes. "Well, I suppose I could go without. If you, you know, promise not to look."

Ford can tell I'm not serious, and his eyes dilate with a fresh wave of need. "I can't promise that, sweetness."

"Well, good, because I won't promise that either. If you're naked, I'm definitely going to be peeking."

He chuckles. "Yeah?"

"Mmhmm," I mumble, right before I press my lips—and my chest—against his.

Strong arms wrap around my waist, lifting me into the air as he devours my mouth. My ankles lock at his lower back, my core spread wide open for him. I can feel the head of his cock pressing directly against the place I need him most. The sensation rips a moan of pleasure from my lips as I gently rock forward, seeking sweet friction.

"You can stop this at any time, Shayne. All you have to do is say the words. I didn't necessarily bring you here to fuck you. I'd be okay with just holding you close," he pants, his serious gaze locked with mine.

"I want this. I want you. Please."

Heat flares in those alluring green orbs. Ford nods once before moving us to the bed. He gently lays me back on the bedspread, his large body covering mine. His magical lips press against mine once more in the most delicious of kisses. It's part exploratory, part demanding, and all Ford.

He slowly kisses down my neck, his warm palm grazing against my side as he pushes my shirt up. My nipples pebble against my bra, and it's as if they already know what's to come. Ford helps me take off my shirt, leaving me covered in only thin, soft pink lace. He trails kisses over the mounds of my breasts before flicking his tongue over the first nipple. A jolt of need streaks through my veins, leaving me yearning for more.

When he gets to the second nipple, I eagerly anticipate the flick, only that's not what happens. Ford gently bites down on the hard peak, sending shockwaves of pure pleasure rolling through my body. I moan loudly and rock my hips upward against his erection. He hisses at the contact and clamps down on my nipple a second time. I cry out at the sharp nip of pain, only to have it replaced quickly by bliss as he sucks it into his warm mouth.

"What do you say we take this off?" he asks, his voice husky.

"I say do it quickly," I pant, needing to feel his mouth on me as soon as possible.

Ford chuckles as he reaches back and unfastens my bra, quickly pulling the lace down and completely exposing my breasts. "Fuck, you're beautiful."

Then his mouth returns to my nipples, licking and sucking like it's his job. Big hands come in to play too, cupping and squeezing each one, rolling each bud between his thumb and index finger. The onslaught of sensations has me writhing beneath him, all but begging. I don't know if it's for more or for him to stop torturing me and make me come.

"I-I need..." I murmur, thrashing my head from side to side.

"What do you need, beautiful?" Lick. Suck. I can't think. "Do you want more? Do you want me to take off your pants and taste you? Devour your sweet, wet pussy?"

I whimper.

"Is that a yes? Say the word, Shayne, and I'll make you come."

"Yes, yes, please," I beg, overwhelmed by the pleasure he's creating and the emotions that come with giving him complete control, but I know I'm in good hands. Ford would never do anything to hurt me, physically or emotionally. I trust him wholly.

The realization hits me like a ton of bricks, stealing the oxygen straight out of my lungs. Ford gazes up at me, worry marring his handsome face. "Are you okay? Do I need to stop?" He starts to sit up, releasing my body. I feel the void immediately.

"No," I insist, reaching for his arm as I sit up. "What you're doing..." I have a hard time putting into words what I'm feeling. "It's amazing. I've never felt so good, yet so... cherished at the same time." I can feel the blush on my neck, slowly making its way to my cheeks.

Ford gives me the softest smile. "I want to make you feel good, Shayne."

"You do. I promise."

He nods, but just sits there on his haunches as if waiting for me to make the next move. I decide to take the lead, lying back and unfastening my cutoff shorts. His eyes drop, watching my every move, which gives me the confidence to keep going. Unzipping the shorts, I slowly shimmy them down my hips and thighs. Ford leans back more so I can get the shorts off, helping to relieve me of the clothing as soon as it hits my ankles. Then, I lie back and wait.

He starts with his hand at my knee and slowly runs it up my thigh. It feels like he's leaving a trail of fire in its wake. I spread my legs even wider as his fingers dance along the hem of my panties. Our eyes meet once more, the question shining brightly in the semi-darkened room. I nod, giving him the confirmation he needs.

Painstakingly slow, Ford slips his fingers beneath the hem and starts to pull them down. He leans forward, blazing a trail of openmouthed kisses as he goes, his tongue darting out to taste my skin. I kick off my flip-flops and lift my legs, eager to help get the material off my body, only to be left completely exposed before him. Instead of the embarrassment of being naked in front of him, especially when he's still wearing every piece of his clothing, I feel elation. Sexy. Desired. It's written in his eyes as they drink their fill of my body.

"You are the most beautiful woman I've ever seen." His voice is hoarse, and I can feel the truth in his statement. It lands square in my chest and causes my heart to skip a beat.

Unsure what to say, I'm saved from having to reply when he lowers himself between my legs, throwing one over his shoulder. Ford leans forward, his mouth so very close to where I ache, his eyes land on mine. He holds my gaze as his tongue snakes out and tastes me for the first time. Our joint groans fill the room as he places his palm on my other thigh, holding me open.

Then he devours.

I've had a few guys go down on me before—Rodney included— but never like this. Never this raw, animalistic need radiating from the man between my legs. Never as if he'd die if he didn't get his mouth on me that very moment. That's exactly how it feels to have Ford licking and sucking on my clit. As if he was made for giving me pleasure.

And he does.

Jesus, he takes me straight to the edge of insanity so fast I barely see it coming. In fact, before I know it, I'm ready to come. I rock my hips into his face, seeking out the glorious friction of his tongue against my clit. A moan fills the hotel room, surprising even me. Mostly because it actually came from my mouth.

Ford teases my entrance with a finger, and I whimper. I need to feel him filling me. I need it more than I need air.

"Shhh, beautiful. I got you," he murmurs against my flesh, slowly sliding a single finger into my body. "Fuck, you are so tight. I can't wait until this is my cock," he adds, gingerly pulling it out and adding a second digit.

His mouth latches back onto my clit as he slides both fingers deep inside my pussy. When he shifts his hand and arches his fingers upward, he grazes against that magical place deep inside me. I cry out, my orgasm looming just within reach. I try to grasp it, but he won't let me move. All I can do is lie here, completely at his mercy, and wait for him to take me there.

He spreads my thighs even farther, his broad shoulders holding me open for his consumption. His two fingers pick up the pace, and my body rocks against him, riding out each thrust. He reaches up with his unoccupied hand and squeezes a nipple at the exact moment he sucks hard on my clit.

Stars.

Oh, sweet Jesus, I'm flying.

Over the edge of euphoria, riding wave after wave of pleasure, I come so hard, I can barely breathe. He doesn't let up either. He draws out every ounce of gratification he can until there's nothing left of me but a pile of bones. I'm spent. So gloriously sated, I may never be able to move again.

Until I look down and see nothing but hunger in his eyes. His face is covered in my wetness, and all he does is lick his lips and suck on the fingers he just pulled from my lifeless body. That's when I know we're not done. I feel the stir down in my gut.

My internal muscles clench in anticipation as he slowly lifts himself up and moves to cover my body with his. His mouth comes down hard, the taste of me fresh on his lips. I wrap my legs around his hips, begging to feel his hard length against me.

I gasp for air when he breaks the kiss, trailing his lips across my jaw. "I can't wait to be inside of you."

"Yes. That. Now."

He chuckles as he drags his lips down the column of my neck. "You ready for more, beautiful?"

He glances up, our eyes meeting. So much emotion passes. It's so real and heady, I almost tell him right here and now I've fallen in love with him. Not only do I trust him with my body, but with my heart too.

And if I'm not mistaken, I see the same in his eyes too.

Love.

After what feels like the shortest courtship in the history of the world, I realize I'm completely head over heels in love with this man. This incredible soul, who sees what no one else can see, and who treats me as if I were the most important thing in his world. The one who doesn't care about my flaws and my past, and maybe even likes me a little more because of them. Because they made me who I am.

Am I ready for more?

"Yes. I'm ready."

Chapter 19

Ford

I STARE DOWN AT HER. I RUN THE RAMIFICATIONS OF GOING AWOL in my mind. How in the hell am I going to leave her? I know this sounds crazy, insane, and completely unbelievable, but in a matter of days, this woman lying beneath me has stolen my heart.

"Yes, I'm ready," she says with a hunger in her eyes that has my heart flipping over in my chest.

"Shayne, I—" I swallow hard. I was just about to drop that four-letter word, but I can't do that now. Not when I'm getting ready to bury myself balls deep inside her. I know my girl, and she's going to assume it was in the heat of the moment that I would only be saying those words.

With staggering effort, I manage to pull away from her and climb off the bed. Those blue-green eyes follow my every move as I strip out of my clothes, tossing them to the side. My cock is hard and begging for release. Wrapping my fist around the base, I give myself three long strokes, my eyes locked with hers. When she licks her lips, my body shudders.

That's what she does to me.

All it takes is one look.

I need to be inside her. Now.

Blinking hard, I turn to look around the room for our bags. I find them just barely inside the door, where I discarded them without a thought. Rushing to our bags, I pull back the zipper on mine and shove my hand inside, searching for the box of condoms that I packed. When my hand finds the box, I pull them from the bag and notice a slight tremble. I've done and seen things in the army that most men and women, hell most humans wouldn't be able to process. Now here I am, ready to have sex with a woman who I know without a shadow of a doubt that I'm in love with, and my fucking hands are shaking. I don't know if I'm nervous or excited. I'm thinking a little bit of both.

"Ford?"

I turn to look over my shoulder to find her eyes on me. I hold up the box of condoms like a fumbling teenager. "I promised I'd keep you safe."

"I guess we should have that talk, huh?" She sits up on her elbows.

"It's been a long damn time for me," I confess.

"Me too. I'm um. I'm not on birth control. I didn't see the point if I wasn't sleeping with anyone, and I didn't expect you. I didn't expect this."

"That's why we have these." I hold up the box of condoms.

"Do you need me to help you put it on?"

"No." I shake my head and chuckle. "Baby, if you touch me right now, I'm going to lose my damn mind." I grip my cock and squeeze hard at the base. Her eyes follow my movements, and she licks her lips. "Shayne." My tone is a warning. "That's not helping."

The vixen lies back on the bed and spreads her legs for me. There is a blush that coats her cheeks, but she holds my gaze. "I'm ready."

"Fuck yes, you are." Ripping into the box, I tear off a little foil pack and let the rest fall to the floor. Bringing the small wrapper to my teeth, I tear it open and sheath my cock. The tremble in my hand has made its way to my knees as I make my way back to the bed. I crawl on and settle between her thighs.

"Kiss me," she demands, and who am I to deny this beauty anything? Bracing my hands on either side of her head to hold my weight, I bend my head, my mouth meeting hers. She quickly takes control as her tongue invades my mouth, exploring, tasting, and taking what she wants.

Me.

She wants me.

"Please," she murmurs.

Transferring my weight to one elbow resting on the bed, I slide my hand between us and trace my fingers over her wet pussy, stopping to massage her clit with my thumb.

"Tease," she pants.

"Is this what you want?" Gripping my cock, I trace it through her folds.

"Ford," she whines, lifting her hips, and arching her back.

Staring down at her, I want to memorize this moment. I know it's going to change the course of my life forever. She's changing my life, and I never want to forget it. After everything she's been through, her trust is a gift that I will always hold close to my chest.

"What's wrong?" she asks, resting her palm against my cheek.

"Nothing. I just don't ever want to forget this moment."

"Oh, Ford." She smiles but blinks hard to keep the tears shining in her eyes at bay. "You're unlike any man I've ever met."

"Good." I kiss the tip of her nose. Putting us both out of our misery, I align myself at her entrance and push home. We both gasp at the feeling of being connected for the first time.

"So full," she exhales, moving her hands to my biceps and holding on, her nails marking my skin.

"Fuck, you're so tight," I whisper as I rest my forehead against hers. We lie here, just relishing the feel of one another until she finally speaks.

"Are you waiting for permission?"

Lifting my head, I find a smile tilting her lips. "Tell me what you want, Shayne."

"I want you to move."

"Come on, baby. You can do better than that. Tell me," I urge her.

"Move," she says again, lifting her hips.

"Say it. What are we doing here, Shay? Tell me what this is, and I'll give you what you want."

"I want you to fu—" She stops and swallows hard. I see a storm of emotions flash in her eyes. "Make love to me, Ford. Please."

Those six words seal our fate. I will forever only ever make love to her. She's my endgame, and I'm about to show her what it means to be mine. Pulling back, I let my cock slide out, almost to the tip, before pushing back in. She closes her eyes and moans, a sound emitting from deep in her throat.

Over and over again, I repeat the same torturous slide of my cock in and out of her tight pussy until we set a good rhythm. Her hands roam my body, and her legs lock behind my back. "Faster," she breathes.

"I can't," I say through gritted teeth. "I'm barely hanging on." It's a confession that no man wants to tell his woman, but it's facts all the same. She's tight and wet and so damn sexy. I wasn't lying when I said it had been a while for me.

"I'm so close," she says, pulling me deeper with her legs that are locked around my waist.

"Tell me what you need, Shayne." Her hands land on my chest as she pushes me away. I'm startled for a minute until I realize what she's doing. She moves to where she's on all fours, backing her ass up to my cock. "Fuck me. You're perfect."

"I love your sweet, Ford Gregory, but I need you to fuck me. Take what you need from me. You've given me so much, I just—Take me."

"Are you sure this is what you want? I'm not going to last like this," I say, grabbing a handful of ass cheek. Damn this woman.

"I want you to fuck me."

"My girl gets what she wants," I grunt as I grip her hips and push inside. "Jesus." I tilt my head back and take a deep breath. "Touch yourself, Shayne."

"Already ahead of you, soldier," she says, and I see that she indeed has her hand between her legs.

"That's so hot."

"Less talking, more thrusting," she says, and I can hear the humor in her voice.

I'm not a man who sleeps around. It's never been my thing, and I don't have a hell of a lot of experience being deployed more often than not in the last three years. However, I can tell you that I've never been with a woman who is playful, sexy, thoughtful, and sweet all at the same time. To joke while having sex is every man's dream. She doesn't know that I love her, and if I weren't already certain on the fact, that comment would have sealed the deal. To have her trust, to know she can speak freely and ask for what she wants, that's what you need to build a strong relationship.

Hands tightening on her hips, I unleash everything that I'm feeling. Love for her, the passion that ignites between us, anger that I have to leave her, and sadness that she won't be curled up in my arms every night when she falls asleep. Thrust after thrust in a feverish rhythm, I give us what we both need.

"There. Right there," she pants. Both of her hands clasp the sheets as I give her everything. My grip on her hips is so tight I'm sure I'll leave a bruise, but I can't stop. She's begging me not to stop. "I'm close, baby. Get there," I tell her.

"I—Oh, God." A deep, throaty, sexy-as-fuck moan falls from her lips, and I let go. Her pussy is squeezing me, as I spill my release inside her with a grunt and a moan of my own.

Sated, I grip the condom at the base of my cock and pull out of her. She whines, and I chuckle. "Let me take care of the condom. I'll be right back." I place a kiss on each ass cheek and the base of her spine before standing on shaking legs and disappearing into the bathroom. I handle my business before washing my hands. Snagging a washcloth from the counter, I run it through warm water and take it back to the bed to clean her up.

"What are you doing?" she asks. She's now lying on her back. Her head lifted, watching me.

"Taking care of you."

"I'm pretty sure you just did that."

"You're good for my ego." I wink, then toss the washcloth into the bathroom, where it lands on the floor with a plop. "Are you okay?" I ask, lying down on the bed next to her.

"More than okay. I think I just had an out-of-body experience."

"Go on, keep those compliments coming," I tease.

She giggles and rolls over to bury her face in my chest. "Seriously, Ford. I have two words for you. Life. Altering."

"Me too, beautiful. Me too."

"When can we do that again?" she asks, tracing her hands over my abs.

"I need a little recovery time. Are you trying to kill me?"

She giggles and sits up, smiling at me. "You know what we should do?"

"What's that?" I reach up to push her hair out of her eyes.

"We should go grab some snacks from the vending machine."

"You want to get dressed and go get snacks from the vending machine?"

"Yeah, I mean, you can't perform yet." Her eyes glance at my cock before coming back to my face. "It will give us something to do in the meantime."

"Apparently, I don't need as much time as I thought." I nod where my cock is standing at attention. "Just one look from you is all it seems to take."

"So, again?"

"Again."

She climbs off the bed and grabs another condom. This time it's her who places the small package in her mouth and tears it open with her teeth. She bounces back to the bed and straddles my hips. I watch as she bites down on her bottom lip in deep concentration as she covers my cock.

"Can I try something?"

Clasping my hands together behind my head, I smile at her. "I'm all yours." With a nod, she grips my cock and slowly lowers herself until I'm buried deep inside her.

"Oh," she moans. As if that sound alone wasn't enough, she tilts her head back and cups her breasts in her hands, tweaking her nipples, all while grinding her hips.

My hands that were casually behind my head fall to the bed and grip the sheets. This is her show, and I'm just along for the ride.

Hours later, after she rode me to ecstasy, both hers and mine, and about twenty dollars' worth of vending machine snacks later, we're showered and back in bed. Her back is to my front as I hold her. My eyes are heavy, but I can't seem to let them close. I miss her already, which I know is impossible. She's here in the flesh in my arms, but it's true. The thought of being away from her is killing me inside.

I don't know how the guys who are married do it—missing their wives, missing the birth of their children. I know that's what I signed up for, and I'm still honored to be serving my country, but that was all before Shayne. I can't help but wonder if I still would have enlisted if it was her I was dating in high school and not Sara. My gut tells me probably not. Not with the way I'm feeling right now.

Then again, maybe I wasn't ready for this then. Everything happens for a reason, and maybe it was always meant to be this way. I know without a shadow of a doubt that Shayne is strong enough to endure me being gone. She has the courage and the will to be an army wife. I know I'm jumping ahead of myself, but it's good to know that she has what it takes. She's already put up with so much shit from her small town, and yet she's still there. Slinging drinks no matter how many dirty looks or snide comments are thrown her way.

My girl is already army strong and doesn't even realize it.

"I can practically hear you thinking," Shayne says into the darkness of our room.

"I'm going to miss you."

"I know." Her voice is soft, and I detect a slight tremor.

"Can I tell you something?"

"Of course you can."

"I want you to keep an open mind. This isn't something that I take lightly, and I feel as though I need to tell you."

"Is everything okay?" She tries to turn to look at me, but I keep my arms locked around her, preventing her from moving.

"Everything is perfect."

"You can tell me anything."

"Shayne," I say, my lips just a kiss away from her ear. "I love you."

She gasps and turns to face me. This time I let her. "What?"

"I love you. I'm in love with you. I know it's soon, but I'm telling you this is real. The way my heart misses a beat when I hear your name. The way it races when you walk into a room." I press my lips to hers. "The way your pussy feels gripping my cock. All of it. Everything from the moment I laid eyes on you is overwhelming and real, and it's... everything. You're everything."

"Ford, I—" I stop her with another kiss.

"I know you've been through so much, and I know this is fast. I just can't drive away from you tomorrow without telling you what's in my heart. I don't expect you to say it back. I don't expect for you to feel this strongly, but I refuse to run from it. I just need you to know that I'm in love with you."

Her arms fly around my neck as she pulls me into an awkward hug. Her grip is fierce as she presses her face into mine. I can feel her tears, and even in the dark of the room, I know they're not tears of sadness. They're tears of joy. We're that in tune with one another.

"Shayne?"

"I love you too," she says, her voice cracking. "I love you, and it scares the hell out of me. I don't know why I trust you so easily, but from day one, my guard has been down when it comes to you. I want you to know that I'm going to be here waiting for you. I don't care if it's a two-day leave or ten. I'm going to be here. No matter where you are in the world, I need you to know that my heart is with you, and I'm going to be right here waiting for you. I'm going to try and shift my schedule for some three-day weekends so I can come and visit, and I'll send you care packages, and I promise you we're going to do this, Ford. We're going to kill this long-distance thing."

"Fuck yes, we are." I kiss her hard. I put everything into this kiss that I want to say but can't seem to find the words. Her words are like a fist around my heart. I had once thought that Sara would be the one saying those words to me, but that didn't happen. I often wondered where she and I went wrong, and now I know.

It was because of Shayne.

I was always meant to meet her. It was always supposed to be us in each other's corner. I may not know the meaning of life, but I sure as hell know the meaning of mine.

Her name is Shayne Danner.

Chapter 20

Shayne

"WHAT HAPPENS TODAY?" I ask over breakfast, almost afraid to find out the truth. It's Sunday morning, which means at some point, Ford and Chad return to base so they can report first thing tomorrow morning.

And I return to Kentucky.

"Well, I was thinking about that while you were showering off the early morning jacuzzi water," he says, between bites of bacon, smirking in satisfaction at taking me in the jacuzzi tub about the same time the sun came up. "We have to report at 0600 tomorrow morning. It's not too long of a drive, but we were talking about heading there later this afternoon."

"Oh." I swallow over the thickness in my throat. "That soon?" I don't know what I thought. Of course he has to return today.

He wipes his hands off on the napkin on his lap and reaches for my hand. The pancakes I just consumed sit like a lead brick in my stomach. "We could drive it in the morning, but neither of us think that's a good idea. That calls for an early departure, and even though traffic will be light, we risk running into a delay. So, we decided to go today. I'm hoping you'll go too."

"Me?" I ask, confused by what he's saying.

"One night isn't enough, Shayne. I want to spend every last possible second with you before I have to return, so if we get a hotel just off base, we can stay there and be practically next door in the morning. We won't have to leave nearly as early."

I can't help but grin. "You want to spend another night in a hotel with me? What kinda girl do you think I am?"

He smiles widely and brings my hand to his lips. "My girl, that's what kind you are. So what do you say? Want to drive to Fort Campbell with me? We can take your car so it's there. It's actually not too far from you. Only about two hours from base."

"One more night with you in a hotel? I'm all yours until you have to leave in the morning," I whisper, the words getting caught in my throat. God, that hurts to say.

His grin is sad as he links our fingers. "Thank you. I'd let you go back today, but I'll admit, I'm selfish. I want every second I can get. But if you want to head back today, just say the words, Shayne."

I'm already shaking my head. "No, I want to be here—or there—wherever. With you."

He nods. "Okay, sounds good. Let's finish eating, and then we'll head back to my folks' place. Mom is preparing lunch before we head out."

"Okay."

And it is. I love spending time with his parents and sister. They welcomed me into their home without knowing me from Adam. They invited me to their dinner table and let me stay in their son's bedroom. They are the kind of parents I had in my dreams. Attentive, supportive, and loving. Ones I've always longed to have for my own.

"Eat that," he says, pointing to what's left on my plate. With a wink, he adds, "You're going to need all your strength later."

"I'm going to miss you," Beth whispers just loud enough I can hear.

"Gonna miss you too, Mom," he replies, hugging her tightly against his chest.

When he sets her back down on the ground, she wipes tears from her cheeks before she places both palms against her son's cheeks. "You be careful, you hear me, Ford Andrew?"

"I hear you, ma'am. I'll be careful, I promise."

She nods and gives him a kiss on his cheek before standing up straight and stepping aside. As she heads my way, Todd steps up to bid goodbye to his son. "You come by for a visit any time, you hear me?" she asks, reaching up and running a hand along the side of my head. I can picture her doing that often to Faith as a child. It's a very motherly gesture.

I nod, fighting the emotions clogging my throat. "Thank you."

"I see a lot of goodness in your eyes, Shayne. There's a lot of light and love. I see it when you look at my son," she states, a tender smile on her pretty face. "I also see a touch of hurt and pain when you think no one is looking."

I open my mouth, but nothing comes out. How does she know? Did Ford tell her about my past?

She instantly starts shaking her head, as if she knows what I was thinking. "No one has said anything, sweetie. Your secrets are your own. Just know that they don't define you. Embrace the hurt you've felt in the past and grow from it. It may be your roots, but only you get to decide how you blossom."

Air seems lodged in my lungs, unable to move. It isn't until she leans in and pulls me into a warm hug that I'm finally able to breathe again. Ford mentioned to me all the wisdom his mom has bestowed on him over the years, and I never understood the importance of receiving it until now.

This is what it's like to have a real mother.

"Thank you for allowing me to stay here. I've had a wonderful time with your family," I say.

Beth squeezes my hands. "You're welcome anytime, Shayne. Please don't be a stranger. In fact, I'd love for you to get my cell number from Ford before he returns to base and keep in touch. I promise to reply, but not overwhelm you with messages. Not like the kids these days do. I don't know what TYVM or FML means," she states.

"Mom, why are saying fuck my life?" Faith asks, caught between laughter and shock.

"What? That's what that means?" Beth shakes her head in dismay. "What a horrible thing to say. Anyway, give me one final hug. It looks like the guys are almost ready."

After a few long seconds, she releases me from the embrace. I turn to give Faith a hug as well, only to have her say, "I'm going to ride along with Chad, Mom. I'll bring the rental back tomorrow morning and turn it in."

Beth gives her daughter a knowing grin. "Call me when you get back to town, and I'll pick you up."

"'Kay," Faith replies as the sound of a car pulling onto the gravel driveway grabs our attention. "What is she doing here?"

"Who?" I ask, following everyone's line of sight.

"Sara."

Beth sighs. "I hope she's not here to stir up trouble."

My eyes move to Ford, who seems tense all of a sudden. He watches as Sara pulls up to where we all stand and parks beside the rental. She's slow to get out, but when she does, she's just as put together today as she was yesterday. Long blonde hair with perfect beach-wave curls, flawlessly executed makeup, and clothing that looks like she spilled off the pages of *Vogue* magazine.

"Hi," she says, coming around the front of her car and fidgeting a little when she realizes all eyes are on her. "I was hoping I could talk to Ford for a moment."

He crosses his muscular arms over his broad chest. "I'm not so sure that's a good idea. We're getting ready to leave, and there isn't anything left to say."

Her eyes shift to me. "Actually, I think there is. Please, Ford. Just a minute."

He sighs and meets my gaze. I can see the conflict and feel the uncertainty. He doesn't want to, but he's also a good enough guy to not completely ignore her or send her packing in front of his family. His shoulders fall and he takes a step forward. "Fine. One minute."

I watch him walk toward her, nodding for her to follow him. He leads her about thirty yards away, over to his dad's shop. I try not to stare, but it's hard, especially since everyone else is watching too.

His demeanor is rigid, his features guarded as he stands and listens to whatever she's saying. Sara's an animated speaker, her hands constantly moving while she's talking. Beth, Todd, and Faith move together and talk, though their gazes are never too far from Ford and Sara.

Chad comes over and stands beside me. "Wonder what that's about."

"No clue." I swallow hard, hating the jealousy and rage I feel toward that woman. She made Ford's life hell when he enlisted and was horrible to us yesterday.

"He mentioned before you guys left last night that you ran into her, and she was a total bitch."

I mumble something that sounds like an agreement and return my gaze to where the man I love stands with his ex. After a few more minutes, I hear him chuckle, the sweet sound carried across the yard in the breeze, and while I love the sound of his laugh, the fact it's aimed at that toxic witch doesn't sit well with me.

Sara steps forward, goes up on her tiptoes, and kisses Ford on the cheek, and the only thing keeping me where I stand is the fact Ford doesn't move a muscle. He stands there, his arms crossed over his chest, and not making it easy for his ex.

"Easy there, tiger. She's leaving," my cousin whispers.

"What?"

He laughs. "You growled when she kissed him."

"Oh. Well, I…," I stammer, shoving my hands in my pockets and turning away from the scene by the shop. "I'm not a fan."

Chad snorts. "I wouldn't be either if she said the things to me she said to you. But you don't have to worry about Ford, okay? He's got it bad for you, Shay."

I can't help but smile. "I kinda got it bad for him too. We both said we loved each other last night."

Chad grins from ear to ear. "Yeah? The *L* word?" he asks, pulling me into his arms. "I'm so happy for you."

"Thanks," I mumble against my cousin's chest.

"Hands off my girl, Anthony."

I smile at the familiar voice and the sternness behind his words.

"She's my cousin, dude. Don't be gross."

Ford pries me from Chad's hug—who hangs on a little longer just to piss off Ford—and takes my hand. "Ready?"

I nod, feeling lighter and more at ease now that he's beside me. "Ready."

We say final goodbyes to his parents before climbing into my car, as Chad and Faith get in the rental. They follow us as we pull out of the driveway and onto the road, a quick blast of the horn to punctuate our departure.

With our fingers entwined on my thigh, we set out for Hopkinsville, Kentucky.

To another goodbye.

"Go ahead and ask."

"What?" I ask, sucking on the vanilla milkshake we grabbed along the way.

"Sara. I know you're curious."

I shift in my seat, slurping up my sugary drink with gusto. "It's okay. If you want to tell me, I'll listen, but if not, that's okay too."

After a few long seconds, he says, "She wanted to apologize."

Okay, I wasn't expecting that.

"Really?"

He seems just as surprised as I do. "Yeah. Not just to me, but to you too. She said she thought about what I said, and I was right. We weren't meant for each other. I'm pretty sure she almost choked on the words, but she got them all out. She even wished me luck and told me to be careful out there."

I take in his words, wondering if he believes her or not. To be honest, I'm not sure I really believe her, not after she was so horrible yesterday, saying the meanest thing. "Wow, do you believe her?"

He sighs, merging into the passing lane on the interstate. "I guess. She seemed remorseful and mentioned a guy she just started seeing, and to be honest, I just want to put her and our past where it belongs. Behind me. Maybe hearing her apologize was what I needed to really put our time together to rest and embrace the future. Embrace you."

The smile on my lips is small, but there's so much meaning and emotion behind it. I bring his hand to my mouth and place kisses on his scarred knuckles. "We have less than fifteen hours, Ford Gregory, before you have to report to base. We have a lot of embracing to get in before you go."

His chuckle is low and deep, sending volts of electricity through my veins and landing straight between my legs. "We could probably take the next exit and… embrace."

I shake my head and pull a face. "No embracing in rest stops."

"Good point." He kisses my wrist. "Let's get to the hotel. I can't wait to hold you in my arms."

Me either.

Especially since the clock seems to be getting faster and faster with each passing second. Before I know it, and way before I'm ready, he'll be leaving. Again. And I'll be heading home.

Without Ford.

Without my heart.

Because there's no way it's going anywhere but with him.

It's forever his.

Chapter 21

Ford

THE ALARM ON MY PHONE BLARES AT 5:00 A.M., AND I RUSH TO turn it off. Shayne and I didn't fall asleep until well after one this morning, and I know I'm going to be dragging ass today. That's okay. It was worth it. Anytime spent with her is worth a few hours of lost sleep. I'm glad we have the room until eleven so she can sleep a little longer before her drive home.

Chad and Faith stayed in the room across the hall from ours, and I'm sure he's going through something similar right now. They might not be where we are exchanging promises of love, but I know he's into my sister, and she him.

Shayne is sleeping peacefully, and I hate to wake her, but I promised her I would. I decide to shower first and get ready to head back to base. As carefully as possible, I slide out of bed and quietly make my way to the bathroom.

The hot water feels good against my tired muscles and helps wake me up. Closing my eyes, I tilt my head back, letting the water flow over my face. I'm trying really hard not to think about her driving away from me today. Hell, it's going to be me walking away from her as we report at 0600. I never knew how hard it would be to walk away from my heart.

Hands around my waist startle me, but I know it's her. "Hey, baby." I turn to face her, and there are tears streaming down her face. "Don't cry, Shay. It tears me up inside."

"I can't stop," she says. "I'm going to miss you so much."

"I'm right here, baby." I place my hand over her heart. "I won't be able to hold you every night, but I promise you that's what I'll be thinking about as I lie in my bunk alone."

"What if I move here? Then can I see you?"

"Yeah, but I can't move off base for another year. I have to have four years of service in before we can do that."

"Okay. So one year. That's not so bad."

"No, but what about when I'm deployed? I hate the thought of you being here all alone when I'm thousands of miles away."

"I don't know, Ford. All I know is that my heart feels like it's shattering, and I don't know how to fix it."

My hug is fierce, but I don't dare let go. Not when I can feel her body shaking and the sounds of her sobs over the running water. I don't know how to make this better for her. I don't know what to do when it's not just her heart that's breaking. It's mine too.

"Shayne." I pull back and cradle her face in the palm of my hands. "I love you. Do you hear me? I love you. Not just for today, or the past two weeks, I love you enough for a lifetime. Our lifetime. The next year is going to be hard, but I promise you that we'll get through it. I need to know that you're going to be there for me when I get home. I know that's selfish of me to even ask that of you, but I need you, Shayne." I sound desperate, but I can't find it in me to care.

I am desperate. I'm desperate for her.

For my Shayne.

"One year or ten years, I'll be here. I know this has been a whirl-wind romance, but I love you, Ford. I don't care how long it takes. I just want to be with you."

"I have a year left."

"I know, but you said this was always meant to be your career. The goodbyes, they'll get easier, right? I mean, this one is hard because we just found one another, and we need more time."

"I don't know, baby. I know that no other goodbye has been this hard for me. I know that the army used to be what I saw when I thought about my future, and now all I see is you. I promise you, no matter what I decide to do once this year is up, we'll talk about it and come to a decision together."

I hold her close while the warm water cascades around us. Closing my eyes, I commit this very moment to memory. The feel of her body pressed against mine. Like the rest of the last two weeks, this moment is burned into my memory for safekeeping.

"We should get out. I need to get dressed and ready to go."

"Okay." She nods. She leans in and presses her lips to my chest, then pulls open the shower door and steps out.

Turning off the water, I step out of the shower and take the towel she offers me. "I think you should stay and try to get a few more hours of sleep before you drive home."

"I don't know if I can."

"Try for me? And text me as soon as you get home. Hell, text me whenever you want. If I don't respond, it's because I can't, but I will as soon as I'm able. I promise you I'm not ignoring you."

"I'll text you." She nods.

Once we're dried off, we step out of the bathroom, and my eyes go to the clock. It's already five thirty. I need to get dressed, pack up my stuff, and get to the base. Walking to the side of the bed, I call Chad to make sure he's up. "Hey, man, just making sure you're awake. We need to leave here in fifteen."

"Yeah, I know." He sounds about as thrilled as I am to have to go back. I'm pretty sure it has everything to do with my little sister and nothing about the job.

We both love what we do, but sometimes there is something or someone who comes along to take its spot. I freeze when I remember that's what Dad told me several years ago. He always intended to have a career in the army, but he served eight and was done. He told me he found something he loved more than serving his country. At the time, I didn't realize it, but he was talking about Mom. And us. He missed us being born, and six months later, he was home for good.

Now I understand.

"All right, man, I'll see you in the hall in fifteen."

"Roger that."

"I'm not ready," Shayne says, shaking her head.

I swallow hard past the lump in my throat. "I love you," I tell her. Reaching for my bag, I toss my shit inside, not caring how it's packed. I just need this shit done so I can hold her until the very last second. Slipping into my clothes, I take a quick glance around the room. Satisfied I have everything, well, everything that will fit into my bag, I zip it shut and hold my arms open. My girl comes willingly. She, too, is dressed, her wet hair pulled back in a bun.

"I love you."

"I love you too," she whispers.

Sitting on the bed, I pull her into my lap and hold her with everything I have. I kiss her temple, her cheeks, her forehead, and finally, her lips. I try to show her without words what she means to me. I know that words are hard for her to trust with her past, and so I make this one count. I kiss her with all the passion and love I have for her. I just hope it's enough. I wasn't enough for Sara, and I can't help but wonder if I'm enough for Shayne. I trust her, and she's so damn strong. I know she can handle this. I know she can handle me being away, but will she want to? It's a lot to ask of her, but the heart wants what the heart wants.

"Baby, I need to go."

She lifts her head, and I tap her thigh, giving her the signal to stand. When she does, I guide us to the window, where the sun is meeting the horizon.

Standing behind her, I wrap my arms around her waist and rest my chin on top of her head. "Whenever you miss me, just look up at the stars. I'm staring at the same sky every night."

"I love that we can share that, something we can do jointly when we're not together." She turns to look at me, and I press my lips to hers.

"I have to go," I say, my voice cracking.

"I know."

"I don't want to. If I had the choice, I would stay here with you. I would never leave you, Shayne."

"I know that. You're doing your job, Ford. I support you. You do what you have to do and be safe doing it. Don't worry about me. I'm going to be here. Waiting for you," she says as tears coat her cheeks.

"Thank you, Shay. You don't know how much that means to me." I kiss her softly and then pull away. "I need to go."

"Okay."

I grab my bag, and she walks me to the door. Outside in the hallway, I find Chad and my sister locked in a tight hug. "Ford," Faith cries and rushes toward me. I drop Shayne's hand just in time to catch her in my arms. "I love you, brother," she says through her tears.

"I love you too. Kick this last year of school's ass. You've got this," I tell her, placing her back on her feet. She looks up at me and gives me a watery smile. "Will you check up on her for me?"

She nods. "You two take care of each other," she says, giving me one more hug before going to Chad, who is releasing his hold on Shayne.

She rushes back to my side, and I hold her tight. "Will you check in on her for me?" I repeat my question to my sister to Shayne. I'm hoping the two of them can lean on each other this next year.

"Yes." There's no hesitation in her agreement to check in on my sister.

"We need to go," Chad says solemnly.

"Come here." I drop my bag and pull Shayne into a hug. "I love you. I'll see you again soon."

"I love you."

With more effort than I knew I could muster, I pull away from her, pick up my bag, and lean in for one more quick kiss before taking a step back from both of them. "You ladies, behave and take care of each other. I love you both."

"What he said," Chad says, and Faith's eyes go wide. "Take care of each other and behave." He points at each of them.

With a nod, I turn my back on the love of my life and my sister as my feet carry me to the elevator. I don't look back while I'm waiting for the doors to open. I can't. I'm too afraid that I won't step on. My heart feels as though it's being crushed in a vise. When the doors finally open, Chad and I step on and turn to face them. They're hugging one another in the middle of the hallway, tears streaming down their faces as they give us one final wave.

I take a step forward, but Chad's hand on my arm stops me. "Ford."

"Fuck," I mutter as the doors slide shut. "I don't know if I can do this," I whisper the confession to my best friend.

"You don't have a choice, brother," he says, his hand landing on my shoulder. "It's one year. We can make it through one year."

"I don't know if I can."

"You have to, for her. What happens if you go AWOL? You want her to come and visit you behind bars?"

"Fuck. No, that's not what I want, but dammit, it's harder to leave her than I thought it would be."

"One year, Gregory. You've got one year. And we have ten minutes to get our asses checked back in at the base."

Luckily our hotel is just outside the base, so we make it in time.

Once in our room, my phone vibrates. When I see it's from Shayne, I smile.

> **Shayne:** You do what you need to do, Ford Gregory. You do it safely and then come home to me.
>
> **Me:** Yes, ma'am.
>
> **Shayne:** I love you.
>
> **Me:** I love you too.

I don't know how she knew that I needed to hear that from her, but I did. Her words pull me back into the headspace I need to be in. I miss the hell out of her, but I'm going to do exactly what she says. I'm going to do what I need to do. Then I'm coming home to her, for good. I found something in life, someone I love more than serving my country.

I have one year. Twelve months.

We've got this.

Chapter 22

Shayne

Dear Ford,

    You've been gone a day. One. That leaves about 364 to go, give or take. I realized this notebook only has 150 sheets of paper, so I'm going to have to pick up another one if I'm going to write you a letter a day. And that's my plan. I'm going to write every single day we're apart. I know it's a little dated to write letters so much, especially since we'll probably text and talk on the phone dozens of times before you get this, but I don't know. I just like the idea of taking the time to sit and write. We've already texted this morning, and I know we're planning a FaceTime date later in the week, but there's something about putting it all down on paper that makes me smile.

    After you left yesterday morning, Faith and I went back to our room and cried together. She was able to nod off to sleep, but I wasn't so lucky. I just kept thinking about how damn proud I am of you and Chad, and while

I was so incredibly sad, I was honored too. Honored to have our love and know there are men like you out there protecting people like me.

You'll be happy to know Faith and I have remained in contact. I know, I know, it's only been a day, but it still means something to me that she's taken time out of her day to check on me. And to chat. It's been a while since I've had a friend, and I find she's easy to talk to. Must be a twin thing. She reminds me of you.

I had to work last night, and it was hard. I tried to be brave and not cry, but a Garth Brooks come on the jukebox about jumping in a truck and getting it on all night in a field, and suddenly, I was bawling like a baby. Which is nuts, because it's not a sad song. The regulars thought I was crazy. I overheard Jet mumble something about emotional chicks and their periods. HAHAHAHA!

I'm working again tonight, and I think I'm glad. When I'm in this apartment, the walls feel so close. It makes it hard to breathe sometimes, but then I slip on that US Army T-shirt I stole from you, and I can feel you. And smell your deodorant. It's really strong, and when I'm all alone, I don't have to worry about you catching me sniffing it. I don't ever want to wash it. Ever. In fact, you may have to send me a fresh supply of lightly worn shirts. Maybe once a week? A new one to get me by? No? Too weird? You love my weirdness.

Anyway, it's only midafternoon and I'm already waiting for night because that means I can gaze up at the stars. Last night, the sky was so clear, I swore I could see all the constellations. I only know a few though, so I'm probably going to have to order a book to learn them all. I'm sure there's more than just the Big and Little Dipper, Orion, and Taurus. That's the bull, by the way. Google says there are 88 total, which means I have a lot more to learn!

Oh, before I forget to tell you, I texted your mom today. She said I could message her anytime and she'd reply. I hope that's still OK. I told her I had made it back home safely and was working to stay busy. Those little bubbles appeared almost instantly, and I admit, I was so grateful for it. She bestowed some of that famous Beth Gregory Hallmark wisdom on me and had me cracking up by the time our conversation was done. You're pretty lucky to have such an awesome woman in your corner.

Anyway, I should probably go. I need to shower before I head downstairs for work, and I have got to do something about these bags under my eyes. I look like I'm packing for a weekend getaway. HEHEHEHE

I hope this letter finds you well. Know that I am doing as well as I can. I miss you. So much. Some moments I think it's not so bad, but then others, it's hard to breathe. Those are the times I wonder if I'll ever survive a whole year without you. But I know I can. I will. Because I have your love to carry me through. And I have a picture of you that I snapped while you were sleeping one night, like the true nutty stalker I am. I had no idea I had this crazy side of myself. First the shirt sniffing, and now the phone. Last night I fell asleep with my phone lying on the pillow beside me, that picture of you filling the screen. It was like you were there, hogging my pillow, just like you did when you were in here. Then I woke up and my battery was dead because I forgot to plug it in.

I won't make that mistake twice.

Plug in phone, THEN stare at picture all night long of cute boyfriend sleeping.

I'm going to go now and get ready for work. I'll write again tomorrow. Even though we'll text or talk on the phone later tonight, I'll still write to you because each time I do it, that's one day closer to you being home.

Take care and be safe. Oh, and don't let Chad take all your money in poker. He likes to bluff when he only has a low pair.

Thinking of you constantly and loving you always,
Shayne

Chapter 23

Ford

THE FIRST DAY BACK ON BASE IS FULL OF MEETINGS AND workouts, and of course, my ass is dragging. It was worth it, though. Spending all night with Shayne in my arms, being able to make love to her and hold her just a little longer, was definitely worth the hell of today. It's just after eight, and Chad, me, and a few of the other guys just got back from a late dinner. I'm almost too tired to eat, but I know that I needed the fuel, and I need sleep. I definitely need sleep.

Dropping down on my bed, I pull out my phone and read through my messages with Shayne today.

> Shayne: We're checking out of the hotel now. Headed home.

> Shayne: Stopped to get gas and saw an older gentleman with a Veterans hat on his head, and I can't help but wonder if that will be you and Chad in forty years.

> Shayne: Made it home. My apartment isn't the same without you.

> Shayne: Just woke up from a much-needed nap. I'm heading downstairs to work.

My reply didn't come until a few hours ago, when we were finally released for the day.

> Me: Hey, babe. I'm glad you made it home safe. It's been killing me that I couldn't check in with you.

> Me: I could totally rock a Veterans hat now and in forty years.

> Me: Good. You needed the rest. Have a good night. I won't be up when you get off. We have to be up at the ass-crack of dawn.

> Shayne: Taking a quick break. Just wanted to say I miss you. Love you!

That one she sent about twenty minutes ago and was delivered with a selfie of her standing behind the bar, I stare at the screen, looking at her breathtaking eyes. She literally makes it hard to breathe when I look at her.

I can barely keep my eyes open, but I need to tell her goodnight. She might not get it until the end of her shift, but at least she'll know that I'm thinking about her.

I'm always thinking about her.

> Me: I'm calling it a night. I love you, be safe. Text me when you get into your apartment safe. It won't wake me up. I'm exhausted—Miss you, Shay.

Plugging my phone into the charger, I strip down, and I'm asleep as soon as my head hits the pillow.

I groan when the alarm goes off at four. We have to be on the field for a workout at five. Tossing off the covers, I reach for my phone. Sure enough, there are a couple of messages from Shayne.

> Shayne: I'm home. It was a hard night, but I made it through. Everything made me think of you.

> Shayne: You've turned me into a sap, Gregory!

Those were both sent just after midnight. About a half hour later, she sent her last one of the night.

> Shayne: Night, Ford. I love you, and I miss you. I spent some time with stars tonight. XO

Right below was a picture that I'm sure was taken from her bedroom window of the starry sky. Fuck me, I miss her something fierce, and this is my first full day without her.

Tossing my phone on my bed, I make my way to the bathroom to handle my business and brush my teeth. There is no point in showering. The workout is going to be grueling, and I'll just need another after.

Once I'm dressed and have my bed made, I have about fifteen minutes before I have to report. Making my way to the window, I stare up at the star-filled sky and smile. I know my girl was looking at the same sky when she texted me last night. Pulling my phone out of my pocket, I snap a picture and send it to her.

> Me: Morning, beautiful. This is my view early this morning. I can't stop thinking about you. I love you too, and I miss you. Have a good day.

I'm sliding my phone back into my pocket when Chad and the guys call out for me. I run to catch up with them as we do our mandatory morning workout and five-mile run. The two-week break we got spoiled me. Then again, maybe it was just Shayne that spoiled me and sleeping next to her. I don't mind working out. It's been my daily routine for the last three years, either here on the base or deployed. We never miss a workout. It not only keeps us in shape, but it also keeps our minds clear and us healthy. That's important in any line of work, but especially ours.

Dear Shayne,

The mail came today, and color me surprised when I got your letter. It was dated for the first day back at base, so I can only hope that I'll get the others soon. I can't tell you how excited I was to receive that envelope. I wasn't expecting it, and it was a welcome surprise.

The days are counting down, baby. We've got this. As far as the notebook, I've got you. You can expect a shipment of notebooks, pens, stamps, and envelopes. Whatever it takes to keep getting these handwritten treasures from you.

I hate that you cried for me, but I'm glad that you and my sister had one another. I'm glad the two of you are keeping in touch. Thank you for your words, but I'm the one who is honored. To know that I have your love, that means more to me than you will ever know. I'm proud of you too, baby. You're strong, and I know it's hard for you to trust, yet you've given me the gift of yours, and I promise you I will cherish it always. Oh, and Garth Brooks, he can be one swoony fucker, I get it. I'm man enough to admit. He's got me choked up a time or two. As far as the regulars, you know how I feel about them. That's all I'll say about that.

I hate that you feel as though the walls are closing in on you when you are in your apartment. Think about it like this. That was our place. That's where we fell in love. I might not be there in the flesh, but my heart is there. It's you, in case you're wondering. You are my heart, Shayne. And the smelling my shirt thing, well, I can help you out with that too. Expect more to come your way soon. Speaking of smelling, and since we're confessing our weirdness, I might have sniffed your letter. I swear I can smell you on the paper.

I miss you.

It looks like I need to do my homework on the constellations. I had no idea there were 88. Hey, I have an idea. Why don't you teach me? We can learn together. Something we can share even though we're not together. And let me tell you, I am definitely hot for teacher. (See what I did there!)

My parents love you. I'm glad you got to experience the Beth Gregory effect. Mom is definitely one of a kind, and I'm lucky to have her and my dad. Lean on them, Shayne. If you need someone and you can't reach me, call them. They will be there for you. I know that you have your aunt and uncle and Cassie, but I want you to know that you have my family too. Who knows, maybe one day soon, they'll be yours too. (Yes, that means what you think it means.)

I love that I'm the last person that you see when you fall asleep, even if it is a picture. I'm honored to hold that position in your life, and I promise I don't take it lightly. I, too, sometimes find it hard to breathe from missing you. I feel guilty that I even pursued you and asked you to wait for me, but my need for you in my life outweighs the guilt. I'm selfish when it comes to you, Shayne. I promise after this year is up, you get your turn. College, travel whatever you want to do, we'll do it. Hell, if that's something you want. Do it now. I'll hate to miss you kicking ass and taking names like I know you will, but you will have my unwavering support and my never-ending love with you always.

It's getting late, so I need to get to bed. I need to text you and tell you goodnight, and I need to drop this off in the mail. I hope it finds you soon. I'm doing well here. I miss the hell out of you, and I love you more today than I did yesterday.

Take care of yourself, Shayne. Lean on my family and yours until I'm home to offer you my shoulders once again.

You're never not on my mind.

All my love.

Ford

P.S. Chad doesn't have a chance at beating me at poker. I know all his tells.

P.P.S. I love you.

Chapter 24

Shayne

Me: I got the BEST box in the mail today!!

Ford: Oh, yeah? Something from an admirer?

Me: Yeah, some hot guy. He sent me stamps and pens and all kinds of goodies to write letters.

Me: AND… his lightly worn yet deliciously sexy shirt!!

Ford: Have you already sniffed it?

Me: Are you kidding? I'm already wearing it.

Ford: You sure know how to make a man smile, angel. How's your day going?

Me: OK. I met Aunt Joan at the café for lunch. Daphne was our server again, but since Aunt Joan was there, she was nice. At least to my face. She kept throwing daggers at me when my aunt wasn't looking.

Ford: Ugh! What a bitch! I hate that you have to deal with her and everyone else in that town.

Me: It's OK. I'm used to it.

Ford: But you shouldn't have to be. It pisses me off! *insert angry emoji*

Me: I know. So, tell me how your day has been. I wasn't expecting you to reply until later.

Ford: I'm in the mess hall eating an early dinner. We're doing some night training later.

Ford: Chad says hi.

Me: Hello, Chad. I can let you go so you can eat.

Ford: I can do both. I like being able to talk to you now. We'll probably miss each other later. Last time we did night training, we didn't finish until two.

Me: What are you eating? Anything good?

Ford: Spaghetti and meatballs. I wouldn't exactly classify it as good, but it's sustenance. And I know we'll need the carbs and protein for what's coming later tonight.

Me: I had chicken salad on a croissant for lunch. It was really good. The café puts grapes in it.

Ford: Interesting. I think I'd like that.

Me: Next time you're here, we'll go and order it.

Ford: Next time I'm there, it'll have to be delivered because we won't be leaving the bedroom.

Me: *giggles*

Ford: I miss that sound.

Me: I miss you.

Ford: Not as much as I miss you.

Me: Impossible.

Ford: We're almost out of time. I need to wolf down the rest of this food. If I didn't need to fuel so much, I'd say screw it and spend my last four minutes of dinner talking to you.

Me: Go. Eat.

Ford: Text me when you get home so I know you're safe.

Me: You do the same. Love you.

Ford: Love you most. Have a good night at work.

Me: You too.

Dear Ford,

I did a thing. I wanted to tell you last night, but I didn't want to do it in a text. I'm not sure a letter is much better, but it seems right. Remember when you mentioned me going back to school or doing whatever I wanted?

Well… I've been doing a lot of thinking. A lot. Especially when it's a slow night downstairs. I might have checked into that. Today in the mail, I received my information packet for the Kentucky School of Cosmetology. It's about forty-five minutes away but won't be too bad a drive. Jet has agreed to work with me on my schedule, if I decide to pursue it. I'm still torn. I mean, a part of me wants to do it. It might be my ticket out of here. And when I was in high school, and they did career day, it was the only thing I could see myself doing. But with a mom who wasn't paying the bills, all my money went to that, but over the last few years, I've been able to save a bit. Plus, when I was filling out some stuff online, I might have qualified for tuition assistance.

Anyway, this packet is staring at me while I sit to write this letter. I don't know if I'll fill it out or not. I probably shouldn't even have said anything, but I've been dying to tell you.

So there. My big news. We'll see if I actually fill out all those forms or not.

I've also been talking to Faith a lot. We're considering a girls' trip soon. Somewhere close, but a long weekend somewhere. Maybe somewhere between the two of us, we'll see if something transpires from those discussions, but I kinda hope it does. I really like your sister.

Oh, guess what! Aunt Joan told me at lunch that my mom showed up at her house over the weekend. She said she was just there for a visit, but she eventually asked for money. Mom swore it wasn't for drugs, but I could tell Aunt Joan didn't believe her. I just wish things were different, you know?

Anyway, enough of that doom and gloom.

I was just checking the weather forecast, and we're supposed to have storms later. That means no stars. But I'll still look up, pretending they're there. We're on Scorpius. It's prime time to see it, but probably not tonight. The next clear, hot summer night, we'll find it.

Well, I should go. I have to change out of your shirt before work. But no worries! I'll put it back on before bed tonight.

Oh... I also just realized it's been two weeks! Two weeks apart, but now two weeks closer to your release. We've got this!!

LOVE YOU!!!!!!!!!!!!!!!!!!!!!!
(Yes, my love required 22 !'s)

Shayne

I reach for my body spray and give it a little spritz, making sure some of the moisture falls onto the paper. Smiling, I carefully fold the paper, picturing the moment when he brings the paper to his nose and inhales. Once it's ready, I slip it into the envelope, lick the tab, and place the stamp in the upper-righthand corner. Then, like a complete loon, I kiss the name I had already printed across the front.

"Love you," I whisper, setting the letter aside and making a note to run it to the mailbox down on the corner first thing in the morning.

Just as I jump up to get ready for work, a text comes through my phone. Thinking it's Ford, I reach for the device and tap on the screen. It's my uncle.

> **Uncle Henry:** Hey, kiddo, I'm downstairs with pie. Are you upstairs or in the bar?
>
> **Me:** Upstairs! I'll come down and unlock the door.

I toss my phone onto the couch and make a beeline for the stairs with a grin on my face. As soon as the door is open, he grins and spreads his arms. I step forward, pressing against his familiar chest, and squeeze as his arms wrap around me. "How's my favorite niece?"

I snicker. "I'm your only niece."

When I step aside, Uncle Henry secures the door and follows me up to my apartment. "Apparently, your aunt had a hankering for a strawberry rhubarb pie. She whipped up six pies this afternoon after picking rhubarb from the garden and asked me to deliver them."

"Why'd she make so many?" I ask, taking the dessert and placing it on the counter.

"She's used to feeding Chad, remember?" he teases, making me laugh.

"Man, that boy can eat," I quip, taking a quick peek under the plastic wrap and inhaling the sweet scent of homemade pie.

"That he can. What's this?"

I glance his way and find Uncle Henry standing over the folder of information I left on the coffee table. The packet from the cosmetology school. "Oh. That. Just something I... picked up."

He glances at the cover letter and flips to the financial assistance sheet. "Are you enrolling?" he asks, his eyes full of excitement.

I shrug. "I'm not sure yet. It's just something I've been thinking about lately."

He sets it back down and smiles. "I'm proud of you, sweetie."

"Thanks. Well, it's not official or anything. There's a lot to think about. The closest school's forty-five minutes away," I reason, shifting on my feet.

"I think it's a wonderful idea," he says, coming over and pulling me into another hug. "I'm proud of you."

My chest tightens and my stomach churns. "I haven't done anything yet," I whisper, breathing in the familiar scent clinging to his shirt. Hay, horses, and sweat. It brings as much comfort today as it did when I was younger.

"You'll do what's right for you, and your aunt and I will help." He places a kiss on top of my forehead.

"I can't ask you to do that."

"You didn't ask. I volunteered."

I give him a genuine smile and squeeze his hand. "Thank you for the offer, but…" I start, stopping to take a deep breath. "…if I do this, I want to do it on my own. I've been saving some money. Plus, there's a scholarship I qualify for. That would help a lot."

He nods and hugs me once more. "I'm so damn proud of you, Shayne. Not just because of the schooling thing, but proud of the woman you've become. You're going places, Shayne. Remember, this place," he says, waving his hand around the small apartment, "is just a stop, not your destination."

I close my eyes and just breathe him in. "Thank you."

"You're welcome, sweetie." Once he pulls back, he continues, "I better go. I know you probably have to work soon, and I have two more pies to deliver."

We walk back down the stairs and step out into the hot, summer sun. "I'll text Aunt Joan a thank you shortly, but also thanks to you for delivering. You're the best."

He waves off the compliment. "You're welcome. See you soon."

I watch as he gets into his big truck and pulls out of the lot before I head back up to get ready for work. The packet of information sits on the table, a glaring reminder that I own my own future. I also can't help but wonder what Ford will say when he reads that letter.

Chapter 25

Ford

"YOU COMING, FORD?" CHAD ASKS ME.

"Nah, I got a call to make." I hold up my cell phone.

"Tell Shayne I said hi," he says, standing from his bed.

"Pussy," Barnes barks out. "Your girl's got you whipped, Gregory." He holds up his pinky and pretends to be wrapping something around it.

"Fuck off." I chuckle. "You just wait until you find a girl. Payback's a bitch!" I call after them. He flips me the bird, the sound of their laughter following them out the door.

Before Shayne, I would have been with them. A few beers at the local bar in town on our night off is exactly what I would have wanted. Now, well, things are different. All I want is her. And right now, our scheduled phone call and the sound of her voice is the best I can do, and I'll take what I can get.

Two minutes until I call her. Standing, I grab my bottle of Gatorade and make my way outside. There's a picnic table just outside our barracks and that's where I'm headed. I want to have a clear view of the stars when I'm talking to her. Lying back on the picnic table, I stare at the screen on my phone until it turns to eight o'clock on the dot. I press her name on my favorites list, and it barely rings when I finally hear her voice.

"Hey."

"Fuck, it's good to hear your voice."

"I miss you."

"I miss you too, baby. How was work?"

"Good. We're actually slammed, so I'm still here."

"Damn," I mutter. I was really looking forward to some time with her tonight.

"I know. I'm sorry. The extra money is nice, and Jet is so nice to me. I wanted to help him. The new girl he hired called out for the second time. I think he's going to fire her."

"He should. He can't keep asking you to work double shifts."

"I'm fine. I was only on from two until eight. I told him I had to have a break at eight or else I couldn't do it."

"Well, at least there's that. How much time do we have?"

"Maybe fifteen minutes," she mumbles. "Sorry, I'm eating."

"I don't care. It's so good to get to actually talk to you."

"How are things?" she asks.

"Same old. I've been spending more time in the gym. The guys went to a local bar for a few beers, so I'll probably hit the gym again when we get off the phone."

"Why don't you meet up with them?"

"Not really into that scene."

"I work in a bar."

"I know. I didn't mean anything by it. There are usually a ton of girls there trying to latch on to one of us, and all I see is you."

"I love you."

"I love you too, baby."

"I talked to Faith earlier today. She's getting ready for classes. She's excited for her final year of college."

"She's going to make a great teacher. She definitely has more patience out of the two of us."

"I don't know... you're patient with me."

"Because I love you."

"True." She laughs. I close my eyes and soak up the sound.

Slowly, I open my eyes. "The sky is clear here tonight."

"Yeah. And it's a full moon."

"Hopefully it doesn't bring out the crazies."

"You and me both," she agrees. "Luckily, Jet only needs me until eleven."

"That's good. Hey, I sent you a package. Did you get it?"

"I did. Thank you. I'm sorry, but I need to get back down there."

"We knew this would be tough."

"Yeah," she whispers. "I love you, Ford. You've changed my life in so many ways in such a short amount of time. I don't know how to thank you for that."

"You just did. You love me, Shayne. That's all I want and need."

"I miss you."

"I miss you too. Let me know when you can get a three-day weekend. I need to see you."

"When can you get away?"

"I could meet up with you Friday night, and if it's a weekend I'm off, I wouldn't have to report back until Monday morning."

"We could get our same hotel room."

"Yes. I'll look to see when I'm off, and you try to coordinate that with your schedule, and yeah."

"It's a plan."

"Text me when you get home."

"I will. Love you."

"Love you too, baby."

I end the call and rush back to my room to look over my schedule and immediately text her a few options for long weekends.

Shayne: Thanks! I'll get with Jet and let you know.

Me: Perfect!

Placing my phone on the small nightstand, I see an envelope. I know immediately it's a letter from Shayne. Chad must have left it when he went to check his mail. Tearing it open, I bring the paper to my face and inhale her floral scent. I read it three times before reaching for my notebook and pen. I might as well take advantage of the guys not being here and write my girl back.

Dear Shayne,

I just talked to you and came back to my room to find a letter from you. It was like hitting the lottery. I have the place all to myself. I read it three times, and now here I am writing you back.

Baby, I am so fucking proud of you. I wish I would have known this when we talked so I could have told you. You control your future, and if cosmetology is what you want, I support you. Free haircuts for life. LOL. In all seriousness, just reaching out to the school was a huge step for you, and I couldn't be prouder. I want this for you. I want you to follow your dreams. If there is anything I can do, let me know. I have money saved, pretty much everything I've made over the last three years minus a few beers and some wings on the weekends. It's yours. Whatever we need to do to make this happen, I'm all in.

Fill it out, Shayne! You've got this!

I hate that your mom isn't a mother to you. I am grateful for your Aunt Joan, and now you have my mom too. She texted me the other day and told me you were a keeper. I'm not sure if it was Mom-speak or more Hallmark-talk, but either way, I agreed with her. I think I'll keep you.

Hopefully, your mom doesn't come knocking on your door next. I hate the thought of that happening and that I'm not there to support you through it. I know that you're strong, and you can handle it. Hell, you've handled it your entire life, but you're not alone anymore. We're a team, and I feel like I'm not pulling my weight. I'll have a lot to make up for when this year is over.

A girls' trip sounds fun. Maybe you all can find your way to Fort Campbell? Just saying. Whatever the two of you decide to do, please be safe and enjoy yourself. You deserve all the joys in life.

I love that you're sleeping in my shirt. You need to send me a pillowcase or something, so I can sleep with your scent too. That sounds creepy now that I read it back, but I'm going to roll with it. I'm desperate to feel closer to you.

I know we talked tonight about a long weekend, and I hope we can make that happen soon. I'll cover the room and whatever else you need while you're here. Hell, I'll fly you if you don't want to drive. I just need to see you.

In your letter, we were at two weeks, and now we're at three—forty-nine to go. I've decided that once this year is up, I'm done. I want a life with you. After three weeks, I know that distance between us isn't what I want. I want to fall asleep with you in my arms and wake up to your smiling face. So, mark your calendar, beautiful. In forty-nine short weeks, I'm coming home for good.

LOVE YOU!!!!!!!!!!!!!!!!!!!!!!!!

(I'll see your 22! And raise you 1!)

Forever yours,
Ford

Chapter 26

Shayne

"I'll take another Jack and Coke and a sex on the beach for the lady!" Connor hollers, his eyes dropping to the cleavage of the woman standing beside him, chatting animatedly with her friend. She barely looks a day over twenty-one, and if it weren't for Jet already carding her and her friend when they arrived, I'd be doing it now.

I roll my eyes at the fruity girly drinks. Yep, definitely twenty-one.

"Aww, don't be jealous, Shayne. You're still my number-one girl. I can stop by later tonight, after I'm done with Sydni," he adds, waggling his eyebrows suggestively.

I'm about to roll my eyes again, ignoring his nasty comment, when my stomach pitches. It's been doing that all night, every time I catch a whiff of something sour. Like beer. I have to hold my breath with every draft I pour. It's not exactly sour, but it's definitely not sweet, and for some reason, it's turning my stomach.

Ignoring Connor's lewd offer, I make his drink and mix up one for his friend. When I add the cranberry juice, my stomach pitches hard, dropping to my shoes. I barely have enough time to cover my mouth before I'm bolting from behind the bar. The public restroom is closer, but there's no way I'm using that tonight, not when my dinner from earlier is about to make a reappearance.

Pushing through the swinging doors for the kitchen, I run to the small employee bathroom back by Jet's office. I don't even have time to flip on the light before I'm dropping to my knees and hurling my guts up.

Just as I get the heaves to subside, I sit back against the wall and greedily suck in oxygen.

"You all right, kid?" I glance to the doorway and see Jet standing there, a concerned look on his face.

"I'm okay. I think I just ate something funny when I took my break." I can feel the clamminess on my skin subsiding and the color starting to return. "I scarfed it down in like four minutes, so I'm sure it just didn't settle right."

Jet sighs. "I'm sorry to have to work you so much lately. It's hard to get reliable help. I'm sure I can cover the last few hours, if you want to head up now."

I'm already shaking my head. "Not necessary. It's passing. I feel much better. I'll stay."

Jet watches me for a few long seconds before adding, "If you start to feel sick again, head home. I can handle it. And if not, they'll just have to hold their damn horses until I get to them."

I can't help but smile. "That's not good for tips."

Jet chuckles. "When have I ever worried about making sure I get tips?"

Never.

In fact, for the first several months I worked here, I'm pretty sure he gave me all the tips at the end of the night, not just my half.

"Give me a quick second to wash my face and rinse my mouth, and I'll be out, okay?"

He stares at me a few long seconds before he nods. "All right. Take your time."

Then he leaves me in the tiny employee bathroom alone.

I quickly flush the toilet and grab a Clorox wipe to clean around the bowl and seat. Once that's done, I wash my hands and pat my face with cool water. I can see a flush to my cheeks, but I don't feel fevered. Clearly, it was something I ate earlier. Once my mouth is rinsed out, I flip off the light and return to the bar.

Connor isn't where I left him, which tells me Jet must have finished his order, thankfully. I jump in and serve drinks, staying on the side of the bar closest to the bathroom, just in case. The yucky feeling from earlier has passed, and I'm actually starting to feel good.

By the time Jet hollers last call, the queasy feeling has gone completely, and all I can think about is closing down and getting something in my stomach. In fact, there's a can of condensed chicken noodle soup in my cabinet upstairs that's calling my name. Maybe I'll even write another letter to Ford while I'm eating it.

Tonight didn't go as planned. I was only supposed to work until eleven, but we were so busy, I ended up staying until close. Since Ford is working tonight, I know I'm not missing anything from him yet. My attention is behind the bar, emptying and washing glasses when Jet yells from his end. I glance over to see what's up, and my heart drops into my shoes. It's the last person I expected to show up here.

Tonight.

My mom.

At first glance, she looks… good. Her smile is hesitant, and for good reason. The last time we spoke, it didn't exactly end well, so of course she'd be a little uncertain about my reaction. That's probably also why she decided to spring a visit on me here, where I'm least likely to make a scene.

Taking a deep breath and steeling my back, I head her way. "Hi."

"Hi, Shayne. You look good."

I just stand here, waiting, and take in her appearance. Her hair is somewhat clean, and she doesn't look strung out on whatever drug was readily available earlier in the evening. She's wearing a black T-shirt, which hangs loosely on her boney frame. What really catches my attention is the sadness in her eyes.

"What can I do for you, Mom? I'm working."

"Oh, I know," she says with an awkward chuckle. "I was just in the area."

My eyebrows draw together. "You were?"

She nods but looks away. The familiar tell comes back, and I have to swallow against the bile threatening to rise once more. Her painful lies are one of the main reasons I finally left. It wasn't just the drugs that destroyed her, but the lies she told to get what she needed, when she needed it. Even after every rehab stint, I could tell by the look in her eyes that she'd spiral out of control once more, sooner rather than later.

"I just…" she starts, glancing around to see who's listening.

I do the same, realizing everyone else is leaving for the night. The only one paying attention to our conversation is Jet, who knows all about my history with my mom. He's not even pretending to not eavesdrop either, but it doesn't bother me because I know his nosiness comes from the heart. He's protecting me, ready to step in at a moment's notice.

"I shouldn't have come," she whispers, turning toward the door.

"Wait!" I don't know what makes me say it, but the word's out of my mouth before I can even stop it. "Where's Bull?" I ask, the question chalky in my throat.

Bull Wagner is the town dealer. He's been arrested more times than I can count for various offenses. My mom hooked up with him years ago, when I was still in high school. He had money but wouldn't give it to her to spend on anything other than drugs. So while I sat at home, often with no heat in the middle of winter, he was across town living high off his cash cow. And she was right there with him.

"I, uh, left him."

Her words have my complete attention now. "What? When?"

She sighs and closes her eyes. "A few days ago. He… he wasn't a good man."

I can't stop the snort. "You don't say," I mumble sarcastically. "What tipped you off?" I ask, crossing my arms over my chest.

She holds up her arm to show me the casted wrist. "He wasn't happy when one of his associates didn't show for a meeting. He, uh, took it out on me."

My stomach falls once more. Even though I've washed my hands of my mom, doesn't mean I want anything to happen to her. In fact, I've pretty much lived my entire life waiting for something *to* happen to her. "I'm sorry, but I'm glad you got away from him. He was bad news."

She gives me a small nod in agreement and glances at the door. "Well, I should go. You're getting ready to close. I was just…" She stops and takes a deep breath. "I just wanted to see you."

I watch as she shifts on her feet and turns her back to me. I can see her shoulder blades through the material of her top, a reminder of how unhealthy she is.

Just as she reaches for the heavy door to push it open, I speak again. "Wait. Where are you going?"

She glances back and gives me a sad smile. "I'll be fine, sweet pea. Don't you worry about me." Then she pushes out the door and disappears.

My heart stops beating in my chest and plummets south while my feet start moving, hurrying to the place she just exited. When I hit the sidewalk outside, I find her only a few businesses down the walk. "Mom!"

She stops and turns around.

"Why don't you come inside? You can sit at the bar while I finish closing up, and then come upstairs. I was planning to make some canned soup."

"Oh, no, I can't," Mom insists, shaking her head. "I can't impose on you, Shayne." Then she starts doing something I've never witnessed in all my twenty-three years on this earth. She starts to cry. "I've been a horrible mother to you."

I don't argue. I can't. She's not wrong, but clearly, she needs a little assistance, and if I'm being honest, I want to help her. If she's sober, drug-free, and has left Bull, maybe she's ready to change her life. I know coming here wasn't easy for her. We don't have a good relationship or an okay one at that. For years, I've resented her—hated her even.

So why am I inviting her into my life right now?

Because of hope.

I can't help but hope she's a different person than she was before, and maybe, just maybe, there's hope for us too.

Seeing Ford with his family only reiterated the fact I don't have one. At least not in the traditional sense of loving, caring parents, and maybe a part of me craves what he has.

Am I setting myself up for heartache?

Probably.

That's why I'll guard myself when she's here, only offering enough help to get her through the detox and break-up part, and then she's on her way. She can find a job, pay her own bills, and finally become an upstanding part of society.

There is hope for her.

But she has to want it.

I pull two bowls of chicken noodle soup from the microwave and set them at the two-seater table in my kitchen.

"That smells amazing," Mom says, grinning at the yellow broth and noodles.

"It's just canned soup," I state.

"I know," she starts, grabbing her spoon, "but I haven't had much in the last few days." She takes a small slurp of hot broth.

"Much? To eat?" My stomach growls for food but gurgles at the same time with uncertainty.

She shrugs. "I stayed one night with a friend, and I ate spaghetti with her. It was good, but I didn't want to impose, so last night I slept in my car."

I swallow hard. "You slept in your car?"

She waves off my concern. "It's fine. Not the first time, unfortunately. In fact, when Bull was in prison two years ago, I lived in my car for about six months."

I push my soup away, suddenly not hungry.

"Enough about me though, tell me what's happening with you?"

I clear my throat, trying to buy myself a little more time. How much do I want to give away about my life? About Ford?

"Well, I'm working a lot, and it's going well. And... I met someone," I whisper.

"Really? Tell me about him? Is he from here?"

"No, he's in the army. He was in town a while back with Chad. They're friends."

"Wow," she says, her eyes full of excitement, "that's terrific. Can I meet him?"

Even if he wasn't in the military, that's a big no. She's not exactly the bring-a-guy-home kinda mom. In fact, she's not really a mom except on paper. "He lives on base."

"So it's a long-distance thing then, huh? Well, be careful. Long-distance relationships rarely work out, especially for a military man. Many think with their dicks, not their heads," she states, taking bigger bites of the soup now that it's cooled off a little.

Funny, when I consider her statement, it's not the thought of Ford cheating on me that catches my attention. Even in such a short amount of time, he's become one of the few people I have faith in. I trust him completely.

I can't help but think of what Ford would say right now. Well, actually, I'm pretty sure I know exactly what he'd say, and it wouldn't be good. He's not a fan of hers, and I imagine me telling him I allowed her to come up to my apartment would probably worry him.

And he'd be right.

It's not smart.

I know this.

Yet, here I am, sitting at my kitchen table with her, because I want her to be different. I want our situation to be normal, to be what most everyone else has, including Ford. So even though he wouldn't like of this, especially since he's not here with me, I'm sure he'd understand.

At least, I hope.

Right now, that's all I have.

Chapter 27

Ford

I'T'S FRIDAY NIGHT, AND IT'S BEEN A LONG-ASS WEEK. NOT ONLY
has it been a long week, I haven't talked to Shayne since Monday.
We keep missing each other at our opportune times to talk, and it's
making me cranky as fuck. Her text messages tell me that she's okay, but
I want to talk to her, to hear her voice, and be my own judge.

I understand why she offered to let her mom stay with her. I get
it. I do. However, I still worry about her. I don't know her mother, and
honestly, at this stage in the game, I don't want to know her. Not after
the way she treated her daughter. Her flesh and blood. I couldn't hold
my tongue, and I told her that I didn't think it was the best idea, but that
she had my support no matter what. She does. Always. However, when
we talked last, she said that her mom seemed to be doing well, and she
was still staying with her. It's been four days since I've heard her voice,
and it's kind of tripping me out a little. I let my imagination run wild.

I mean, her mom has been there almost three weeks. Surely, if she was being malicious in her intent, it would have shown by now.

"You coming?" Chad asks.

"No."

"Why the hell not?"

"I'm not in the mood for the bar."

"You've never not been in the mood for the bar."

"I'm going to stay home and try like hell to get ahold of Shayne."

He nods. "Fine. You know where we'll be if you change your mind."

"Thanks, man." With a wave, he walks out the door, and I'm finally alone. Pulling my phone out of my pocket, I dial Shayne. And much to my dismay, it goes to voice mail. "Hey, babe. It's me. I really need to hear your voice. I don't care what time it is when you get this, call me. I'm off this weekend, so don't worry about interrupting my sleep. I miss you. I love you." Ending the call, I drop my phone on the bed beside me.

I don't know how long I lie here looking at the ceiling before my phone alerts me to a new message.

Shayne: Hey! Sorry, I'm working. I miss you. Love you!

Me: I just need to hear your voice, Shayne. Thirty seconds, babe. Just need to hear it.

I am completely aware I sound like an irrational, jealous asshole. I own that. I just hate that she's had her mother staying with her, and I'm not there. I told her I would be there to support her, and yet I'm stuck here. I hate the distance between us, and as the days and the weeks wear on, it gets harder and harder not to be there with her.

I fucking hate the distance.

I'm in the middle of pleading my case when my phone rings. "Hello."

"Hey, sorry, it's really loud in here tonight. Is everything okay?"

"Yeah, babe. It is now. I just… I was worried about your mom staying with you, and I hadn't actually gotten to talk to you since that night, and well, not hearing your voice kind of put me in this funk. I was afraid that you needed me, and I'm not there, and yeah…" I say, ending my rambling.

"That's just one of the many reasons I fell in love with you. I'm sorry I've been so busy. I've been working and going through the packet for school."

"Yeah?"

"I really want to do it."

"Do it. You can do anything you want, Shay."

"I would never have even considered it or gotten this far without you," she says as Jet calls out for her. "Sorry, it's really busy tonight. I'll call you when I get off work."

"I'm off this weekend, so yes, do that. I don't care what time it is. You call me."

"Okay. I love you. I miss you like crazy."

"I miss you too, babe. I'll talk to you soon."

Phone in hand, I pull up my pictures and flip through the many that I took during our time together as well as those I've saved that she's sent me during our time apart. I don't know that I can do another year. I hate being away from her. I know she has Chad's family there, but I want her closer to me. Hell, I want to be closer to her. I know there's not a damn thing I can do about it.

The thought has crossed my mind to ask her to move here, but that's selfish. If we get shipped out again, and the chances that we do are pretty high, she'll be here all by herself. At least she has some allies where she is. I just hope her mother really does have her shit together this time.

I'm lying awake with my phone clutched in my hand. As soon as I feel the vibration, I hit Accept and place it to my ear. "Give me two seconds, babe." Climbing out of bed, trying not to disturb the others, I make my way outside to the picnic table. "How was your night?"

"Exhausting. I don't know why but all week I've felt drained."

"Are you sleeping okay?"

"Yes. I think it's just the changes, you know? I mean, Mom is still staying here, you're gone, I'm getting ready to apply to school, and I've been picking up extra shifts."

"Do you need money? I can send you whatever you need."

"No. I'm good, but I love you for asking. For the fact that you want to take care of me. Jet needs the help, and I thought it might be nice to grow my savings for when I'm in school in case I need to cut back."

"I told you I would help with that."

"I know you did."

She doesn't say anything else, but she doesn't need to. I already know she's going to be stubborn and try to do this on her own. Soon she'll realize that she's not alone anymore, and she never will be. Not as long as I have breath in my lungs. I don't push her. Instead, I change the subject. "How are things with your mom?"

She sighs. "Good, I think. I've been working more hours, but the apartment is clean, and her eyes are clear. I don't see any kind of track marks, and she's been going out every day applying for jobs."

"That's good."

"Yeah," she agrees. "Maybe this time will be the time. Maybe she's finally getting clean for good."

I want to tell her not to get her hopes up, but I hear it in her voice. She's the same little girl who wanted nothing but her mother's love. I have a feeling that if this goes south, it's going to crush her. I also know my girl, and this will be the final straw for her mother ever getting a chance to be a part of her life.

"Sorry I was so needy earlier. I just needed to hear for myself that you were okay."

"I'm fine. Everything is good. Well, as good as it can be without you here with me."

"Damn, Shay. There's an ache in the center of my chest that never seems to go away."

"The stars are bright tonight."

"They are," I say, looking up. We're both quiet for the longest time, happy to just listen to the other breathe. "Hey, Shayne?"

"Yeah?"

"Have you ever thought about what you want your wedding to be like?"

"Sure. Don't all girls think about finding the love of their life and changing their last name? Why?"

"You should probably start thinking about the details, not just the day in general."

"You think so?" she asks. I can hear the smile in her voice.

"I know so."

"Ford Gregory, are you asking me to marry you?"

"No. I'm not asking you, but I will. Right now, though, I'm telling you that it's going to happen, and I want it to be exactly as you want it to be. So, start thinking, making lists, cutting out magazines, whatever it is you need to do. I want it to be a day you will never forget."

"It will be because it will be you."

"Damn right," I say, feeling myself start to get choked up. "I never knew I could love this deep or this hard."

"You taught me that."

Her words are like a vise squeezing my heart. "I'll show you too. Every day. I promise you that."

"I'm holding you to that," she says over a yawn.

"Get some rest, beautiful. Call me tomorrow?"

"Definitely. I picked up a shift, but just for a few hours in the afternoon. Sweet dreams, Ford."

"Sweet dreams, beautiful."

Ending the call, I take a few minutes to force the smile from my lips. If there's even a slight chance the guys are awake, and I come in smiling like a love-sick fool, they'll never let me live it down. Once a little of the euphoria from our call drifts off into the night, I head back to my room. Everyone is still asleep. Placing my phone on the charger, I crawl back into bed, and I don't need a mirror to know I drift off to sleep with a smile on my face.

Dear Shayne,

It's been too damn long since I've held you in my arms. I knew this would be hard. I knew being away from you was going to suck, but I didn't understand how much.

I miss you.

Every second of every damn day, I miss you. The guys are telling me I'm whipped, and maybe I am. I'd like to think it's not being whipped, but that the love I have for you is so deep, so raw, and so real that it consumes me. I'm okay with that, in case you're wondering. I want to be consumed by you.

I want to hold you.

I want to kiss you.

I want to fall asleep next to you.

I want to feel your skin next to mine.

I want to taste your lips.

I want you.

Forty-five more weeks.

We've got this. Some days are harder than others, but I know we'll make it through. Tonight, well, tonight, as I glance up at the stars, I'm missing you even more than usual. In fact, I just saw a falling star, something I rarely ever see. I hope that you were looking up and caught it as well. I hope that beneath the fallen stars, you're thinking of me.

All my love.
Ford

Chapter 28

Shayne

Dear Ford,

Guess what?! I did it! I just opened a letter from the Kentucky School of Cosmetology, and I'm accepted into this fall's class. I start in two weeks; can you believe it?!?!?!?!?!

This isn't the best day of my life, since that is reserved for the day I met you, but it ranks up there pretty high. Finally, something for me, and I have you to thank. You've been the best boyfriend ever, even all the way down there in Kentucky.

So, Mom got a job at the grocery store in town. She's working the register. The money isn't great, but it's a start. I'm super proud of her. I haven't seen her yet to see how her first day went, but I'm sure I will soon. She insisted on walking, even though I offered her my car since hers is out of gas, so it'll take her a little longer to get back here.

Next step is her getting her own place. This apartment is so small, we're starting to get under each other's skin. She's been sleeping on the couch, but complaining it's been bothering her back. The last few nights, when I've gotten home, she's been in my bed. She was sleeping so peacefully, I didn't want to disturb her, so I left her sleeping. The next morning, it was my back that was sore, so maybe it's time to upgrade the ol' couch to something a little more comfortable.

Oh... I know I'll tell you this sooner than you'll read it here, but I still want to make sure I include it in my letter. Jet gave me the weekend off in two weeks! Faith and I will meet near the base and wait for you! I can't believe it! After what feels like FOREVER, I finally get to see you face-to-face. Less than two weeks, and you're mine, Gregory. I hope you're ready.

You won't sleep much. HEHEHEHEHE

Anyway, I should go. Work calls, but fortunately, it's a short shift. Jet's training the new guy tonight, so I'm helping four to eight to get through the dinner rush.

Love and miss you!!

And more anxious to see you now more than ever!!

Shayne

I glance at the clock. Again. Mom was supposed to be home after her shift ended at three, but I have yet to see her. It's just after seven. Even if she was asked to stay after, it wouldn't be this late. Not on her first day. I keep running through different scenarios, but I keep coming back to the same one.

Drugs.

Even though she's been doing well, I don't trust her. Not the way I should, and that thought is so heartbreaking.

Reaching for a glass, I feel a sharp pain in my lower abdomen. It hurts so hard and fast that I find myself doubled over, trying to catch my breath. The cramping steadily grows until I can barely move. All I can think about is getting up to my apartment, but I'm not sure I can actually make it there.

"Hey," Jet says, bending over beside me. "What's wrong?"

I suck in a deep breath and try to stand up. "I don't know."

When I'm upright, he gives me a once-over before his eyes widen in horror. "Shit, Shayne, you're bleeding."

"What?" I gasp, glancing down and taking in the blood running down my legs. "I need to go upstairs," I whisper, pushing off his arm and heading for the back stairs. I need to get to some feminine products as soon as possible.

"No, I don't think so," he says, helping me walk out of the main bar. "You need to go to the hospital."

I open my mouth to argue, but another cramp grips my body and squeezes, and that's when I feel the rush of blood. It feels like I wet my pants, and suddenly, I know. This isn't a period. This is worse.

Because I have no clue what to do in this situation, I just look at Jet and let the tears fall. "I can probably drive myself."

He immediately starts shaking his head. "I don't think so," he states, grabbing a towel from the kitchen and guiding me to the back hallway. His eyes are full of understanding and compassion as he adds, "I don't know much about female... stuff, but this isn't just monthly problems, is it?"

I shake my head, my tears falling harder. "I don't think so."

Jet pulls me into a hug, something completely out of character for the older, gruff man. "What should I do?"

"I wish I knew. I guess I should go to the hospital, but I don't want to call an ambulance."

He nods in understanding. "Then who should I call? Your mom?"

I think about his question. My first thought is Ford, but what good would that do me? He's hours away and working. He probably wouldn't even be able to leave. Then there's my mom. She should be home but isn't, and if I'm being honest, she wasn't even the second person I thought to call right now. "Cassie." I grab my phone from my pocket, knowing she's at her parents' house.

Jet takes the phone from my hand, insisting on doing it himself. "I'll call her. Take a seat, okay?" he suggests, sliding a stool over to me.

I do as instructed as he puts the phone to his ear and calls. Jet steps away, talking quietly to my cousin when she answers. A few seconds later, he holds out the phone for me and says, "She's on her way." Then he runs up the stairs to gather my purse, leaving me alone in the warm hallway, sitting on a towel quickly soaking in blood.

My mind races as I try to grapple with understanding.

I'm having a miscarriage. The knowledge hits me hard.

I'm losing a baby I didn't even realize I was carrying. The sadness hits me square in the chest, and the tears start to fall all over again.

Jet returns a few seconds later, setting my purse by the stool. "I'm going to check up front and be right back."

"You don't have to stay with me. I know you have to get back up front to train."

But he's not hearing it. "I'm not leaving you back here alone," he states bluntly before slipping back up front to check on the situation.

He returns a few minutes later, just as a hard knock sounds on the back door. Once he opens it, Cassie flies inside, her eyes wide with worry. "Let's go."

I gingerly stand as she comes over and places her arm around my back, leading me out the door, my purse and phone cradled under my arm. "Let's take my car," I instruct once we're outside. When she gives me a questioning look, I whisper, "I don't want to get blood on your seat."

She waves off my concern. "I don't even care about that. Get in," she demands, holding open the passenger door.

The ride to the hospital is short, especially with Mario Andretti behind the wheel. I try to reassure her I'm fine, but the words sound uncertain, even to my own ears, so I don't blame her for driving her car like she stole it.

Cassie pulls up in front of the emergency department and stops the car. I get out, cradling the towel between my legs, and go inside, my cousin hot on my heels. "May I help you?" the woman at the counter asks.

"I think I'm having a miscarriage," I whisper, the words feeling like they're choking me.

"Okay. I need your insurance information," she says, typing in her computer.

"I don't have any."

She looks up and blinks. "Oh. Okay, well, I'll have some paperwork for you to fill out," she starts, reaching for a clipboard and stack of papers.

"Can she do that in a bit? She's bleeding all over your floor," Cassie counters with a clipped tone.

"Oh. Yes, of course," the woman stutters, gathering up the necessary paperwork and handing over the clipboard. "Please fill these out and return them when they're complete."

I'm ushered through a doorway and led to a room.

The next thirty minutes are a blur. My blood is drawn to confirm what I already know. I'm still bleeding and cramping heavily, even after a pain reliever was administered. My aunt arrived not too long after we got here and has been standing at my side, holding my hand the entire time. The mood is stoic as we wait for word on what's happening.

"Shayne, good evening," a woman says as she enters my room. "I'm Dr. Lewis, an OB-GYN. I'd like to take a quick look at your uterus with an ultrasound, if that's all right? I'm a little concerned about the heavy bleeding," she adds as a nurse enters the room with the machine.

"What's the concern?" Aunt Joan asks, taking charge.

"Well, it could be nothing, but it might also mean infection, or the tissue isn't shedding completely. If that's the case, we'll schedule her for a D&C as quickly as possible."

I blink away the wetness in my eyes and try to focus on her words. She explains the process for a D&C, but my mind just seems to struggle to catch up and grasp her words. It hurts to concentrate when your heart is aching, so I finally just close my eyes and let my aunt handle the doctor.

I go through an exam and ultrasound, all while trying to keep it together. I find myself focusing on Ford. On his smile and easy laughter. On the way it felt to be in his arms. I try not to think about what's happening or what it'll be like to tell him about it. Those thoughts are too painful to comprehend.

"You said you've been spotting for a few days, right? You thought it was a menstrual cycle?" Dr. Lewis asks as she finishes up what she's doing.

I nod in confirmation. I had been late, but I figured it was due to the stress. Between Ford leaving and my mom returning, I've had plenty of anxiety lately. When the spotting started, I just assumed it was my period finally arriving several weeks late.

She gives me a small smile. "I'd like to go ahead and do a D&C. You'll be able to go home afterward, but you'll need to take it easy for a few days. Drink lots of fluids. You'll experience some mild cramping and bleeding, which could last a week or two. The nurse will go over what to watch for before you go back for the procedure. Do you have any questions?"

I can't think of any, so I shake my head.

At least none that she can answer.

My question is this: How will I tell Ford?

How will I explain that I lost our child? One I didn't even know existed until it was too late. What kind of mother am I? How will he ever forgive me?

And my biggest question of all: How will I ever forgive myself?

When I wake, I'm groggy and tired. My lower abdomen feels tight, but there isn't any pain. At least none there. All the ache remains in my chest.

"Hey," Aunt Joan whispers, her eyes swollen and tired. "You did great." She leans over my bed and kisses my forehead, much like she did when I was a child and would show up at her house hoping to eat.

I look around, noticing we're alone in the small room. "Cassie?"

My aunt flashes me a quick look. "Well, she's in the hall, talking to Chad on the phone."

"Chad?" I whisper, my voice raw and hoarse.

She nods. "Yeah, she called him. Your phone has been blowing up with texts from Ford. A bit ago, he called too, but I missed the call before it went to voice mail. Since I don't know your password, I wasn't able to call him back. The texts have been getting increasingly urgent, so I told Cass to call Chad. I hope I didn't overstep, but I knew how much that boy must be worrying about you."

I close my eyes for a moment and fight against the fatigue. The clock on the wall reads three in the morning, and I can only imagine what Ford must be feeling. Even though I'd much rather tell him myself what's going on, I wouldn't want to keep him in the dark any longer than necessary. "No, it's okay."

"Chad will tell him you're okay," she reassures, rubbing my hand. "He'll have Ford call you at our house later after you've gotten some rest."

"I can stay at my apartment. Mom must be worried," I reply, catching the look that crosses her face. "What?"

Aunt Joan sighs. "Well, your mom was here, sweetie."

"She was?" I ask, glancing around.

She nods. "I sent her away."

Her words are quiet yet pack a punch. "You did?"

"I did. She showed up looking for your keys so she could get into the apartment. She was…" Aunt Joan closes her eyes for a second, but when she opens them, I already know what she's going to say. I can feel the remorse ebbing from her small frame. "She was pretty strung out, and she kept saying she needed to get inside to get her things. Bull was with her."

And just like that, I'm crying all over again. My body aches with a familiar pain, one I've grown so accustomed to carrying, yet it engulfs me, taking me by surprise all the same. Why? Because I had hope. I had hoped this time would be different.

That *she* would be different.

"Security escorted them from the building, and Jet was going to make sure they didn't gain access to your apartment. Uncle Henry will gather her things and meet her somewhere away from you. We won't let them hurt you again," my aunt vows, but we both know it's already too late for that.

The damage is done.

She's hurt me all over again.

"Shayne, we're getting you set for discharge," Dr. Lewis says, entering the room. She takes a seat beside me and goes over post-op instructions. The nurse removes my IV and helps me change into a T-shirt and pair of cotton shorts that Cassie brought me, and before I know it, we're on our way.

A part of me wants to insist I go home to my own bed in my own space, but a bigger part doesn't want to be alone. I don't want to be there if my mom or Bull shows up, so I don't fight it when I'm placed in my aunt's car and driven out of town, toward their farm.

Once we arrive, Uncle Henry meets us at the car and helps me out. He never leaves my side as he escorts me to the house and up the stairs. I'm led to Chad's room, where his bed beckons me. I'm suddenly so exhausted, I feel like I could sleep for days.

They say their goodnights and promise to check in on me regularly. I can tell by the look in Aunt Joan's worried eyes, she probably won't be getting much rest, even though she's been up all night.

That's love.

I climb into bed and curl up against the soft sheets. I can hear the whispered murmurs down the hall and Cassie's muffled crying as she tells them about talking to Chad. I hate that I've caused pain for those I love.

Especially Ford.

I want to feel his arms around me and hear his reassurance that everything is going to be okay.

To hear him whisper he loves me and to hold me while I cry.

I close my eyes and welcome the coolness of the sheets against my skin. When I open them, I stare out the window and find a sky full of stars. Bright and sparkly ones. I can't help but smile. Because even though I'm alone and filled with a horrible sadness, I can't help but feel like I'm not. That beneath these stars is a man gazing up at them and wishing he was by my side.

As I drift off to sleep, it's with pictures of Ford accompanying me, of us together under those very stars, his arms wrapped firmly and protectively around me.

And only then do I feel like I'm truly home.

Chapter 29

Ford

SHE'S NOT ANSWERING HER PHONE. IT'S BEEN HOURS SINCE
I've heard from her. I know she's working, but it was a four-
hour shift, and it was before then that I talked to her. She never
goes this long without responding to my messages. I understand that
I'm a little over the top when it comes to Shayne, but that woman is
my heart. I can't stop worrying about her. If I were there, close to her, I
wouldn't worry as much, at least that's what I tell myself.

"I'm sure she's fine," Chad assures me from his bed across the
room.

"She was supposed to be off work thirty minutes ago. It never
takes her this long to call."

"She's probably staying over. She's fine," he says. He's confident in
his statement, but something in my gut tells me she's not. I can't explain it, but there is this churning of anxiety that tells me something
else is going on. Is it her mother? Someone from town giving her shit

again? I clench my fists at my sides as I pace across the room. I want more than anything to get her out of that town. That's not fair to her, but damn, I hate that she's there facing the scrutiny all on her own.

Dialing her number, I call her again. "Voice mail," I mutter. I wait for her to tell me to leave a message and leave yet another. "Hey, Shay, baby, I'm starting to get worried. No, I am worried. You're not replying to messages or answering your phone. Call me or reply, please. I love you," I say, hitting End Call on the small screen.

"Something doesn't feel right," I tell Chad. "Seriously, man."

"You miss her," he says, sitting up in his bed. "That's what this is. I get it, I do, but you can't be blowing her up while she's working. She doesn't do that shit to you."

"I know, but..." I rake my fingers over my shaved head. "This is different."

"How do you know, Ford? You're not there. You're stressing yourself out. Look, man. I know that you love her. I get it, but you can't drive yourself crazy like this."

I nod, plopping down on my bed and resting my elbows on my knees. My phone is still gripped tightly in my hands as I wait for her call. "Come on, baby," I murmur, willing her to call me.

"Come on, man, let's play." He tosses the PlayStation controller to me. "Distract yourself. She's going to call."

Nodding, I take the controller and play him in a game of Madden. He wins, but to be fair, my head's not in it. In between games, I text her again with no reply. Chad beats my ass in the second game of Madden, and I'm done. I can't focus.

"Let's go grab something to eat."

"I don't know—" I start, and he pins me with a stare.

"You have your phone on you. You won't miss her if she calls. You need to eat. Maybe getting out of this room will help."

"Maybe," I say, but I don't believe it. I text her again as we're walking out the door.

Me: I'm worried. Please reply or call me back. If you're working, I get it. I just need to know that you're okay. I love you.

Me: Chad and I are going to run out and grab something to eat, but I have my phone with me.

We go to the small mom-and-pop diner just off base. We both order bacon cheeseburgers and fries with chocolate shakes. I'm sure to keep my phone face up on the table, and the ringer is turned all the way up. I know it's rude, but I can seem to find it in me to care.

"Maybe it's my phone. Call me," I tell Chad.

He rolls his eyes but does as I ask, and the shrill ring of my phone echoes throughout the small diner. "I wonder what's up?" he asks.

"I thought you said she was fine?" I ask, trying not to let my panic show.

"I'm sure she's fine," he assures me. "But this is unlike her."

I nod as the waitress drops off our food. He tries to distract me with random small talk, but it's hard to focus or even eat. I force it down, knowing I need the sustenance, but I don't taste it.

A few minutes before eleven, Chad's phone rings. "It's Cass," he says, placing the phone to his ear. "What's up?"

I can see it on his face. Something is wrong. I fucking knew it. Standing from my bed, I begin to pace the room again. "Is she okay?" I ask. It's rude as fuck to ask him while he's on the phone, but I can't find it in me to care.

He ignores me. "Okay. Yeah. I'll tell him. Can you call us when it's over?" He's quiet while she replies. "Thanks, Cass. Love you."

"Tell me," I say, standing with my hands on my hips.

"I'm going to need you to sit down."

"No. Just tell me. Is she okay? Is it her mom? What did she do? Fuck, I should be there."

"Ford!" he says, much louder than he should have to. "Sit your ass down."

I do as he says, closing my eyes and pulling air into my lungs. With a slow exhale, I open my eyes and nod. "Tell me."

"She's okay," he starts, and I feel my shoulders relax just a little. "She was at work and having some cramping and belly pain. There was some bleeding. Jet took care of her. Called Cass, and she drove her to the hospital."

"What caused it? You said she was okay. Can I talk to her? Why can't I talk to her? Fuck. She's my girlfriend."

"What does that have to do with anything?" he asks.

"We're not married. That means I can't get leave. I can't go see her." My mind is racing, and I'm wondering if I should do something like break my arm or my leg, something to get me home to her. I'm desperate. I can't go AWOL. Being in jail won't help her, but I need to get there. I think I might be losing it.

"Ford. I need you to listen to me."

Shaking out of my thoughts, I give him my full attention.

"She's in surgery."

"Tell me." I know he's holding something back. "What's wrong with my heart?"

"She didn't know," he says cryptically.

"What didn't she know, Chad? Please stop talking in fucking riddles and just spit it out."

"She was pregnant, Ford. She didn't know, and she lost the baby. I'm sorry, man."

"W-What?"

Pregnant.

She lost the baby.

I swallow hard. "Repeat that," I say, my voice not sounding like my own.

"I'm so sorry. They have to do a procedure, and that's where she is now. My mom and sister are both there with her."

"Fuck. I can't leave, Chad. I have to wait until tomorrow to ask for emergency leave. Will they even let me? We're not married, but that was—" I swallow down the bile in my throat. "That was my baby." My voice cracks.

Hot tears burn behind my eyes, and I know no matter how hard I try, I'm not going to be able to keep them at bay. My Shayne, our baby. She's in the hospital dealing with all of this without me. If I didn't already know, I do now: I'm not signing up for more time. I can't. This distance, not being able to be there with her, it's killing me. My chest is tight, and it's hard to breathe.

"I'm so fucking sorry," Chad says. I feel his arms engulf me in a hug, and the dam breaks. Tears fall unchecked, and I hug him back.

My baby.

"When can I talk to her?" I ask him.

"Cass said she would call after the procedure. She and Mom are staying with her. They're taking good care of her."

"I know, but it should be me. I should be there to hold her and tell her that we'll try again."

"Wait? Were you trying?"

"No. But that doesn't mean I don't want to. I want everything life has to offer us. That includes marriage and kids, and anything else she could ever want."

He nods. "Why don't you pack? You're going to need to plead your case, and I don't know how much time they'll give you. A few days, maybe a week, but you need to be ready when they do so you can get on the road."

"I need to rent a car," I tell him as I pull my phone out of my pocket and pull up the rental car site. I secure a car for a week, not caring if I don't really need it that long. "Chad?"

"Yeah?" he answers, clearing his throat.

"What if they won't let me go? What if I can't go see her?"

"We just got back, so they're not shipping us off again for at least a few more months. They're going to let you go. I just don't know how long they're going to give you."

I nod and begin to pack a bag. I don't know what I'm packing, and honestly, I don't care. If I forget something, I'll buy it when I get there. All I care about is getting to her.

I just need to get to her.

Chad spends the next couple of hours trying to distract me. He also keeps me updated, thanks to messages from his sister. Finally, at three, she calls. Chad puts the call on speaker this time so we can both hear what she has to say.

"Hey, Cass," he greets her. "You're on speaker."

"How is she?"

"She just got out of the procedure. She's in her room resting. They're going to release her in a few hours."

"Cassie, I'm going to have Chad send you my number. I can't ask for emergency leave until eight in the morning. As soon as I get cleared, I'm headed your way. I'm going to need you to keep me updated on where she's staying and how she's doing. Can you do that for me?"

"Of course."

"Can you do me one more favor?"

"Anything."

"Tell her I love her."

"I can do that. I'm sure she's going to want to talk to you when she wakes up. I don't know if she's going to be upset that she's not the one who got to tell you, but you were blowing up her phone, and we didn't get to it to answer in time, and it's locked with a password. We knew you had to be worried sick, so let's just hope she's not mad at me."

"She won't be mad at you," Chad and I say at the same time.

"Cassie, if she wakes up and wants to talk to me, you call me. I don't care what time it is. If she refuses because of the time, you call me anyway and hand her the phone."

"You're a good man, Ford Gregory. I'm so glad that she has you."

"I'm the lucky one," I tell her.

Chad and Cassie talk for a few more minutes while I move to the window and look up at the stars. Maybe when she wakes up, she'll be able to see them and feel me there with her.

Fucking bureaucratic red tape kept me from getting on the road until after ten. I had to have a doctor's statement about the miscarriage as well as a statement from Shayne stating that I'm the father because we're not married. To make matters worse, I had to call Cassie to get her to have Shayne approve the request because Shayne's phone is dead. I'm going to remedy that situation as soon as fucking possible.

So, here I am, finally on the road at half past ten, headed to see my girl. With about an hour left in the drive, I can't take it any longer and try to call Shayne's cell. It goes straight to voice mail, so I call Cassie.

"Hey, Ford."

"How is she?"

"Doing as good as can be expected. She's in the shower now."

"I'm about an hour away."

"Good, she'll be happy to see you."

"You have no idea," I tell her. I was granted five days of leave, and I'm already dreading that day I have to come back to base. It's going to tear my heart to shreds.

"You want me to have her call you when she gets out of the shower?"

"Nah, I'll be there soon. I mean, if she wants to, she can. I imagine she's moving slow." At least I think she is. I don't know the procedure other than what I read online last night when I couldn't sleep. I don't know how to handle any of this. The only thing I am certain of is that I can love her through it.

"Okay. See you soon," Cassie says, ending the call.

Tossing my phone into the cupholder, I press a little harder on the gas pedal, sending up a silent prayer that I don't get pulled over.

Forty-five minutes later, I'm pulling into Chad's parents' driveway. The car is barely in Park before I'm tearing open the door and jogging to the house. Before I can knock, the front door opens, and Cassie waves me inside.

"She's upstairs in Chad's room."

"Thanks, Cass." I squeeze her shoulder as I pass her and take the stairs two at a time. I don't stop when I reach the door, and I don't bother to knock. Nothing else is going to keep me from her for another damn minute. When I push open the door, she looks up from where she's lying on the bed, and tears instantly spring to her eyes.

Closing the door, I kick off my shoes and lie down next to her, pulling her into my arms. "I'm so sorry," I whisper.

"I'm sorry," she counters. "I didn't know, Ford. I promise I didn't know."

"Shh, baby, I know. I believe you." I can feel her relax in my arms, and it hits me that she's worried about history repeating itself. She's worried I'm going to assume that she knew and blame her. Just like this entire fucking town, excluding Chad's immediate family, assumed she knew that man she was seeing was married.

"I love you. I love you so much," I whisper, placing a kiss on her temple. "I've never been more scared in my entire life. I'm in the army, Shayne. I've been in some situations, but this... *this* is the worst of them all. Knowing that you needed me and I didn't know if I would be able to be here. We're not married, hence all the hoops that we had to jump through. I hate that we had to do that. I'm sorry. I wish I could have been here sooner."

"That's a situation out of your control, and you're here now."

"Do you know? I mean, was it a boy or a girl?" I ask the question that's been running through my mind since the moment I found out.

"They're not sure. I wasn't very far along. They had to send the—" She swallows hard. "They have to do lab work to see if there was anything genetic or otherwise. It will depend on the development if they can tell us the gender."

"Are you okay?"

"My heart hurts, but I'm okay. Better now that you're here." She snuggles close. "I was worried about maybe not being able to have more in the future. The doctors have assured me that shouldn't be an issue, but they will know for sure when the pathology comes back. I need to follow up with my OB-GYN in a few days."

"Good. I'm glad I can be there with you."

"How long are you here for?"

"They gave me five days. I don't know if you want to do a memorial or something? I mean, I don't know how all of this works."

"I don't know either. I don't think so. Maybe at some point, but I'm still adjusting to the idea that I found out I was pregnant and lost the baby all in the same day."

"I'm so sorry I wasn't here."

"You're here now, and I know that if you could have been, you would have." She yawns.

"You tired?"

"Yeah. They have me on a mild painkiller, and they always make me sleepy."

"I'm drained. I didn't sleep last night, so why don't we take a nap?"

"Will you hold me?"

"Try to stop me." Kissing her lips softly before climbing out of bed,

I pull the blinds, and strip out of my jeans and move to lie next to her, sliding under the covers.

"Not the visit we were hoping for," she says with sadness in her voice.

"No. But you're in my arms, Shayne. I can feel your breath on my neck and your heartbeat beneath my palm. I wanted our baby. The minute I heard what happened, I was devastated for what we lost, but we still have each other, and we will get through this. I promise you that."

"Together," she mumbles.

"Together," I repeat. I don't want to sleep. I want to hold her and just be with her, but exhaustion wins as I drift off with her safe in my arms.

Chapter 30

Shayne

"**Y**OU READY?" FORD ASKS, SQUEEZING MY HAND.

We're standing outside the bar, the stairs leading to my apartment before us. It's been less than twenty-four hours since I was last here, yet it feels like a lifetime ago.

Uncle Henry came early this morning and gathered my mom's stuff. He tried to do it without me knowing, but I overheard him and Aunt Joan talking in the kitchen after I woke up. When I went downstairs, he tried to change the subject, but I wouldn't let him. He ended up sharing his plan to gather her belongings and drop them off at Bull's place, explaining that he didn't want to cause me more pain. I love him more because of it.

"I think so," I finally reply, gazing up at the stairs.

Ford leads me to the door and holds it open. As I step over the threshold, I find Jet waiting. "Hey, kid," he says, instantly pulling me into his tattoo-covered arms.

I go willingly, so grateful for the gruff older man who has become a friend, an extension of my family. "Thank you," I whisper, my face pressed against his chest.

He pulls back and gives me a small smile as he releases me. "I've got you." Then he takes Ford's hand and gives it a few pumps.

"Appreciate all you do for her."

Jet grins. "She's a good kid. You take care of her, or you'll have to deal with me."

Their exchange has tears welling in my eyes, my emotions all over the place since everything happened last night.

"Come on, Shayne. Let's get settled," Ford instructs, placing a warm hand on my lower back and guiding me to the stairs.

"I took you off the schedule for a week. If you need more time, just say the word." Jet nods and disappears through the kitchen entrance, making sure the door is secured behind him.

We go up the stairs, and I unlock my apartment door. It feels the same when I enter, yet nothing is right. I look around and see the place my mom kept her small bag of clothes, the spot on the counter where her purse sat, and the used cups lining the sink. Yet it feels foreign and wrong.

It doesn't feel like home.

Ford drops the rental keys on the counter and guides me toward my bedroom. The bedding is different, which tells me Uncle Henry took care of changing the sheets after he cleared my mom out of my space. I snuggle into my bed, seeking out the comforts of home. It's only when Ford crawls into the bed and wraps his arms around me do I finally feel the peace settle in.

"You sure you're okay to stay here tonight? We can go back to your aunt and uncle's place, or even get a hotel." He runs his hand down my arm, and like a balm, soothes the anxiety in my chest.

"No, I'm good here," I reassure him, slipping my fingers into his and holding on tight.

"But…" When I glance over my shoulder at him, he just smiles and adds, "I could tell there's more to it." His voice is gentle, calm, and patient.

I sigh and close my eyes, just lying here and feeling his body pressed to my back, reveling in the sound of his even breathing. I smile as I inhale, taking in his familiar scent. "I can smell you," I whisper.

Ford sniffs my hair and groans. "You're my favorite scent ever. I've missed this."

I let him hold me before I take us back to our original conversation. He knows what happened with my mom and would have come with my uncle to deliver her stuff if he had been there. I can imagine he has a few choice words for her as well. "I'm good here, Ford, but I don't think I'm happy."

I feel him tense and quickly realize my words could be taken out of context. "I'm not happy here. In this apartment. In this town. I'm comfortable, but this isn't what I want out of my life. I feel like I was starting to gain a little perspective on what that might be when I filled out those school papers. I thought I was doing something for me, you know? This is what I wanted. It felt right.

"If I hadn't met you, I'd be fine living in this place, working in the bar, and ignoring the town chatter behind my back. But now, now that you're a part of my life, I realize all of it is just a stepping-stone. I want more, and for the first time in my life, I'm not afraid to grab it. That's because of you. You're so brave, and you defend our country with such pride and strength. I can tell you love what you do, and I want that," I whisper, swallowing hard over the lump and swiping at falling tears.

"I never thought I'd want to be a mother because I was sure I'd be a terrible one. I mean, look at my example. But when we met, and you asked me about it, I realized I did want that. I want to have a family someday. I want to experience that part of life and show a child exactly what it feels like to be loved unconditionally by a mother. I want to prove to myself, and maybe to everyone who doubts me, that I can do it. That I'm better than where I came from."

I'm moving before I even realize what's happening. Ford pulls me firmly against his chest and holds me while I cry. I let go completely, unleashing years of anger and pent-up sadness, letting it wash from my body one tear at a time.

"I wanted that baby," I whisper, opening my eyes to find his wet and overflowing with his own grief.

"Me too." His words are hoarse. When he clears his throat, he adds, "I never knew it was possible to love something so quickly and then lose it at the same time. When you were in surgery, it was the scariest moment of my life. I was terrified of something happening to you too, but worse, distraught I wasn't there to help you."

I give him a faint smile. "I'm sorry."

"Stop," he insists, shaking his head. "You did nothing wrong. I don't want to hear you say another apology, okay? It was out of our hands, you got me? And it doesn't reflect on us. Google says a miscarriage happens in ten-to-fifteen percent of pregnancies. Hell, my mom had one before she got pregnant with me and Faith. There's no rhyme or reason behind it."

I place my cheek against his chest once more and just listen to the steady thunder of his heartbeat. I'm not sure if this guilt will ever go away, but I do feel better talking to Ford. I wish I could have stopped it. I wish I had known. I wish it wouldn't have taken a tragic turn before I was even allowed to experience the joys of motherhood.

But it wasn't in the cards.

At least not now.

After several minutes, I finally say, "I think I want to move."

He pulls back and meets my gaze. "Yeah?"

I nod. "I've been talking to Faith a lot lately. Her roommate moved out a few weeks ago to live with her boyfriend, and well, she hasn't found a new roommate yet. I've been thinking… maybe I could move in with her. I know it's a lot farther away from your base, but—"

"I think it's a wonderful idea," Ford interrupts.

"You do?"

He nods. "I do. All I want in this world is for you to be safe and happy. Getting you out of this town would do both. Plus, you'd have my sister, so you wouldn't be alone."

"Cassie did some research while I was in the shower, and there's actually a school near where Faith lives."

I can see a plethora of emotions cross his features. "Keep going."

"The original course I signed up for was thirteen months, and as long as they offer a similar one, I think I can still work part-time evenings and weekends."

He rubs the outside of my arms and places a small kiss on my nose. "You know you don't have to work, right? I can help you."

I give him a small grin. "I appreciate that, really, but… I need to do this myself."

Ford just smiles back at me. "And I knew you'd say that. Whatever you need, I support you a thousand percent, Shayne," he says as he links our fingers together.

"Maybe tomorrow we can look up the school and check on enrollment," I whisper, snuggling back into his warm, familiar chest.

"I'd love to help. I'm on leave next weekend. Chad and I will move you."

I sigh in complete contentment. "It's not done yet, Ford. I haven't talked to your sister. She may have already gotten a new roommate, and the school might already be full for fall."

"Nope. It'll happen. I know it," he says, turning my chin up and meeting his gaze. "Do you know why I'm so certain?"

I shake my head, already feeling the emotions lodging in my throat.

"Because you're amazing and so fucking strong, and honestly, this is probably a much better idea than the one I was going to suggest," he says, offering me a sheepish grin.

"What's that?"

"You marry me right away and come live with me on the base."

My eyes must resemble something out of a cartoon, because Ford cracks up laughing. "What?"

"Chill, sweet Shayne," he whispers, placing a soft kiss on my lips. "I'd do it in a heartbeat to get you out of here, but that's not the only reason why I'd marry you."

"It's not?" The words feel choked in my throat.

"No. I'd marry you because you're my future, not just my present. Because I want to build a life with you," he says, bringing our joined fingers to his mouth and kissing my knuckles. "Because when I see myself outside of the military in a little house with a wife on the porch watching kids playing in the yard, I see you. From the moment I met you, I knew you were going to change my life forever."

My words are barely audible as I murmur, "I want that too."

Ford grins the most handsome, breathtaking smile. "Then this is what we're going to do. In the morning, we're going to call Faith. If she's already rented the room, we'll find you something else near her. It's a college town. Apartments open up all the time. We'll go online and get you enrolled in school too, so you're all ready for fall."

"You're so confident."

"In us, baby. I'm confident in us. We can get through anything as long as we do it together. This year is going to fly by, and before we know it, I'll be discharged, you'll finish school, and then we can go wherever we want, do whatever." Ford swipes at a few stray tears under my eyes.

"I'd like that."

He kisses me soundly, reiterating his declaration and love through the way he kisses me. It's poignant and tender, yet completely toe-curling passionate at the same time. It's just us.

When I'm completely breathless, he pulls away and asks, "So, what do you want to do? Get ready for bed?"

"Actually," I start, curling on my side against him and raising our hands up. I trace his scarred knuckles with my thumb, memorizing the roughness of his skin and the way it feels in my hand. "I was thinking, since it's such a calm night, maybe we can go outside and look up at the stars. You can show me if you've done your homework and know where Sagittarius is."

He snorts out a laugh. "I'm a quick study, sweetheart. I knew where it was after I got that letter. I had to go outside and find it."

We hop off the bed, don't even bother with shoes, and head downstairs. Once outside, we walk to the back of the parking lot, away from the area used for smoking, and find a little spot between trees and some overgrown hedges. Ford pulls me into his arms, my back pressed firmly against his front, and we both look up.

"It's a gorgeous night."

"It is. I'm just happy to be sharing it with you in person, instead of a few hours away."

"Me too," I confess, my head resting on his chest.

After a few seconds, a star streaks across the sky. "Did you see that?" he asks, wonder and amazement filling his words.

"I did. You have to make a wish."

"Already done," he informs me, kissing the top of my head.

I close my eyes and say my piece. It's more of a prayer than a wish. I figured the star gods wouldn't mind. I pray for peace as I accept the loss of our baby and go through the grieving process. I pray for a smooth transition into whatever my future has in store for me, and I pray for comfort for Ford as he also deals with the emotions he feels concerning the loss of the baby, as well as not being with me when it happened.

"Did you make one?"

I chuckle. "I made three."

"Me too."

"You did?"

He nods. "Want to know what they were?"

"No, because then they won't come true."

"That's a myth. I happen to know, for a fact, we make our own destiny, so sharing my wishes won't hinder the outcome."

I snort out a laugh and turn into his chest. "If you say so."

"I wished for this next year to pass by quickly, so I get back to you as soon as possible. I also wished for peace and comfort for both of us as we grieve, and my third wish was for you to say yes when I finally ask you to marry me."

I blink rapidly, trying to clear the wetness from my eyes, but it's no use. The tears that have seemed to do nothing but fall for the last twenty-four hours are at it again, spilling in earnest from my eyes. "I know for a fact those three wishes will come true."

"Yeah?" he asks, so much hope and happiness reflected in those eyes and echoing in his voice.

"Yep. We're going to get through this because we have each other. And someday, when you decide to ask me to marry you, there'll only be one answer you'll get."

He kisses me soundly once more, holding me close and refusing to let me go. "We've got this, Shayne. Do you know why?"

"Because you love me." My reply is so easy, so natural. When I'm feeling weak, he's my strength. When I'm down, he lifts me up. And vice versa.

"Because I love you," he confirms. "And because you love me. We're a team."

He hugs me against his chest, and I just breathe him in, soaking up his strength, his reassurance, and his love. It pours from his heart and vibrates from his soul, wrapping around me so completely, as if it were always there, lying in wait for us to find each other. Like two pieces searching for the other half. For fear of sounding like a cheesy '90s rom-com movie, he completes me.

If it were possible, I fall even more for Ford Gregory.

Beneath the fallen stars.

The next few days pass in a whirlwind of phone calls and online registrations, but by the time Ford is ready to head back to the base, we're all set for his weekend leave.

Faith was in the process of interviewing potential roommates, but when her brother called and told her my plan, she threw all the applications out the window and insisted I move in. The cosmetology school accepted my application, and I even qualified for financial assistance to help cover some of the costs.

Telling my aunt and uncle was the hardest part. I'm going to miss them terribly. They're my family. They helped raise me, even though I wasn't their responsibility. I truly think they would have taken me from my mother had they had the opportunity. Being hours away from them both is going to be hard, but no one supports me as much as they do.

Except Ford.

He's finally packing his bag after dragging his feet the last few hours. Now, it's almost time for him to get on the road. He has to be on base tonight and ready to rejoin his team tomorrow morning. As hard as it is for him to go, I know it'll only bring us closer to the day we're finally together forever.

As I watch him shove shorts and socks into his bag, an idea pops into my head. I practically jump up off the bed, glancing at the clock to confirm I have time. "I'll be right back!" I yell, turning and making a beeline for the door.

"Where are you going?" he hollers.

"Five minutes. Be right back!" And then I'm out the door and virtually running down the block.

Once I get to the flower shop, I place my order and watch as they fill it. I pay the few bucks and hurry back to my apartment. When I round the building, I find Ford outside by his rental, bags already loaded. "What's that?" he asks, shielding his eyes from the sun.

"Do you remember when you asked if I wanted a memorial or something for the baby? Well, I've been thinking about it, and I thought this was something we can do together. A way to say goodbye," I tell him, my eyes burning with unshed tears.

His green eyes brighten with realization. "Hang on," he says, bolting up the stairs to my apartment. When he returns a minute later, he has my letter-writing notebook and a pen. "Here. We can attach a note."

I watch as he rips a sheet of paper out and sets it on top of the notebook. We walk over to the car and use the hood as a table. Ford hands me the pen and takes the balloon. I lean over the hood and start to write.

Dear Sweet Baby,

Not a day will go by that we won't think of you.

The sobs start slowly, and my hand starts to shake. I can't seem to make myself write anymore. Ford gently takes the pen from my hand and kisses me on the forehead and finishes the note.

Until the day we can finally hold you in our arms, we will hold you in our hearts. Mommy and Daddy love you more than you'll ever know.

"It's perfect," I whisper, sniffling and wiping my eyes.

Ford nods and sets the pen down. He takes my hand in his and guides me to the far end of the lot where there are no trees. He ties the little note to the end of the balloon and holds it out for me to grab on. "Until we meet in heaven," he whispers, his tear-filled eyes locked on mine.

"In heaven," I murmur.

Together, we let go of the balloon and watch it float higher and higher until it's no longer in sight. A calmness washes over me, bathing me in peace. I close my eyes, still grieving our loss, and whisper, "I love you, sweet baby. I'll never forget you."

Ford pulls me against his chest and sighs. "I really don't want to leave, but I have to get on the road."

I nod. "You can't be late," I confirm, knowing he's already going to be pushing it for returning when required.

"But hey, we're going to be seeing each other soon. Chad and I will be here to help you move."

"Yep," I mutter, pasting on my best, most confident smile.

He pulls me back against him, threads his fingers into my hair, and kisses my lips. "I'll text you as soon as I get back."

"'Kay."

"I love you most," he murmurs, sliding his lips across mine and savoring the connection.

I snicker at his comment. "Love you so much."

"See you soon, Shayne."

Nodding, I watch as he climbs into the car, starts it up, and closes the door. He puts the shifter into Drive and starts to pull away, mouthing, "I love you," as he goes.

I wave, giving him a reassuring smile, yet I can't stop the overwhelming feeling of sadness as he drives away. Only this time, I know there's a light at the end of the tunnel. Soon, he'll be back, helping me move to my new apartment in a new city in a new state. And with each day that passes, we're one more closer to our forever.

Epilogue

Ford

I CAN'T SLEEP. THIS IS THE FIRST NIGHT SINCE I'VE BEEN DISCHARGED from the army that I've had that problem. Normally, with Shayne curled up beside me with her head resting on my chest, sleep finds me easily. Tonight, that's not the case.

I've been home for two months, and it's been the best two months of my entire life. The year that we spent apart was hell, but at the same time, I think it was good for us. Good for her. Shayne grew into the person she wanted to be, and I got to witness it firsthand. Sure, it was mostly video calls and pictures, but I was there for it.

All of it.

I can still remember her first day of school. She called me as soon as she was in her car, and luckily, it was a time I could talk. She went on and on about how much she loved it and how excited she was. I don't think there has been a single day since she started classes that I've heard her complain. My girl has found her calling, and I couldn't be prouder of her.

I missed her like crazy, but we made it work. Our love is built on a solid foundation. We wrote many letters about the loss of our baby and what we wanted for our future. It sounds crazy, but I feel as though I know her better than I know myself. I have the distance to thank for that. Sure, this would have happened with time. The distance fast-tracked us, and I'm good with it. In fact, it's worked in my favor.

I know she looks forward to the nights that we gaze up at the stars. I know she wants to be a mother more than anything. She wants to prove that she's breaking the cycle, and like her, I can't wait to be a father.

We will always mourn the baby we lost, but we are both looking forward to the day when we hold a tiny human in our arms that's a piece of both of us.

I know Shayne's favorite color is pink. She hates onions, loves Doritos, and chocolate cake. I know that the stars tattooed on her shoulder blade are a reminder of the life we're building together and that no matter where we are or have been in the world, we're still always together.

I know without a shadow of a doubt that she is the absolute love of my life. My future is with her. She's going to be the mother of my children, the smile I come home to, and everything in between. I know she loves me as much as I love her, and the future we talked about all those months ago while I was away is happening now.

Tomorrow, the woman lying in my arms, the love of my life, graduates from college. I can't tell you how fucking proud I am of her. For the last two months, since I've been home, I've been staying with her and my sister, Faith. It's been good, but I'm ready for us to have our own space. We've talked a lot about what that would look like, and part of the reason I can't sleep is that tomorrow, I get to give Shayne her graduation present.

The present isn't just for her, which is kind of a dick move, but I know she's going to love it. It's for us—our first house. We've been looking online, and there was one house a few weeks ago that she fell in love with. I went to look at it, and it's everything we both want. Lucky for me,

I saved most of the money I made while in the Army, which allowed me to have the down payment, and some cash left over for furniture, which the two of us will pick out together.

For now, there is an air mattress and bedding in the master bedroom waiting for our first night there. It's not the most romantic gesture, but the double lounge chair on the back deck is. I want to be able to lie under the stars with her anytime I want. We've spent enough time looking at them separately. For the rest of our forever, I want to hold her in my arms as we stare up at the twinkling night sky.

I told Faith she could stay with us until she got on her feet. She's a substitute teacher right now, but she's applying for full-time positions closer to our parents. I love our parents, but moving home after not living there for four years would have been tough. Faith was worried about Shayne not wanting a house guest so soon, but we both know the worry isn't needed. Those two have become as thick as thieves over the last few months. I'm thrilled they get along so well, considering Shayne is about to be her new sister-in-law.

I wish I could say that taking her to our home, which is close to my parents, and her graduation is the only reason I'm lying awake tonight. However, there is a little black box hidden away in the closet of my sister's bedroom that says otherwise. I'm going to ask her to marry me. I'm not nervous. I'm not worried that she's going to say no. I know that we're solid and that the love we have for one another is deep and true. No, I can't sleep because I'm excited. Finally, we are both at the same stage of our lives. We no longer have the army or college hanging over us. We're ready to move forward with our next chapter.

There was a slight transition for me coming back to civilian life, but I'd like to think that I adjusted well. I got a job at a local car manufacturing plant as an operations manager. I was excited to see that my skills from the army could carry over into my civilian life.

As for Shayne, she still needs to sit for her state boards, but I know my girl, and she's got this. There is already a salon in town, the one my mom goes to, and my sister did as well before going to college, that has offered her a position. She'll be answering phones and other odds and ends until she passes her test. I'm so damn proud of her for reaching for her dreams.

Shayne snuggles closer and releases a sigh of contentment. I tighten my hold on her and close my eyes, savoring the feeling of her lying on my chest. It's an action I will never take for granted. Having her here and having her close. Knowing that I'm holding my forever, I finally drift off to sleep.

Shayne

"You did it," my uncle Henry proclaims as he pulls me into a hug.

"We're so proud of you, sweetie," Aunt Joan announces happily as she patiently waits for her turn.

We're gathering at a local restaurant with family to celebrate my official graduation from cosmetology school. It was a fun thirteen months, and I'm anxious to take my state test so I can start my new career. I'm lucky to have been offered a station in a small salon in Cooper with three other stylists, two having worked in the industry for more than two decades each. It's going to be great learning from their experience as I grow my skills and my clientele.

My aunt, uncle, and cousin Cassie made the trip here, along with Chad, who took a weekend leave to come. He decided to stay in the army, signing for another two years after Ford left. There's been talk of him transferring to a different base in the near future, so I'm glad to steal a little time with him.

In addition to my family, Ford's mom and dad, as well as his sister are here. It's the first time Faith and Chad have seen each other in a few months. I'm not really sure what happened with them. They were gung-ho about keeping in touch, but then all of a sudden, it just stopped. Someone put on the brakes, but neither of them are really saying much. All Faith has really said is that if they were meant to be, they'd find a way.

After dinner today, everyone is going back to our apartment to finish packing the U-Haul. We leave bright and early in the morning, heading back to Cooper. Ford said he found an apartment for us that'll work until something bigger and better comes along, and Faith is moving in with their parents for the same reason. She says she doesn't want to commit to an apartment until she finds a job. Especially since she's searching within an hour radius of where her parents live. She'll want to live wherever she works, which makes sense to me.

"Hey!" Chad offers a wide smile and a warm hug the moment he steps inside the restaurant. His hair is cut in the familiar buzz I've grown accustomed to, but there's something different about his eyes. They're sad.

"What's wrong?" I whisper as soon as his arms are around me.

"Nothing," he insists, shooting me a reassuring grin, but I don't buy it. I've known him too long to not spot his tells.

My eyebrows arch together in question, and my arms cross over my chest.

Chad is saved from answering as Ford comes over to say hello to his best friend. "Hey, man," he offers, foregoing the handshakes and offering a hug. "What's the matter?"

I can't help but smile in victory. Even Ford knows something's up.

Chad sighs. "Now's not the time, okay?" he whispers, glancing around until he spies Faith. Something washes over him as a slow grin spreads across his lips.

"You'll tell us later?" I ask, trying not to draw attention to his discomfort.

"Yeah. Listen, I'm going to go say hello, okay?" And then he's gone, heading straight for Faith.

We enjoy dinner and visit for much longer than we should,

considering we're at a restaurant until the party eventually breaks up. Everyone is staying at a local hotel for the evening and will be meeting us at the apartment at eight tomorrow morning for the big move.

"I'm going to ride with Chad," Faith mutters as we all head for the exit, our bellies full of amazing food.

I can't help but grin. "Oh, you are, are you?" I waggle my eyebrows suggestively, making her laugh.

"Stop it. We're going to talk. He says he has something to tell me," She replies nervously. "I hope everything's okay."

"I'm sure it is," I encourage, giving her a quick hug. "Thank you for helping organize this dinner."

"Well, we're all so proud of you. I just hope I get a teaching job close to you so I can get free haircuts for the rest of my life," Faith teases, winking. She was my favorite guinea pig while in school but always insisted on paying for the service, even when it was supposed to be free.

I laugh. "You got it."

When everyone else takes off to head to their hotels, Ford takes my hand and guides me away from where his truck is parked. "Where are we going?"

"It's a surprise," he announces as we cut across the street and head for a park.

A bark of laughter spills from my lips. "Ha! Last time you gave me a surprise, I wound up naked in the shower."

He grins suggestively. "Oh, I remember. Vividly."

We head to the center of a large grassy area. Ford takes my hands in his and turns me so I'm facing him. He smiles one of those breathtaking grins I can't help but love more and more every day. Then, he drops one hand and pulls an envelope out of his pocket. "I got you a gift."

I smile. "We said no presents," I remind him, even though I kind of knew he'd get me something. That's the type of man he is. He'll stop and grab flowers on his way home from the plant or make sure to have dinner waiting when I had a late class. He's the most thoughtful, loving person I've ever known, and I still can't quite believe he's mine.

"Open it," he whispers, his voice so full of excitement.

I pull open the white envelope and unfold the sheet of paper. My eyes read over the words, but they barely register. I stop and start over again, stuck on the words "offer accepted." "What offer?" I ask, glancing up and finding him watching me intently.

"You remember that tri-level home we looked at online? The one with the huge fenced-in backyard and the room over the garage?" He takes a deep breath. "Well, I put in an offer to buy it a few weeks ago, and it was accepted. We have a home."

Tears gather in my eyes as my own smile stretches across my lips. "We have a home? The one with the big kitchen and little breakfast nook?"

"That very one, sweetheart. It's all ours."

I squeal and leap into his arms, wrapping myself around him like a spider monkey. He catches me easily. "I can't believe you did this."

He inhales against my neck, his warm breath so familiar and comforting against my skin. "For us. I did it for us."

"Thank you," I murmur, pressing my lips firmly against his.

"You're welcome." He holds me against his chest and kisses me until my lips are swollen and tender.

"We should head back and celebrate," I announce, making him laugh.

"We should."

"Faith is gone with Chad, so we might have the place to ourselves for a few hours."

He sets me down on my feet and takes my hand. I turn to head back the way we came but am stopped when he doesn't follow. Just as I look over my shoulder, he drops to one knee. It takes a second for me to register what's happening.

Ford releases my hand and reaches into his pocket. He pulls a little black box out and flips open the lid. I gasp as I gape down at the most gorgeous diamond ring nestled in black velvet.

"Shayne Danner, you're everything I never knew I wanted in this life. You're kind and brave and so strong. You make me want to be a better person every day, to be the type of man worthy of your love. I want to share my life with you, become parents, and grow old together. Marry me, Shayne. Make me the happiest man in the world and be my wife."

"Yes," I practically yell, not even sure if he's done speaking or not. All I know is I need to get my answer out as soon as possible.

He takes my hand and slips that gorgeous ring on my finger, sealing the deal. Ford jumps up, threads his fingers into my hair, and kisses me. Every ounce of love he possesses pours into this kiss.

"Thank you," he whispers, nibbling on my bottom lip.

"Hey, that's my line."

"Nope. For the rest of my life, I'll be saying it. Thank you for agreeing to go on a date with me, even though you knew I was only in town for a week. Thank you for not giving up on me every time I had to return to base. Thank you for loving me, Shayne, for completing my life."

I sigh in contentment as he turns me in his arms, my back pressed against his front. We gaze up, eyeing the darkening sky. "I think we should get married at night, outside. We fell in love beneath the stars, and I think it would be perfect if we became husband and wife there too."

He kisses my neck and threads our fingers together. "That sounds perfect, but I have to say, I'd marry you whenever, wherever. As long as you're my wife at the end of the day, that's all I need."

"And I just need you."

We stand here, together, and gaze up at the stars. The very ones that kept us linked even when we were apart. They represent so much more than just lights in the sky. They were our compass, our solace in a world tattered by distance and separation. Our link to each other. We found friendship and love and fought to keep it together.

Now, we celebrate that love beneath the fallen stars.

Thank you for reading *Beneath the Fallen Stars.*

Want more from the Never Too Far Series? Chad and Faith's story, *Beneath the Desert Sun,* releases in July 2024.

MORE FROM LACEY BLACK

Bound Together Series:
Submerged | Profited | Entwined

Rivers Edge Series:
Trust Me | Fight Me | Expect Me | Promise Me: Novella
Protect Me | Boss Me | Trust Us
With Me (Christmas Novella)

Summer Sisters Series:
My Kinda Kisses | My Kinda Night |My Kinda Song
My Kinda Mess | My Kinda Player | My Kinda Forever
My Kinda Wedding

Rockland Falls Series:
Love and Pancakes |Love and Lingerie
Love and Landscape | Love and Neckties

Standalone Titles:
Music Notes | Ex's and Ho, Ho, Ho's
A Place To Call Home | Pants on Fire

Burgers and Brew Crew Series:
Kickstart My Heart | Don't Go Away Mad
Same Ol' Situation | Wild Side| What's It Gonna Take
Home Sweet Home | Too Young To Fall In Love
Without You

Co-written with Kaylee Ryan:
It's Not Over | Just Getting Started
Can't Fight It

MORE FROM KAYLEE RYAN

With You Series:
Anywhere with You | More with You
Everything with You

Soul Serenade Series:
Emphatic | Assured
Definite | Insistent

Southern Heart Series:
Southern Pleasure | Southern Desire
Southern Attraction | Southern Devotion

Unexpected Arrivals Series
Unexpected Reality |Unexpected Fight
Unexpected Fall | Unexpected Bond
Unexpected Odds

Riggins Brothers Series:
Play by Play / Layer by Layer
Piece by Piece / Kiss by Kiss
Touch by Touch | Beat by Beat

Standalone Titles:
Tempting Tatum | Unwrapping Tatum | Levitate
Just Say When | I Just Want You
Reminding Avery
Hey, Whiskey
Pull You Through
Remedy | The Difference
Trust the Push | Forever After All
Misconception | Never with Me

Entangled Hearts Duet:
Agony | Bliss

Cocky Hero Club:
Lucky Bastard

Mason Creek Series:
Perfect Embrace

The Kissing Games Series:
Kissing the Rival

Out of Reach Series:
Beyond the Bases / Beyond the Game
Beyond the Play /

Kincaid Brothers Series:
Stay Always / Stay Over
Stay Forever / Stay Tonight
Stay Together / Stay Wild

Co-written with Lacey Black:

Fair Lakes Series:
It's Not Over | Just Getting Started
Can't Fight It

Standalone Titles:
Boy Trouble
Home to You
Beneath the Fallen Stars
Tell Me A Story

Acknowledgements

To our Beta readers: Sandra Shipman, Joanne Thompson, Stacy Hahn, Lauren Fields, and Jamie Bourgeois. You ladies are the glue that helps hold us together. Thank you for taking the time from your lives, your families to read our words. Your time and input are invaluable to us. We will be forever grateful.

To our team: There are so many people to thank. We apologize if we've missed anyone. Here goes: Hot Tree Editing (Becky Johnson), Opium House Cover Design (Sarah Paige), Kimberly Anne, Kara Hildebrand, Tempting Illustrations (Gel Yatz), Deaton Author Services (Julie Deaton), and the entire crew at Give Me Books. It truly takes a team and we're glad that you're a part of ours.

Bloggers: Thank you for doing what you do. We know that you take time from your lives and your families to promote our work and we appreciate that more than you will ever know. Thank you for taking a part in the release of Just Getting Started.

Readers: Thank you for taking a chance on us. We are truly thankful to each of you.

To our reader groups: Lacey's Ladies and Kaylee's Crew. You are our tribe! Thank you for your never-ending support.